owya

Hold Me Down

Also by Calvin Slater

Lovers & Haters

Published by Dafina Books

Hold Me Down

A Coleman High Novel

Calvin Slater

Dafina Books

KENSINGTON PUBLISHING CORP.

www.kensingtonbooks.com

DAFINA BOOKS are published by

Kensington Publishing Corp.
119 West 40th Street
New York, NY 10018

All Kensington titles, imprints, and distributed lines are available at special quantity discounts for bulk purchases for sales promotion, premiums, fund-raising, and educational or institutional use.

Special book excerpts or customized printings can also be created to fit specific needs. For details, write or phone the office of the Kensington Special Sales Manager: Kensington Publishing Corp., 119 West 40th Street, New York, NY 10018. Attn. Special Sales Department. Phone: 1-800-221-2647.

Dafina and the Dafina logo Reg. U.S. Pat. & TM Off.

ISBN-13: 978-1-61773-134-1
ISBN-10: 1-61773-134-X
First Kensington Trade Paperback Printing: March 2015

eISBN-13: 978-1-61773-135-8
eISBN-10: 1-61773-135-8
First Kensington Electronic Edition: March 2015

10 9 8 7 6 5 4 3 2 1

Printed in the United States of America

This book is for Mary Slater and Jermaine Slater, Jr.

Acknowledgments

First, I would like to start out by thanking my Lord and Savior. It's because of Him that I am able to give you my best!

Mercedes Fernandez—I have to thank you! Thank you for believing in me at a time when I was ready to throw in the towel. You are a consummate professional, and the very best at what you do!

Claudia, you are the absolute best at making things happen behind the scenes!

To my family—my beautiful sister Gloria, my brother Wayne, and baby brother Jermain . . . y'all are the best siblings a brotha can have!

To Roger Jones— thanks for always being there!

Dwayne Patton, thank you for being so genuine! The talk you gave lifted my spirit more than you know. I love you, brah.

I'd like to thank all of my readers and supporters! Without you, there wouldn't be a Coleman High series. I hope you guys are enjoying the stories!

Oh, I'd be in serious trouble if I left out my auntie Eddie Mae Hicks, and best friend Ms. Ola Mae Watts! I love you both!

Prologue

THE VISIT

SATURDAY, JULY 26
7:00 A.M.

On the bus ride to MacSalle State Prison, Xavier's first impression was that the place looked like a huge automotive plant surrounded by razor wire. The prison towers were occupied by armed guards, a stark reminder of what kind of place he was visiting. Sickness came on immediately. He started feeling queasy and his blood was running cold. These had to have been the same feelings experienced by those unruly teenagers in the *Beyond Scared Straight* television series, nervously anticipating the conditions waiting on them inside the prison gates. But he wasn't here to be scared out of his wits. Even though the place was immensely intimidating, Xavier had come here to see his father.

The only thing on his mind as he stepped off the bus

was that he hadn't laid eyes on his old man since he was six. The fact was that he couldn't remember his father's face. In a few moments Xavier would be sitting in front of a man he didn't even know. But first he had to go through security. Xavier walked along with other visitors through the front door and checked in with a fat, bald, white deputy at the desk.

Xavier took his time filling out the paperwork. His stomach felt as though he was going over the first huge drop of a roller coaster. The butterflies were flying. He was nervous, jittery. Not knowing what to say or how the conversation would go was adding to the anxiety building up inside of his body.

Billy had wanted to drive him to the prison, but Xavier told his mentor that this was something he had to do alone. Since his mother went to jail, Billy had been as-signed as temporary guardian of Xavier and his little brother Alfonso. Both boys were now living at Billy's house until a more permanent situation became avail-able. Alfonso, had wanted to come but he stayed behind with a head cold. How things went with this visit would determine whether Alfonso could come on the next trip. Xavier wanted to see where Noah's head was before re-uniting the boy with his father.

He looked around the waiting area. So many sad faces. It made him glad that he'd made the decision to stop run-ning with Zulu last school year. All he'd wanted was some loot so he could get Samantha Fox, the hottest girl in the school to look his way. It was all good when Xavier was just boosting cars for Slick Eddie, but when Slick Eddie got his homie, Romello Anderson, to push drugs inside Coleman High, Xavier knew he had to leave Zulu behind. He could've very well ended up in a place like this if he had continued on that path. His short stay in the Quentin Juvenile Correctional Facility a month ago had been enough for him. The little room with the open toilet was way too degrading.

He finished up the visitor forms and took them up to the deputy at the desk. The correctional officer collected the forms and took Xavier's school ID. He was then given a key to one of the lockers over by the vending machines and water fountain. The locker was for his personal items. Cell phones, wallets, belts, purses—none of these were allowed in the visitation room. Paper currency was prohibited, so visitors were only allowed to exchange dollars for coins at a few change machines—up to twenty-five dollars' worth.

Xavier collected his coins and went back to sit down. Kids were everywhere. No doubt anxious to see their loved ones. He would've been the same way if his mother hadn't been so caught up in her selfishness that she never took him to visit his father. So many years he'd missed, not really knowing the truth about his dad. His mom, Ne Ne, was now in jail and serving a three-year prison sentence for attempted kidnapping because before he stopped running with Zulu, he did get cash—enough to catch Samantha's eye. But after a disastrous dinner involving his mother, her boyfriend, Nathaniel, and Samantha's parents, Ne Ne got a crazy plan to go after Samantha and make her life a nightmare. But Ne Ne and Nate took their plan too far at a school dance when they tried to kidnap her. The cops were called, and the rest is history. Ne Ne testified that Nate had been the one stalking Samantha and was the one responsible for the tons of prank calls Samantha had received. He was sentenced to eight years. Xavier wasn't trying to be cruel, but the two idiots should've gotten more. They'd put Samantha and her family through so much unnecessary stress that it was ridiculous. The trial had played out like a circus, with Ne Ne passing out as the judge handed out the sentence.

After the trial, Mr. Fox, Samantha's dad, had also gone nuclear and warned Xavier that he'd put him behind bars if he ever went near Samantha again. His threat did nothing to stop true love. Only encouraged it. Every chance they had the two teens were on their cell phones texting back and forth.

After waiting thirty minutes, Xavier was called with the group to be searched. He walked through a metal detector, was patted down like a criminal, and had to take his shoes and socks off and wiggle his toes—that was the routine. His hand was stamped and he walked with the group behind another tree trunk of a correctional officer until they reached the visiting room. There was so much activity in this place that Xavier was hesitant to go in at first. People were everywhere, laughing, playing card games, and reading newspapers.

The bright orange and army-green jumpsuits made it easy to identify the prisoners in the room, but there was no way to begin to track down his father in the crowd. It had been so long since he'd seen his dad, he wasn't sure if he'd recognize him. A light-skinned guy standing by a book rack was watching Xavier's every movement. Could it be him? But it wasn't his dad because a woman and a small kid walked up to him. Probably the guy's wife and child.

Xavier was about to go up to the chubby black guard sitting behind a desk, to inquire about his dad, when he felt a hand on the back of his left shoulder. He turned around and looked up into the face of a light-skinned, smiling giant. Xavier didn't want to rush to judgment. So he waited on this dude to make a move first.

"All of these years I've been waiting to see you, son," Noah Hunter said, smiling with tears welling up in his eyes. Before Xavier could respond he was grabbed up in an embrace. "Praise God Almighty that my son is here to see me. I have favor on this day and God's love is so good."

Xavier didn't know what to say. Tears were in his eyes as he hugged his father back.

"My baby boy was too sick to get up here and see his old man, huh?" Noah said, releasing Xavier.

"Yup. The dude is wrestling with a summer cold. I told him about playing up a sweat outside in this hot July weather and then running back inside to get in front of the fan. The boy is hardheaded."

Noah playfully rubbed Xavier's head. "Look who's talking. Before I got into this trouble, you were one of the most hardheaded little boys I'd ever seen." Noah walked over to the book rack and retrieved a terribly worn Bible. "Follow me and let's go grab a seat. We have some catching up to do."

Xavier followed his dad, not believing the sheer size of the guy. Noah was six-foot-six, his shoulders looked like mountain ranges of muscle, and he could've easily weighed 230 pounds. Xavier was jealous because he hadn't inherited his father's height, but he did look like his old man, albeit a darker version; but it was all good.

They grabbed a table in the corner.

Noah said, "So tell me all about yourself, son."

Xavier sifted through his life, highlighting achievements only. "Yup. I'm on the dean's list at school. Held a 4.0 GPA up to this point. This coming school year I'll be a junior."

Then he thought to himself, *Provided I'm not rubbed out for snitching out Slick Eddie and Romello.* Xavier had to snitch on them once he found out they were pushing drugs at Coleman High. But even behind bars, Eddie was still powerful and he had that kind of influence to make folks go missing. Xavier wasn't going there with his father. Didn't know the man well enough to be dropping heavy knowledge on him.

"Great, son," he said excitedly. "Your aunties all have their degrees. God is good. You're smart just like my side of the family."

Wow! Was that a diss directed at Ne Ne? Xavier wondered. It was funny because Xavier could remember Ne Ne telling him that he'd inherited intelligence from her side.

Noah went on to say, "I bet you Alfonso's brilliant even though he's special needs."

"Yeah, the little knucklehead's special all right. Can be a special pain in the butt."

"How's your mother?"

Xavier measured his response. Biologically Noah might've been his father but he was still an outsider to

Xavier. Even though Ne Ne was the biggest moron inside of Detroit city limits and didn't deserve any mercy, Xavier had no right to tell his father her business. Including that she'd tried to kidnap Samantha.

"Ne Ne . . . Ne Ne is good," he lied.

Noah's brow wrinkled. "Son, you call your mother by her first name?"

In trying not to air his mother's dirty laundry, he'd accidentally run his mouth. Noah opened the Bible and flipped some pages. He stopped and quoted, " 'Honor your father and your mother . . .' "

Xavier was stuck, scratching his head. "We weren't disrespecting her. That's what she told us to call her. 'Cause she said calling her 'mother' made her sound old."

"Jesus and Mother Mary," Noah said as he closed the book and laid it on the table. "What has gotten into your mother? What else has she done that you're not telling me?"

Xavier rubbed a hand across his head. He hated starting out with his father by lying. Ne Ne hadn't been all that as a mother, but she still deserved some dignity.

"My Lord," Noah prattled on. "I was gonna save this until you got ready to leave this evening. It was supposed to be a surprise, son. They're letting your father out August first. And by the looks of it—thank You, Jehovah!—it's right on time. Boys shouldn't be without a dad or a spiritual leader. When I come home we're gonna become a family united under Christ." He picked up the Bible and held it out in plain view. "I know I made some mistakes in my life, but this right here is gonna make sure that I stand strong to shepherd you guys through this life."

Xavier had a dazed look on his face. This man belonged in a church, preaching to a congregation. He'd heard about criminals going to prison and coming out holier than thou. Xavier just didn't think his father would be one of those guys. Noah had left an incredible legacy behind in the game, too. Who would've imagined?

"Thank You, Jesus," Noah praised. "You've been so good to me. And, son, when I come home I want to share God's teachings with you and Alfonso. I want to offer you God's salvation right now. Let's close our eyes and pray." His father took Xavier's hand and started praying, loudly.

Xavier's right eye was closed but he was peeping around out of his left. Folks sitting around that area looked so irritated by his father's lack of consideration. Xavier was confused. He was partly embarrassed by the number of people who were rolling their eyes in their direction. Ne Ne had been selfish and let her greed land her into a bed of corruption. She wasn't an ideal parent. She smoked marijuana, drank beer, and partied with her boyfriend, Nate, until they could hardly stand. Xavier was familiar with that lifestyle. But the squeaky clean one that his father was promising sounded more like something that was going to be the stuff of Wednesday night Bible study, Saturday morning choir rehearsals, and being forced into attending double services on Sunday. It wasn't gonna fly with Xavier. He wasn't cut out to be an altar boy. Couldn't see himself holding bake sales to raise money for the church's building fund. There was too much roughneck in him. Even though he was happy for his father, Xavier was now dreading the old man's release date. Aside from worrying about Slick Eddie's revenge, there was also a new worry on the horizon. Nobody was going to force him into doing anything he didn't want to do. Not even his father. There was going be conflict between them. Xavier could just feel it.

1

THURSDAY, AUGUST 28
5:30 A.M.

The alarm clock app went off on Xavier's cell phone. It was the first day of school and Xavier was thanking God for it!

Right on cue his father yelled from somewhere in the house, "Praise God! Xavier, get up and wash yourself. It's time to give God the first fruit of your day, boy!"

Noah, Xavier's father, was light-skinned, stood six-six and had crazy upper body strength. It seemed like he'd done his prison time in the gym, getting ripped. The dude's legs looked like massive tree trunks and his shoulders were huge and full of muscle.

But the guy was getting on Xavier's nerves, real bad. He hadn't been home one full month and already Xavier was over him. Once his father was out, he and Alfonso left Billy's and moved in with Noah. But it was just like he'd thought when he'd gone to see the old man in the joint. Up there Xavier had only received a microscopic dose of his father's fanatic religious beliefs. The dude was now home from prison, and with him he'd brought the wrath of God. When Noah wasn't talking about the Lord, dude was humming his praises around the house, and when he wasn't singing praises, he was voraciously racing through the pages of the Bible as if the book was set to spontaneously combust into flames if he didn't read it fast enough.

Noah said from behind Xavier's closed bedroom door, "Let's meet the sunrise by worshiping the Lord, son. Get up and hurry!"

Xavier couldn't do anything but shake his head. All of these new changes. But this "prayer before sunrise" was the icing on the cake. Though Alfonso had serious issues with the change of pace around the crib, the boy couldn't voice his opinion. Besides, he was too happy to see his father home. He'd been an itty-bitty baby when the old dude went off to prison, and had no memories of him. But to a cat like Xavier, the junk wasn't gonna fly. He was down with God and everything, but not the way that Noah was getting down. The way he'd been acting Xavier would've thought that Noah was hiding angel wings underneath his shirts.

Noah knocked on Xavier's door. "I can hear your alarm still ringing. That means you're not moving around in there, son! God hates laziness."

Why don't you shut up? Xavier thought.

The darkness outside of his bedroom window reminded Xavier of what the upcoming school year could bring if he wasn't careful. He'd pissed a few folks off last school year by snitching on Zulu—under the watchful eye of a fat cat named Slick Eddie. Working side by side to accomplish the deed was his number-one road dog Romello Anderson. Together with Slick Eddie's army of Zulu goons, the two boys had pulled off a miracle and cleaned up the school and got rid of all the scumbags. But unbeknownst to Xavier, Slick Eddie had a different plan for when the two boys had gotten rid of all the competition at Coleman High. When it was all said and done Romello obeyed his boss, Eddie, and went back on his word and double-crossed Xavier. In pursuit of the almighty dollar, Romello Anderson flooded Coleman High with dangerous designer street drugs. Once Xavier found out about the plan, it was too late to stop it from happening. Plus, Romello tried to have Xavier smoked because he wouldn't get on board. Playing rat was the only ace Xavier had in his hand. When he played the card, Slick Eddie's entire criminal empire crumbled. The last words out of Romello's mouth before he was arrested were that Xavier had better watch his back.

Rolling over, Xavier grabbed his phone and shut off the alarm. He had closed his eyes for a few seconds when his bedroom door opened.

Noah stuck his head in to say, "Xavier, it's time to get up. You know we have to start the day by praising God's holy name."

Xavier defiantly pulled the covers up over his head.

"Did you hear me, son?"

"Yeah. I'm good. Getting up right now."

"Also, you and I have to have a little talk about the expensive clothes you wear."

Xavier huffed. "What about my clothes?"

"You shouldn't put too much emphasis on material things. Besides, it's a distraction from your true calling, and that's worshiping God."

After the door closed, Xavier could hear Noah joyfully humming as he went to the next room to wake up Alfonso.

Noah said to Xavier from the hallway, "And don't forget to go and see your probation officer today."

Damn, he'd forgotten about the old, fat, bald white guy named Oliver Meyer. His office was in a smelly, semi-abandoned building six blocks from his high school. This would be the second time seeing his probation officer since getting into trouble last June. On the first visit, Oliver had seemed angry and irritable, and had warned Xavier to toe the line.

"Xavier, are you up yet?" His father's voice came from somewhere on the other side of the door.

This dude is so irritating, Xavier thought.

Xavier took the covers down and sat up on the side of his bed.

Dude was pure crazy if he thought that Xavier was giving up his designer wear because it interfered with worship. The old man had gone so far as to suggest shopping at Kmart for gear that would be less distracting. Xavier thought that his father had been playing when he made the suggestion. But it got real when the old man had pulled up to the parking lot of a Kmart a couple of days ago. He said as long as he was buying clothing for them they would wear what he purchased. Xavier and his dad immediately butted heads. There was no way Xavier was wearing the cheap stuff. He was a designer head and flossed only the best. His pops could kick rocks. The scheme to get Xavier into the cheap stuff was dead on arrival.

Xavier had stayed in the car while his father took poor Alfonso in and came out with shopping bags.

Noah might've been out of his mind at times with his faith, but Xavier had to give him credit. As soon as he'd gotten released, he'd hit the ground running. He managed to find a job and a half, and thanks to a good word from Billy, Noah was able to rent a bungalow from an Arab man, two blocks from the Dearborn city limits. A factory on the east side provided Noah with a full-time gig working days, while he delivered pizzas for a small pizza joint in the evenings. But that's where the respect stopped. The man had another thing coming if he thought that Xavier was coughing up the fancy gear he'd paid a pretty penny for last school year.

Xavier stood from his bed and stretched. He went out into the hall closet and grabbed the ironing board. A crispy pair of True Religion jeans, orange Nautica polo shirt, and white Air Force 1s, trimmed in orange, would be proper for the first day. He set up the board and plugged in the iron. As he put a killer crease in the jeans, Xavier peeked at the eight-by-ten picture of Samantha that sat in a nice frame on his dresser. Despite what they had gone through last semester, Xavier loved that girl. And he couldn't wait to see her in school.

*   *   *

After breakfast, Noah had asked if he could drop them off at school, but Xavier was adamant about doing things his way. Of course Noah could've pulled rank and taken them anyway. But he fell back, allowing Xavier the proper respect that the boy deserved. In Noah's absence, the reality was that Xavier had become the man of the house. There was no way that Noah was going to step on Xavier's toes. So he went to work and Xavier and Alfonso walked three blocks up to Alex Haley Middle School.

After watching Alfonso, wearing his Scarface back-pack, safely file into the school with the rest of the kids, Xavier stood at the bus stop across the street, where he waited for the bus that would take him directly to Coleman High.

The Warren Avenue bus pulled up and Xavier boarded. He took a seat in the rear of the partially filled bus.

He knew damn well that his name still held power, but Zulu wasn't going to have his back this semester like they had done the last. But Xavier still had a few cats willing to stick their necks out and go hard for him if need be, like some of the guys from the football team: Felix Hoover, the top dog of the Second Street gang, and of course Xavier's homeboy Dexter. Yeah, Xavier might've been wearing a leash around his neck in the form of probation, but chumps better step to him correctly. So far, he hadn't heard any gossip about people finding out that he had snitched on his former best friend Romello Anderson. But that didn't mean jack. Somebody had to know something.

When he arrived at school, Xavier was lucky when he went to pick up his course schedule. Just a few students stood in line in the main lobby, so it wasn't a long wait. Four tables were lined up, where three large, plainly dressed women distributed the course schedules for all of the students at Coleman High.

As he climbed the stairs to the third floor, Xavier stole a peek at his schedule: calculus first hour, followed by world history, lab biology next, with a fourth period lunch. English 10 was fifth period. Xavier didn't like phys ed, but it was sixth hour and he had a seventh-hour art appreciation class.

He was rather eager to start this new school year. Put all the craziness he'd been through behind him. A few girls passed him as he walked through the double doors on the third floor. The ladies coldly looked him off. He couldn't believe it. These were the same girls who used to be all up on him, super thirsty to be around him as he walked by them in the hallway last school year. Now they were looking at him as if he was a nobody. Xavier paid them no mind and headed straight to his locker.

If he'd had any questions about students being aware of him snitching on Romello, the answer had been scrawled out in bright red spray paint across the military-green door of his locker: Snitches Get Stitches! Xavier's reputation for being hotheaded was probably the only reason that students were not standing around gawking at his locker, like motorists slowing down to get a better look at a freeway accident. But regardless of how many students were walking by, stealing a glance at the warning in red while keeping it moving, none were foolish enough to be all up in his business—except for his homeboy Dexter.

"Not exactly a proper greeting for Coleman High's favorite son," Dexter stated, standing behind Xavier. It seemed that the boy was sporting a fresh look for the new semester—expensive vintage Cazal eyeglasses, some kind of loud, solid orange shirt, and a red bow tie. But the damn skinny jeans had to go. They hugged him so tight that he'd split his pants with any sudden movement. Oh yeah, his feet were covered by shiny brown penny loafers too.

When Xavier turned around he almost fell to the floor laughing. "Damn, homeboy, who dressed you this morning—Big Bird from *Sesame Street*?"

"Ha ha ha ha," said Dexter, removing his glasses and running a small cloth over the lenses. "Don't get jealous, my brother. I'll have you know that this is the new style this fall."

Xavier chuckled. "For who . . . Kanye West?" He couldn't do anything but shake his head. "Last school year you wanted to be a thug, so you dressed accordingly. I swear, this is ridiculous—I'ma start calling you Kanye Wrong."

Dexter put on his glasses and focused his attention back to the locker. "Enough about me, chuckles. Who the hell is your new fan club?"

"Some prankster looking to get a beat-down."

"Man, you've stepped on a lot of toes. Ain't no telling who's trying to send you a message, homeboy."

Xavier examined the many curious faces of boys and girls walking by.

"Let me get my hands on the fool with the spray can," Xavier said in growing anger. "I'm going to give him something to remember me by."

Dexter asked, "Who do you think did it—Dutch Westwood, Dylan Dallas and his Straight Eight goons?"

Xavier shook his head. "Don't know."

Dexter paused for a second before saying, "Or do you think Romello had anything to do with it?"

"Don't know. But it's gonna be a wrap for homeboy, whoever it is."

At that moment Xavier's sworn enemy Sally Peoples walked up with a sly grin. Xavier couldn't stand her after she tried to embarrass him in Ms. Gorman's English class last year. Surprisingly, Sally looked to have lost a few pounds over the summer break. The girl was wearing her signature bird-nest hairdo, blue jeans that fitted her righteously in all the areas where it counted, and a colorful Nike T-shirt that matched her sneakers.

"Wow, hero," she sarcastically said to Xavier. "I thought you were the *man* around here. Looks like I don't have to waste my precious time getting my brothers to beat you anymore." She gazed up at the locker. "Somebody is about to do it for me." The heifer walked away giggling.

When Dexter figured out that Xavier was gonna give the witch a pass, he put Sally on blast. "Miss us with that garbage, you sea lion–looking troll. I hope a mother eagle nests in your hairdo and raises babies."

Xavier laughed at Dex. " 'Mother eagle nests in your hair'?—I told you, something's wrong with you."

The truth was that Xavier had no time to waste with Sally. The girl hated him as bad as an alcoholic despised drinking water, but this wasn't her MO. She didn't have the heart for this type of job. This semester Xavier would have to grow eyes on the back of his head to ensure his survival. Looking at his locker, he burned with anger. Somebody had violated his space. But somehow he knew that this was only the beginning.

Xavier asked Dexter, "What hour do you have lunch?"

Dex went into his pocket and grabbed his schedule. His mischievous smile said it all. "Fourth hour."

"Cool, that's my lunch hour too. I'll holler at you then, homeboy."

Dex said, "I know you ain't fazed"—he nodded his head toward Xavier's locker—"by this nonsense."

"Man, I'ma have calculus problems this semester that'll come harder than the cowards who wrote this." Xavier rolled his shoulders. "But all the same, I gotta find a janitor to clean this crap up."

Throughout the school day Xavier had been noticing odd looks from other students. Whether he was in class or walking the halls, he would catch them staring at him like he was a marked man—or better yet, a straight-up rat. Last school year, swarms of his classmates used to be all up in his grill, like he was LeBron James signing autographs at a local mall. But the atmosphere around him had totally changed, like everybody already had him dead and buried. Xavier wasn't going out like that. *Whatever*, he thought.

It was weird for him to be all by himself at a corner table in the lunchroom, drinking a vanilla milkshake. Kids sitting at other tables were trying to be slick with low-key glances, but Xavier always managed to catch them staring. He simply shook his head. These were the fools that he had protected last year from bullies, thugs, thieves, and outsiders looking to get inside the school and prey on them.

So far he hadn't seen one Zulu member in the lunchroom, or anywhere around the school for that matter. Because he read more than just the required classroom reading, Xavier had a great deal of understanding about the enemy. *The Art of War* by Sun Tzu had taught him that just because one couldn't see the enemy, that didn't mean they weren't present. He wasn't tripping nor was he scared.

Students were everywhere in the cafeteria, looking fresh in their new school clothes, trying to impress each other with tough talk and even tougher attitudes. Xavier simply laughed. A bunch of phonies. Clowns. If somebody shouted "boo" loud enough, the majority of them would run so fast they'd leave their skeletons behind to get their flesh to safety.

It was strange how life had flipped the script on his boss-dog status, though. It seemed like only yesterday Xavier was walking around carrying absolute power and clocking mad dough, wads of cash stuffed in his pockets making his pants look like they had the mumps. He'd been able to buy all the finest clothes made by the hippest designers.

Samantha walked into the cafeteria through the east doors. She was simply gorgeous. If Beyoncé Knowles ever had a twin, Samantha Fox was her. She approached him, smelling all kinds of good. Her hair was down around her shoulders, and she was wearing a cute black figure-hugging top with *bebe* spelled out across the front in pink rhinestones. Her perfect booty was wrapped up in low-rise jeans from Lucky Brand, and she was wearing white Nikes trimmed in pink.

"You must really like what you see, Xavier," Samantha said with a bright smile. She leaned in to hug him, but Xavier surprised her by suddenly standing and holding her in a powerful yet tender embrace, planting a kiss on her lips.

When the two of them broke contact they found that they had an audience. Almost everybody in the cafeteria stopped to watch, like they were being entertained by the tender side of some drama-filled, high school reality-television show.

"Wow, babe! You must have really missed me, huh?"

Xavier's smile was as charming as ever. One of the things that had made Samantha fall hard for him.

They sat right next to each other at the table.

"You know I did. It's like I haven't seen you in years."

"Stop clowning. It hasn't even been a week."

"Year, month, week, day—hell, it's all too long when you're not near me, girl."

Samantha cracked up. "Was that supposed to be deep? You're a regular Shakespeare from the hood."

Xavier smiled. "You know I have the gift for gab—ain't no denying it. Your Romeo is in full effect."

Samantha smiled and looked away. "What am I going to do with you?"

"You can kiss me before I don't care about you no more."

The two kissed again.

Xavier asked, "Where're your two girls?"

"Who? Jennifer and Tracy?" Samantha smiled. "Both of them should be in class."

"Those are the only two friends I've seen you with, you knucklehead." Xavier looked deeply into her eyes. "Sam, I've been waiting what seemed like years to sniff your perfume and smooch on your big ol' ghetto booty."

Samantha laughed, blushing. "You know you have *pervert* written across your forehead, right?"

"Do I? Is there an exclamation mark at the end of the word?"

Samantha burst out laughing. "What will my daddy think of you feeling on my booty?"

"Go get big, bad Daddy Fox and I'll smooch on his too. With any luck his wallet will pop out and I can take some of that cash and go buy me a Rolex like he has."

"You're disgusting."

"I know. That's why you love me."

"You know I do."

"Will you hold me down—be there for a brotha?"

Samantha grinned. "You know I will, babe. I'll hold you down. Yes, I have your back."

"Will you tickle my feet, and feed me grapes while fanning me with a giant palm leaf?"

Samantha put her hands up to her mouth, trying not to scream out in laughter. "Seriously, what am I going to do with you, Xavier?" That's when she realized her mistake. Xavier's mind stayed in the gutter.

He cozied up next to her and kissed her on the jaw and mischievously wiggled his eyebrows. "Let's find a nice dark broom closet around here and—"

Samantha playfully smacked his face. "Behave."

"You're no fun."

Samantha smiled that pretty smile of hers. "We're not supposed to be having that kind of fun in a cafeteria full of folks. Anyway, do you have any classes with me this semester?"

"Does sex education count?"

"Xavier!"

"Nah, just playing." He removed a folded-up schedule from his pocket and handed it to her.

After Samantha finished unfolding it, she said, "Oo-ee, babe, you have Mrs. Gibson 'The Terrible' for calculus. I heard that lady doesn't have a human soul."

"But she does have a big, bushy, nappy-looking Afro, though—and a set of choppers that could compete with any beaver in a log-cutting contest."

Samantha shook her head. The boy was out of his mind, but she loved his crazy sense of humor and rapid-fire wit. Even though her father didn't approve, there was nothing Samantha would change about her nerdy rough-neck.

Samantha finished reading Xavier's class schedule. "The only period we share together, babe, is this one."

But Xavier was focused on a tall, husky, rough-looking,

charcoal-colored loser, sporting a low fade haircut, big ears, dark Rocawear hoodie, and jeans as he walked through the west doors and seemed to be searching for somebody. Tall and Husky surveyed the crowd of students in the lunch line and walked around, sitting at the tables, until he made eye contact with Xavier. Xavier's antennas went up and he switched into beast mode with the quickness. The boy was a predator and Xavier knew it. Game always recognized game. Tall and Husky continued to stare.

Samantha's babble about Xavier's gorgeous new English teacher, Serena Scott, sounded like it was faraway. Xavier was now focused on one thing: the threat that was intensely staring at him like he was taking measurements for Xavier's casket. Dudes had gotten past security at school before, so there was no way of knowing if Tall and Husky was packing heat. But Xavier was sure about one thing— homeboy was here for him, and he knew it.

The punk walked through the crowd of students, never letting his cold gaze drift too far from Xavier's matching stare. The Grim Reaper was in the house. This moment had Slick Eddie or Romello written all over it. Xavier had never seen this guy before. Dude didn't look like a student but a grown man. If homeboy pulled his tool and started letting off, Samantha and a lot of students would be caught up in the crossfire.

Why can't I have one peaceful moment with the girl of my dreams? Xavier thought. He kept his eyes on Tall and Husky. Why did it always come to this? He recognized that every time he and Samantha had gotten together, his demons always surfaced, putting Samantha in harm's way.

"Hello, are you in there, Xavier?" Samantha asked, playfully rapping on the side of his head.

Xavier was irritated when he turned back to Samantha. "Sam, cut it out!"

He had broken a cardinal rule of never taking his eyes off the enemy. He looked back in the sucka's direction but he wasn't there—it was like he had vanished into thin air.

Samantha snapped, "What rude bug has crawled up in you?"

He collected his breath and let out a much-needed sigh of relief. "I'm sorry, Sam. I just have a lot of things to deal with."

"Like somebody spray painting 'snitches get stitches' on your hall locker."

Xavier ran a hand down his face in frustration. "Boy, I swear there's some big-mouth folks up in this piece. Sam, can we not talk about that now and—"

He was cut off by Brenda Sanders stomping up to his table with an attitude.

"Xavier, me and you need to talk," she said, rolling her neck in Samantha's direction. Brenda was wearing what looked to be a weave ponytail, an oversize sweatshirt and jeans, and some type of cheap-looking leather shoes.

Samantha was the first to put her in check. "We would appreciate it if you could have a little more class in approaching us."

Brenda threw up the "talk to the hand" gesture at Samantha, popped her lips sarcastically and rolled her neck dismissively. "Whatever." She looked at Xavier.

"Anyway, Xavier, we need to talk about our baby." She pulled her sweater tight, to show off her swollen belly.

Samantha was stunned, like she'd been hit by a semi. She'd heard the girl right the first time, but disbelief made her ask, "Did you say *baby*?"

Xavier jumped up defensively. "Sam, don't listen to this little hood rat! She already got one baby and don't know who the daddy is." He said to Brenda, "You better go find one of those suckas you've been hanging out with and quit playing with me."

"So what if I have one baby. What does that have to do with you?"

"That makes you a hood rat. You better go find both of your baby daddies and leave me the hell alone."

"So now I'm easy and a hood rat? You wasn't saying that when you was with me seven months ago," Brenda shouted, stepping to Xavier and pointing in his face. "You 'member that time on my couch?"

Xavier didn't want to but he was forced to grab her finger and push it away. The look on his face said he meant business.

Aggression was in his words when Xavier checked her. "Don't forget who you're talking to, Brenda. You don't have my baby in your belly—don't care what you say! Now get your little rat behind away from me!"

Heeding the anger in Xavier's words and eyes, Brenda began backing up, still talking junk. "You ain't gonna dog me out like I'm some jump-off, Xavier. You will take care of me and mine—because don't forget: Snitches get stitches."

Now Xavier was really fuming. He clenched his jaw and said in a low, menacing voice, "You have anything to do with writing that on my locker?"

At Xavier's sinister tone, Brenda quickly said, "No."

Xavier could be a bastard when he wanted to, a real hard case to deal with, and Brenda didn't want any part of him when he was like that. She walked away but yelled over her shoulder, "You haven't heard the last of me!"

Xavier wiped the saliva from his mouth and was trying to get his anger under control. He couldn't care less about the audience that had gathered around him to witness his fiery exchange with what could potentially be his baby mama. Yeah, he remembered smashing Brenda seven months ago. Right after things went horribly wrong at that Italian restaurant where over dinner Samantha had gotten the bright idea to blend their families. Samantha had sided with her parents and broke it off with Xavier that night. The madness had him stressed out and he needed a way to deal with the drama, so after leaving the restaurant, he'd hailed a cab and gone to visit Brenda Sanders. The same chick who was now claiming to have his bun in her oven.

The lunchroom was buzzing like a beehive with chatter about the drama unfolding. Xavier didn't have to wait long. Samantha put a hand on his shoulder and spun him around.

With tears in her eyes, she folded her arms and demanded, "You have five minutes to explain to me what the hell she was talking about, Xavier Hunter."

Oh no she didn't call me by my government name,

Xavier thought. He prided himself on truthfulness. Xavier might've been a lot of things but he was no liar.

So with a straight face he told the truth. "I'm not saying that this was a good excuse to do what I did, but you put a lot of pressure on me that night at the Italian restaurant and I cracked."

Tears fell down Samantha's face, but somehow she remained calm. "This is a good one—textbook. My boyfriend is having a baby by a hood rat and he's standing in my face blaming me."

"The night you put that dinner together, you knew our families didn't like each other. I told you then it was a bad idea. But you just had to do things your way, which almost led to our folks fighting one another. Yeah, I left the restaurant that evening angry and went over to Brenda's."

"Did you sleep with her?"

Xavier bit his bottom lip and swallowed hard. "Yes, I did, but the baby ain't mine. I swear the rat has been sleeping around."

"Stop. Do you know how stupid you sound?"

Samantha couldn't listen anymore. Xavier was surprised when she pushed him out of the way and tried to walk off. He grabbed her by the shoulder and Samantha slapped away Xavier's hand.

She turned around. "Get your damn hand off me, Xavier!"

He tried to plead his case. "Samantha, it was a mistake but—"

She clapped her hands in his face, sarcastically applauding him. "I commend you for telling the truth,

Xavier. Just when I thought you couldn't stoop any lower. Let me tell you what a mistake is: It's when you go to the store to buy a certain brand of bread and you come back with another. It's when you are taking a test and you know the answer to a certain question but write the wrong answer down instead. Those are mistakes. So you're telling me that anger was the responsible party for you betraying me and sleeping with the hood rat? That's what led to this 'mistake'?"

Xavier couldn't say anything. Hell, if the roles had been reversed, and it was her trying to talk her way out of it, he wouldn't believe Samantha. He would tally it up as a weak lie and then tell her to go kick rocks wearing open-toed sandals.

Like someone who'd been caught up in a lie, Xavier tried to flip the script.

"I'm under a lot of pressure right now and I don't need anybody up in my face talking a whole lot of ying-yang, you feel me?" Xavier said. "And another thing—"

Smack! Samantha's open hand hit Xavier's jaw. She slapped him so hard, she tried to slap the slobber from his mouth. The sound from her smack carried across the lunchroom and oohs and aahs could be heard throughout.

Samantha was crying and Xavier just stood there with a blank expression on his face, holding his jaw. He hadn't seen that one coming. And judging from the stunned looks on the faces around them, they hadn't seen it coming either.

Doug, head of security, had just so happened to be walking into the cafeteria at the precise time of the incident. He didn't waste any time.

He asked Samantha, "Are you all right?"

Even though the tears were flowing freely, Samantha managed to reply, "Yes. I just need to get out of here."

The voices of the crowd seemed to spring to life, gossiping about the drama that had just gone down.

Doug turned to the students, and with a booming voice he said, "Quiet down—right now!"

Doug might've had a friendly nature but could be a beast if provoked. He had a smooth brown complexion, an aggressively receding hairline, stood six-foot-three, and weighed in at a whopping 270 pounds.

Doug removed a small block of sticky-note hall passes and a pen from his right pants pocket. He scribbled something and gave it to Samantha. "Take this hall pass and go to the lavatory to get yourself together." He waited until Samantha was out of earshot before he turned his attention to Xavier. "Mr. Hunter, what was that about?"

Xavier took his seat, inhaling and exhaling out of pure frustration. "Nothing that I can't handle."

"From here it doesn't look like you're handling jack. You want to tell me the real problem, or should we discuss who you think wrote 'snitches get stitches' on your locker?"

"Since you're so informed about current affairs in the school, why don't you tell me who wrote it?"

"This is happening because of last semester, when I told you to leave my job to me. But you had to get in bed with that scumbag Slick Eddie, Romello, and those Zulu dirtbags to try and get rid of the thugs in the school."

"Excuse me, Mr. Head Of Security—no disrespect, but

you knew what would happen when you put my back up against the wall and I had nowhere else to go. You came with the game after Coleman High's precious little golden-boy quarterback overdosed on Ecstasy pills. It was your cop buddies who came with the pressure."

Doug sat in the same seat Samantha had abandoned. "So this is my fault? That's where you're going with this?"

Too many things at one time were knocking Xavier upside the head. He stared at the students sitting at the table on his right. They seemed happy. Probably had lives without the type of drama that simply loved hanging around him like a dark cloud hovering over his head. He would trade places with them in a heartbeat.

Doug asked, "Do you remember me telling you about folks taking the law into their own hands? Your intentions to make the school safe for your fellow students might have been all good, but you went about it the wrong way. You joined Zulu, not me. So from where I'm sitting, you put your own back up against the wall on that one. Yeah, you did what you felt had to be done. Besides, the judge kept to his word and didn't charge you with anything but theft, for the car you stole from the parking lot the night of the last school dance."

"I thought they were supposed to get rid of that charge too. I ended up on probation."

"It could've been worse. Especially after Romello and a number of others tried to testify that you were the head of their car-theft ring."

In his heart, Xavier knew Doug was right.

"I saw your old man at the grocery store a couple weeks back. We didn't get a chance to talk much. Exchanged phone numbers, but with my schedule I haven't had the time to call him. It's good to have him home, though."

Xavier asked Doug with a straight face. "I need a really big favor."

"I'm afraid I have to hear it out before I can say anything."

"At the end of my sophomore year, my mother went to jail. The state gave temporary custody of me and my brother to a friend of the family named Billy Hawkins. Once my father was released we went to stay with him."

"And your favor?"

"If I get into any trouble, please call Billy. My father is a lot different than you remember him. Please call Billy." Xavier scribbled down the number on a napkin and handed it to Doug.

"I can get into trouble if Billy isn't your emergency contact person."

"I understand, but please contact him if anything happens to me."

"Look, Mr. Hunter, I don't think it's safe for you to go to school here any longer. Why don't you talk to your father and ask him if it would be all right for you to change schools?"

Xavier didn't have to think about it. "You know I don't get down like that, you feel me? I ain't running away from these clowns."

Doug merely shook his head. "It's not about you being a coward, Mr. Hunter. We're talking about your life—it's being threatened. And I'm afraid if you stay here—"

"Let me stop you right there. I'm not bowing down like that. I'm no punk."

"And that's going to look real good on your tombstone: 'Here lies Xavier Hunter—he died but he ain't no punk.' "

Xavier dismissively waved his hand at Doug. "Man, miss me with all that crap."

"I asked some of my police friends to come up and sit around the building in marked units when their schedules permit. A few of them told me that they could even walk through the hallways from time to time, just to show police presence."

Dexter walked into the cafeteria with a startled look on his face. It was like the boy was in a trance as he made his way through the crowded lunchroom.

He went straight to Xavier's table and sat down, still looking dazed and confused.

Doug and Xavier both sat patiently, waiting on him to thaw out and speak his mind.

The statement that came out of his mouth was chilling. "Felix Hoover, the big dog of the Second Street Gang, was just murdered."

The three of them could do nothing but stare at each other in shock.

2

In fifth period English class, Xavier was trying desperately to focus on the teacher's lecture, but the news of Hoover's death had sent shockwaves rippling across the school. The circumstances surrounding his brutal murder were still a mystery; the initial report said that he was a victim of a drive-by shooting. Xavier knew of only one crew who got down flexing that kind of muscle—it had to be his old gang, Zulu. But why Felix? Second Street wasn't beefing with Zulu. Felix and his thugs might've pitched in with the football squad to back Xavier in the parking lot that day when Dutch Westwood, Dylan Dallas, and goons from Straight Eight were trying to jump him. But that was it. Felix never had anything going with Zulu.

This thing didn't make any sense. Why Felix? And then there was ol' Tall and Husky in the lunchroom yesterday, the dude with the charcoal skin and big ears, wearing the Rocawear hoodie. Where did he fit into the equation? Was Felix's death connected to him? Xavier didn't get a chance to finish his thought.

"Mr. Hunter," the teacher called. "Can you repeat anything I've just explained?"

"Umm, uh, umm," was all Xavier could utter because he'd been caught red-handed.

"Your tenth-grade teacher Ms. Gorman thinks highly of you, Mr. Hunter. Stands to reason you have to pay attention in my classroom, young man."

Ms. Serena Scott was a brown-sugar Tyra Banks type, with long, curly black hair. Xavier's new English teacher possessed many of the supermodel's voluptuous attributes too. And the lady could dress. Xavier knew expensive clothing when he saw it. Samantha had taught him a few tricks about how to distinguish certain designer giants. The type of print on the teacher's gold and black dress just screamed out the designer's name—Gucci. Her shoes were out cold. Had to be from the same designer because where the gold and black pattern on the dress left off, it picked right back up on the shoes. Her shiny stainless steel and gold bracelet and the black-faced Rolex on her slim wrist solidified the fact that the sista had to have that cake.

Ms. Scott asked her class, "Have any of you read Mark Twain's book, *The Adventures of Huckleberry Finn*?"

A brown-skinned boy who looked like Floyd "Money" Mayweather was the first to raise his hand.

Ms. Scott called on him.

The boy answered, "Huckleberry Finn? Ms. Scott, that sounds like what my drunk uncle had when he staggered up the house steps last night and passed out on the front porch."

The students roared with laughter.

Ms. Scott was quick on her feet. "Another outburst like that will find you in front of Principal Skinner."

Some students laughed but every one of them got the point. This was not a classroom for monkey business.

The student backed down. "Nah, I'll sit back here and chill out. I don't want any parts of old man Skinner."

Xavier raised his hand.

"Yes, Xavier," Ms. Scott said delightedly.

"I haven't read the book, but I know some folks are angry because of the author's use of the N-word throughout the book," Xavier explained.

Heather Larkin sat at the desk behind Xavier. Where Samantha was a certified, sophisticated dime piece, from her body to her elegant clothing and expensive accessories, Heather was the complete opposite. Her clothing looked dusty, more secondhand. She was mixed race and had straight black hair that was pulled back into a ponytail. Both girls were similar in body structure, except Heather had more booty than Samantha. And she wore glasses.

"That's right, Xavier," Ms. Scott praised.

Heather wasn't afraid to speak out of turn. "I see who's bucking for teacher's pet."

Xavier was quick with a comeback. "Those who see 'em must be 'em."

Some chick with closely cropped hair, sitting in the last chair of the last row next to the window said, "Xavier, what the heck did you just say?" She looked from Ms. Scott back to Xavier. "That sounded like some kind of fertility voodoo mess. Ms. Scott, Xavier over there is gonna mess around and get everybody in this room pregnant."

Ms. Scott's earlier threat to send the brown-skin dude packing was still fresh in everybody's mind, so only a handful of students dared to laugh.

Ms. Scott stood in front of the room with the chalkboard at her back, arms folded, intrigued, like she wanted to see where this discussion was headed.

Heather pushed her bifocals up to the bridge of her nose. "If these same so-called black people are having a hard time with the N-word usage in that book, then why did their dollars help make Jamie Foxx's film *Django Unchained* a top grossing movie? People use it all the time, ni—"

She was cut off by Ms. Scott. She slowly approached Heather, stopping and standing over her desk. "Are we going to have a problem? You are never to use that word in my classroom. Do you understand me?"

Heather's facial expression showed a trace of aggression. It was her eyes, though. The intensity in them was cold and threatening. She stared up at Ms. Scott for a few seconds and then whatever anger she might've been feeling abated. Her smile returned.

"You're right, Ms. Scott," Heather relented. "The word is ugly and it shouldn't be used. I apologize if I offended anyone."

The whole scene had played out right behind Xavier.

The boy didn't know what to make of it. But Heather was a very interesting character. She seemed to like living on the edge. Xavier didn't know what it was, but he was attracted—strangely attracted to the anger inside of her passion. This was going to be a very interesting school year—providing he could finish it without getting himself into more trouble.

Xavier was headed to his sixth-hour gym period.

The entire school was still buzzing about the Felix Hoover murder. The brutal killing of the former leader of the Second Street gang had warranted extensive local news coverage. Xavier was sick of seeing footage of the crime scene and hearing crazy rumors and stories.

He entered the locker room, thoughts of Samantha and Brenda heavy on his mind. How could this crap have happened to him—and on the second day of school too? The thought of losing Samantha was horrifying to him. But the fact that Brenda might have his child in her belly scared the living daylights out of him.

When the other boys in the locker room saw Xavier they immediately stopped chatting with each other and hurried up to finish getting dressed. It was funny to Xavier to see dudes getting the hell out, some damn near half-dressed and tripping over untied shoestrings. One punk's gym shorts fell around his ankles but homeboy was still trying to break out. Xavier couldn't really blame them. He would probably be doing the same thing if a dude came around him who he knew had pissed people off and now was a target for revenge.

Rounding a set of lockers, Xavier understood clearly

why the other students were moving like they had heard somebody yell "Free money!" upstairs in the gym. Unlike yesterday when he'd been angry upon seeing the threat spray-painted on his hall locker, this time he was furious. "Snitches Get Stitches" was spray-painted on his gym locker in the same red paint.

Xavier kicked and punched the locker so hard that the punishing blows sounded like cannons going off. He cursed, kicked, and punched until the rage faded from his mind.

Breathing heavily, he dropped and allowed himself to sit on one of many pine-top benches in the locker room. It wasn't gonna be funny, nor pretty, when he caught up to the clown who was trying his best to not let Xavier's fellow students forget about him ratting out Romello and the Zulus. But when he did, he would send a powerful message of his own.

Xavier was seriously tripping, wanting to go upstairs to the gym and force a confession out of someone, when he felt somebody staring at him. Some geeky-looking kid. Standing, peeping out from behind a set of lockers off the main aisleway. Staring through the thick, aquarium-glass-like lenses in the black frames on his face.

"Can I help you?" Xavier asked in a forceful tone. He halfway expected the guy to turn around and bolt.

But the boy stepped into plain view. Dude was dark, short, had a high-top fade, and wore jeans and a butterfly-collar shirt. He wore the kind of cheap sneakers that Xavier had seen guys throw water on the soles just so they'd grip the gym floor.

"Yo," Xavier said to the boy. "You're not some crazy, geeky kid, right?"

The dude looked like he was about to cry over Xavier's comment.

Xavier apologized. "Man, I didn't mean it. Straight up, my bad. It's been rough the last couple of days."

Nerd Boy finally broke his silence, pointing to the spray paint. "Is that your locker?"

Xavier looked at the locker, smiled, and nodded his head. "Yeah. It's mine."

The dude said, "You know"—he looked around the locker room—"this really isn't how I pictured my freshman year. The kids pick on me." He nodded in the direction of Xavier's locker. "They don't refer to me as a snitch, but they call me all types of names. Since I've been here I've been locked inside of lockers, had my face flushed inside a toilet bowl, I've had my glasses hidden from me, and I have almost completely forgotten my mother's real name because of all of the horrible ones she's been called."

Damn. And here Xavier was thinking that he had it bad. His heart went out to the kid. He could feel shortie's pain.

Xavier said, "Sit down. What's your name?"

Nerd Boy tentatively sat down on the bench, with a nice size gap between them, and removed his backpack. "Simon. Simon Templeton."

Figures, Xavier thought.

"Well, Simon, my name is Xavier Hunter."

The young man's face brightened up like he had just

stumbled upon the cure for his sad condition of being chronically bullied.

"You're Xavier?!" Simon enthusiastically asked, like Xavier was some kind of rock star.

"The one and only," Xavier joked, trying to lighten the mood. "Judging by that look on your face, I'd say you've heard of my many heroic exploits, battles, schoolyard scuffles—don't like to brag about myself."

Simon had that look like he wanted to say something but didn't want to get beat up after saying it.

Xavier noticed the kid's struggle. "Go ahead. Speak your mind, homeboy. I can take it."

"Heard that you used to be the man, but now everybody's calling you a snitch."

Judging by the way sneaker soles were squeaking at a frantic pace across the gym floor above them, it was safe to say that gym class had started and the boys were on one side running hoops while the girls were on the other, probably playing volleyball. Xavier wasn't sweating being tardy because he was owed a favor by his gym teacher, Ms. Porter. During Girl Scout cookie season, Xavier had scored the gym teacher a few boxes of thin mints.

He didn't see fit to answer Simon. Instead, he said, "Listen, Simon, don't let anybody bully you. Use your head and fight back."

Simon's face held the look of defeat. The freshman was about to answer before he was cruelly interrupted.

"There's my little Simon Templeton," said some almond-toned dude with extremely nappy locks. The brother was about average height but he had a thick build. Not the body one would get from going hard in the weight room but the frame created by clocking mad hours getting his grub on in the dining section at a local burger joint.

Nappy Locks ignored Xavier and said to Simon, "You know your pockets pay for my lunch. Didn't see you in the lunchroom and I had to go hungry. Little busta, you know how I hate to go hungry. So now you owe me about a month's worth of lunches."

Nappy Locks looked to be a fresh face around Coleman. Xavier had never seen him around. He knew all of his fellow students by name or face. He sat there simply amused. He couldn't believe his eyes. His new friend Simon was being bullied right in front of him.

The bully said, "And if you miss buying my lunch again"—he shoved a fist into Simon's grill—"you're going to get a taste of it."

How corny, Xavier thought, continuing to smile at Nappy Locks's antics.

Simon looked like he was about to cry. He was trembling in fear. "I'm sorry. It'll never happen—"

The bully said coldly, "Zip it." Nappy Locks looked at Xavier like he was a punk. Then he said to Simon, "Can't nobody help you. You're my own personal ATM"—the jerk balled his fist up again and shoved it into Simon's nose—"and this is the pin number."

Xavier had had enough. "Hey. What did you say your name was?"

The guy turned on Xavier. "You don't need to know my name, fam. I don't know you, so just keep it like that. Just sit there and shut up until I get through handling my business. I'll get to you in a second."

"Homeboy," Xavier said, not even bothering to rise

from his seated position, "I hate bullies. Even worse, I hate a bully with nappy dreadlocks who's too broke to get 'em done."

"Is that right?"

Xavier continued, "Because if you knew me, you'd know better than try to jack poor Simon right in front of me."

Nappy Locks raised his arms up like he wanted to do something. "So what you wanna do, huh?" The spray paint on Xavier's locker must've triggered something inside of his head. He turned his body fully in Xavier's direction, taking steps toward him on the sly. "Snap. I know you—you're the one everybody's calling a snitch around Coleman . . ."

Xavier's blood pressure was through the roof right now, but amazingly, he kept himself composed.

"Heard you ratted on your boy," Nappy Locks said, pointing, trying his best to inch closer.

Xavier wasn't born yesterday. He knew the punk's game plan. Dude was trying to get close enough so that he could start swinging. Xavier just sat there, a sinister smile on his face, allowing the bully to come within striking distance.

The bully said, still inching forward, "You know what—I'm about to show you what I do—"

That was about as far as he got before Xavier unleashed a serious right jab to the bully's stomach.

Dude's eyes swelled to the size of dinner plates; his breath escaped his mouth sounding like a balloon suddenly deflating. Xavier popped up from the bench and drove the knuckles on his right hand into his opponent's lips.

Blood spurted.

The bully was dazed and out on his feet.

Simon was still trembling, but there was a little smile of satisfaction on his grill.

Once Xavier felt he had the bully restrained, he laughed, breathing heavily. "Look at you." He took a breath. "What's your name, homeboy?"

"R-R-Rudy," the boy said, struggling, gasping for air.

Simon stepped in and said, "Rudolph. His name is Rudolph Jamerson."

This crap couldn't get any better. Here was one punk with a nerdy name trying to lay the strong-arm game down on a geek who had an even nerdier name. It just couldn't get more comical than this.

Xavier looked over his left shoulder. "Simon, come here."

Simon was shy at first until Xavier yelled at him to come now.

Xavier ordered Simon, "Make a fist."

Simon timidly balled up his fist.

"Homeboy, I'm gonna need you to ball that fist up tight."

Simon did as he was told.

Rudy struggled, asking Xavier, "What you gonna do?"

Xavier looked at Simon. "With that fist, punch this piece of crap in the face."

Simon pleadingly looked at Xavier, because Lord knew he didn't want to punch Rudy. But he had no other choice. He'd rather do as he was told than go against Xavier. So he lined up his fists and swung—connecting.

"Ouch, man!" Rudy yelled out, as if trying to sell the pain of the wimpy blow.

The weak shot drew laughter from Xavier. "Shut up, punk. You know that didn't hurt."

It was the funniest thing to see. Xavier looked like a mother eagle, trying to teach one of her chicks to fly by dropping it out of the nest. But this wasn't a nest. It was Coleman High. One of the rowdiest schools inside the Detroit city limits, a place where you stood up for your rights or surrendered your manhood.

Xavier looked at Simon. "Okay, homeboy, stand back." He turned back to Rudy. "By the way, cuz, my name is Xavier Hunter."

Rudy pleaded, "Xavier, man, I'm sorry. I'll never say anything to Simon again."

Xavier's smile was sinister. "You damn right."

Xavier then pulled Simon aside. "Simon, I need you to go and get Doug and tell him this guy tried to attack you. Tell him the truth. And next time something like this happens, get Doug—he's gonna be the one who can really help you. Aight?"

After school Xavier walked six blocks to the parking lot of a shabby-looking two-story office building named The Hilltop. He hated the place. The hallways were dim, the carpets smelled musty, and three-quarters of the offices were vacant. But for the next year he would have to come here and check in every three months with his probation officer. He was supposed to go yesterday but because of all the drama that went down with Samantha, he was here today instead.

Xavier took one of the shadowy stairwells up to the second floor, with Samantha heavy on his mind. He couldn't believe the situation he'd gotten himself into. And on top of potentially losing the best thing that ever happened to him, there was a small possibility that he might be a baby daddy. To say nothing about the fire and brimstone sermon he'd surely get from his holier-than-thou old man. If Brenda was telling the truth about the baby, Noah would be the last person Xavier told. This was definitely not the life that a student with a 4.0 GPA was supposed to be living.

His probation officer, Oliver Meyer, was a fat slob, wearing a striped button-down shirt with the sleeves pulled up over his hairy forearms. He sat his heavy, hairy body behind the small desk in his cluttered, cramped office. Xavier didn't think the mountain of a man had legs, this being the second time he'd been there and had yet to see homeboy walk around the desk.

Xavier took a seat on a wobbly wooden chair in front of Oliver's desk.

The man was buried behind a stack of paperwork. Oliver didn't even look up when he asked in a dry, impersonal tone, "Name?"

"Xavier Hunter."

"Are you selling or doing drugs?"

"No."

"Any weapons on you?"

"No."

"Have you taken part in any crime within the last twenty-four hours?"

"No."

"I have the right to test you for any substance abuse and if you're in violation, you have violated probation and therefore will be forced to serve out the remainder of your sentence in a juvenile detention center. Do you understand these things?"

"Yes, sir."

"Your next appointment with me is"— the man peered at a calendar on his desk without looking up—"November twenty-fifth. Failure to appear constitutes a violation and you would be forced to serve out the remainder of your sentence in a juvenile detention center. Do you understand these things?"

"Yes, sir."

"Have a good day, Mr. Hunter."

Xavier got up from the chair and left.

3

_____

Xavier had caught the bus over to his friend and mentor's crib. Billy Hawkins was ailing from a bad cold and Xavier rolled through to show the old dog some love.

As usual, Billy's front door was unlocked. Xavier entered, carrying in a recyclable grocery bag. Billy was in the living room laid out on his old mangy sofa underneath a blanket. A humidifier hummed softly on a badly worn coffee table while Billy watched an ancient black-and-white movie on a twenty-seven-inch flat screen television perched atop an old, busted prehistoric floor model color television.

"Got you some chicken noodle soup, old guy," Xavier teased.

"Thank you, young'un," said Billy.

Xavier took the bag into the kitchen and then walked back to the front door and locked it. He stood in front of the television to playfully block Billy's view of the movie.

"Get your LL Cool J–looking behind from up front of the TV, you young punk," snapped Billy, sounding like his nasal passages were completely blocked.

"Geesh, you look and sound terrible," acknowledged Xavier.

Billy didn't deny it. He did look miserable. There was a small piece of tissue paper sticking out of his left nostril and his eyes were watery, red, and swollen. The bags underneath them were huge. Billy's sinuses were so plugged up that he sounded like he was talking through his nose.

"I told you don't be playing with me when there is a good World War Two movie on." He coughed violently.

Xavier laughed off the threat. "Uh-huh, that's what you get. What I tell you about leaving the door unlocked in this neighborhood? You're going senile or sump'n, geezer?"

"Look who's talking. The way you sound, one would think that you've lived a pampered, privileged life, youngster. Don't forget that your little raggedly self lived next door on my property almost a year ago—now you dissin' the neighborhood."

"*Dissing*?" Xavier said, making fun of Billy's efforts to be hip. "You better stop getting slang words from watching Bow Wow and that nice-looking, breezy Keshia Chanté on BET's *106 & Park*."

"Whatever, you little trouser worm. All I know is that any nappy-headed boy walks up in here on me"—Billy reached underneath the sofa cushions and removed a Rambo blade—"Obama health care ain't gonna be able to help 'im." He sneezed violently, blowing the small piece of tissue paper out of his nostril and onto his lap.

Xavier handed him the box of Kleenex that sat by the humidifier. "That's nasty. You're a nasty old man."

Billy jokingly pretended to run the blade over his throat from ear to ear. "This old man is gonna gut you, you little punk, if you don't move your stump from in front of the television, youngster."

Xavier cautiously took a seat on the beat-up armchair next to the sofa that looked like Billy had gone Dumpster-diving for it. "Old man, if I get bedbugs on my clothes I'm burning this dump to the ground."

Billy laughed and blew his nose. "So, you finally came by to visit the old war veteran?"

Xavier didn't say anything. Just had an odd look on his face.

Billy read him like a book. "All right, youngster, out with it."

Xavier exhaled to relieve the ceiling of stress that felt like it was due to come down on his head at any moment. "This girl named Brenda Sanders is claiming to be pregnant by me."

"What happened? The condom break?"

Xavier dropped his head.

Billy said, "You little irresponsible twit. Do you know if it's yours?"

"The chick has a little bit of a reputation. She's had a few partners."

Billy couldn't do anything but laugh.

Xavier was offended. "Have you lost your mind, team geezer? This junk ain't funny."

Billy's laughter melted into just a smile. "Not laughing at you, youngster. The old man has gotten into some trouble himself. You know that little young gal that I let you speak to over the phone eight months ago?"

Xavier nodded his head.

"Well, she's pregnant and she's due to pop in a couple of months. Ain't no denying the baby because it's mine."

"You're so old, do I still congratulate you?"

Billy didn't even crack a smile at Xavier's joke. He looked worried. Xavier had come over here to talk over his problems, but instead, it looked like he would be trying to talk Billy off the ledge.

Billy said, "I don't know how I feel about it either. Hell, I'm in my mid-sixties. When the rug rat turns seventeen, somebody will be pushing around this Depend-wearing, shriveled-up, drooling, dried-up vegetable of a Vietnam vet in a wheelchair at the child's high school graduation."

Xavier had a stunned look on his face. "Okay. You've managed to seriously depress me now."

"Youngster, I'm not trying to depress you. What I'm trying to say is that we have to deal with the consequences of our actions. If the baby is yours then you have to step up and take care of it. I know that's not what you want to hear, but in this life the same experience that teaches us is costly. Unfortunately for me and you, the cost of not wearing protection—well, for you is an unwanted teen pregnancy. Me, I'm too old and set in my ways to be having babies—"

"Don't forget a senile old combat goat."

Billy laughed until he launched into a barrage of wet coughs. He cleared his throat and asked, "Have you told your father and Samantha yet?"

Xavier lowered his head as if he were giving last rites to the idea of telling his Bible-thumping father. "Samantha was there in the lunchroom when the chick stormed up to us and started kicking the claim."

Billy adjusted the blanket around his neck and had that look on his face like he was waiting to be entertained by some intense drama. "What happened?"

Xavier quickly placed a hand on his jaw where Samantha had smacked him. "That junk still stings."

Billy almost hocked up mucus, he was laughing so hard.

"After I told Brenda to beat it, I tried explaining myself, but Sam hauled off. She hit me so hard, the girl almost knocked my shoes off."

Billy had a tissue up to his mouth, cracking up.

"Been texting and calling the girl since it happened. No response."

"Well, that's one of those consequences I was telling you about. But how did Noah take it?"

Xavier let his gaze drift to the television screen. The on-screen war was heating up. German bodies were being blown to smithereens by grenades that had just been tossed, compliments of the US troops.

Billy read Xavier's face right away. "Wait a minute. You did tell your father, right?"

Xavier looked down at his hands in his lap. "The old

dude is different since he came back home from prison. I mean, I was a shortie when he went in, but I remember enough to know what he was like before he left."

"What do you mean by 'acting different'?"

"Praying before sunrise *different*, quoting Bible scriptures like there is nothing else to talk about *different*, and now telling us that we have to go to church at least two Sundays a month—that kind of *different*."

Billy looked confused. "Youngster, you been holding out. When did all of this start?"

"Gradually."

Billy rubbed the whiskers on his chin, like he was about to go deep with wisdom. "Your dad means well. You told me that he used to be heavily involved in the trafficking of narcotics. He was 'the man,' as you put it. There's nothing wrong with a man going to prison and finding God. It shows that he's been doing something constructive with his time while paying his debt to society. Yes, I'll admit that some of those jailhouse preachers can be a little fanatical, but it's better—way better—than what you had before. No disrespect to your mother, but Ne Ne wasn't right in the head. She didn't do right by you and Alfonso. But your dad is, along with trying to make up for all the bad choices in his life that took him away from his sons. So all I'm saying, youngster, is to be patient with him."

Xavier felt like he had gotten a lot off of his chest. And as usual his friend and mentor, Billy Hawkins, had provided the outlet. He just wished he could open up and talk about the growing danger he'd been experiencing at school. But it would lead Xavier to having to explain the whole story to Billy. The entire Zulu story. And that wasn't gonna happen.

Billy asked, "So what are you gonna do about this baby?"

Xavier pursed his lips and furled his brow. "Wait till it gets here. And then have a paternity test done."

"You're not gonna be on the *Maury* show, are you?" Billy laughed.

"Jokes. And your old butt will be right beside me with your baby-mama drama."

"Serious though. Make sure you find that out before you start taking care of it. How far along is she?"

"Told me seven months."

"I suggest you call that girl right now and make sure you tell her your plans about getting the test done."

Xavier had a silly look on his face. "You mean *now*, as of this moment, right *now*?"

"No time like the present."

Xavier removed his cell phone from his pocket and found Brenda's number on his list of contacts. He pushed Call and got an instant busy signal.

"Oops. Uh-oh," Xavier said, looking goofy.

Billy asked, "What do you mean, 'oops uh-oh'?"

"Uh-oh like Metro PCS has cut off my service because I couldn't pay the bill uh-oh."

"I swear, you youngsters and your cell phones. It's called getting a job and being responsible."

Billy held on to the blanket as he stood up and wrapped it around his torso. He walked in the direction of the staircase to the upstairs bedrooms.

Xavier wasn't going to trip. The baby couldn't be his.

His mind shifted to Samantha. The look on her face when she stormed out of the lunchroom. He'd let her down one too many times. And if he ever got another opportunity, Xavier would make it right by her. He promised.

The old man coughed harshly from upstairs somewhere. Xavier could hear him moving around up there, like he was going from room to room searching for something.

Xavier still couldn't believe that Felix Hoover had been taken out. No arrest had been made. No leads. No witnesses. Xavier heard Billy walking down the stairs. He was sniffling as he walked back into the front room with the blanket over his shoulders cascading down his back and hitting the floor like it was a royal robe belonging to a king. The old dude walked over to Xavier and handed him a white business envelope.

Billy turned his back and walked back over to the couch. "There's some money there." He sneezed and grabbed a few tissues. "Should be enough, if you manage it right. Enough to keep you going for a while."

Xavier wanted to feel grateful, but taking handouts wasn't his thing. Having had a taste of independence, taking charity had him feeling some kind of way.

Billy recognized Xavier's struggle. "Don't worry, you can pay it back if you wish. I know that it's hard for you youngsters in today's world. I guess what I'm trying to say is that I don't want you to be another statistic, Xavier. So you might have a baby on the way. I can tell you that you're in for some struggle, but always do what's right, youngster, and right will follow."

Xavier was trying to keep his emotions bottled up, but one lousy tear dropped from his right eye. He went to approach Billy to thank him with a handshake but grabbed and playfully hugged him instead.

Billy's grouchy butt said, "I don't need all that. Get off me."

Xavier took his place back on the armchair. "So what are you gonna do about being a senior-citizen baby daddy?"

Billy cracked a smile. "I guess you will be pushing that shriveled up, diaper-wearing, dried-up vegetable of a Vietnam War veteran around in a wheelchair at the kid's high school graduation."

They both laughed—or at least until the old man nearly coughed himself into a fit.

4

"It's Sunday morning. Can I sleep in instead of going to church?" Xavier asked his father.

"No, son. It's the Lord's day. Time to go to the house of worship and praise Him." Noah carried a garment bag with a dress suit on a wire hanger inside. "Oh, when I was going through your closet of Satan wear, I noticed that you didn't have a dress suit. I took the liberty of purchasing you one. Hurry up and get dressed."

"I don't know about this going to church every Sunday thing." Xavier pulled the covers up over his head.

Noah was quick with a reply. "As long as you live in my house, you will abide by my rules. Besides, you need the Lord in your life. God knows you've been through enough while living with your mother."

"I'm just saying that it's too much."

"It's good that you have some resistance. That way when God breaks you, He'll get the glory," Noah said while hanging Xavier's suit in the closet. "You can't keep avoiding your mother. When are you planning on seeing her?"

"When I forgive her for the foul stuff she's done."

"The Lord is all about forgiveness, son. If He can forgive you, you surely can forgive your mother."

"Whatever," Xavier hissed.

"Well, son, I see I'm just gonna have to pray that God removes that rebellious spirit from you." Noah left the room.

Xavier removed the covers and rolled out of bed.

He stood in front of the closet in his boxers, then grabbed the garment bag and laid it on the bed. He wasn't into dress suits. But he knew enough about material to know when one was old and outdated. Plus, a receipt from the Salvation Army fell to the floor when he unzipped the bag and lifted the hideous-looking thing out.

Noah is snorting hair-spray products if he thinks I'm flexin' in this, Xavier thought, holding up the suit. The black old-school double-breasted would make him look like a friggin' funeral director.

Xavier was standing there holding up the suit when his father walked back into his bedroom. Noah brushed right by his son without saying a word and headed to the closet.

"What are you doing?" Xavier asked.

Noah didn't respond. He just kept going on about his business, like he was taking inventory of his son's many high-priced articles.

Xavier tried to play it off by offering some humor in an awkward situation. "What does Jesus have to say in that Bible about a father invading his son's privacy?"

Xavier was smiling until Noah started spontaneously ripping high-priced items of clothing from hangers and throwing them to the floor.

"What are you doing?" Xavier asked anxiously, as he watched clothes fly through the air. "What is wrong with you?"

Noah shook his son's leather Pelle Pelle jacket in the boy's face. "This right here is the very reason why you can't humble yourself and wear what I buy you. It's this designer junk right here that's gonna keep you from inheriting God's kingdom. You cannot serve two masters, son."

Xavier was trying everything in his power to not go off on Noah.

"All right." Xavier submitted to his dad. "You're right. First thing after church I'll get rid of them. I was thinking about changing my image at school anyway," he lied. He had to buy time some kind of way. At least until he could come up with a plan to move his clothes.

The corners of Noah's lips turned up into a smile. "I knew you would understand, son. Honor thy father and thy mother, Xavier." He handed Xavier the jacket. "Get washed up and dressed and I'll see you and Alfonso at breakfast."

Xavier watched Noah as he walked out. His father must've been out of his mind if he thought for one second Xavier would ditch the only stitches of clothing that were accepted by his peers at school. No way on God's green earth was anything but designer brands touching Xavier's skin. Noah was straight tripping. He'd been locked up for a good part of Xavier's life and now the cat wanted to come in and start laying down the Ten Commandments. His father could miss him with that madness. Getting rid of clothes he didn't spend one slug on. Uh-uh—wasn't going to happen!

But when Alfonso entered Xavier's bedroom Xavier almost fell out laughing at his little brother. Alfonso's condition had the youngster ultrasensitive. Besides, homeboy didn't look too comfortable with his body stuffed into the secondhand suit that fit him more like a Salvation Army straitjacket. Outside of it all, the frown on the boy's face was priceless. Several different shades of misery.

Alfonso gently closed the bedroom door and pulled the tight pants out of his booty before plopping down angrily on Xavier's bed.

Xavier offered his little brother a sneaky grin. "Alfonso, you know I'm not trying to be funny, but those pants look like they got your little coconuts feeling some kind of way."

"Big brah, I don't know how much more I can take of Dad going Jesus on us every second he's around. I know I told you back in the day that I was missing him, but I kinda wish for the old days, even with Ne Ne's trifling foolishness." Alfonso yanked at his black necktie like the thing was alive and trying to choke him.

Xavier sat silently smiling.

Alfonso nodded at Xavier's closet. Empty hangers were still swinging on the closet rod long after Noah had left.

"Let me take a guess: Dad was in here trying to exorcise the demons out of your closet?"

Xavier was still mulling over places to hide his junk. "How'd you guess?"

"They were the same words he used when I was seeing True Religion, Mecca, and Levi's jeans fly through the air out of my closet." Alfonso was dental-floss thin, not much bigger than a leg on a dining room table. The top two buttons on his jacket seemed to be stressed, though. Like any sharp movement would pop them right off his jacket. "I already caught a hard time making friends, but wearing stuff from Salvation Army and Kmart isn't gonna be a good look. Xavier, I don't think I can do it. Kids are already laughing at me."

"You're funny, but I feel you. Same here, little brah. It definitely would be a challenge to maintain my rep at Coleman High dressed cheesy."

"I wanted to bite Dad's kneecaps when he started throwing all of my *Scarface* figures in a black garbage bag. Wanted to make him say 'Say hello to my little friend' for snatching down my *Scarface* posters and curtains, and taking up my Al Pacino comforter with 'The world is mine' printed on the sheets and pillow cases."

"That's what that noise coming out of your bedroom last night was about?"

"Yep. He said that those kinds of toys in my room were inviting in Satan."

"Thank God he's been gone for so long and is not up on technology. Otherwise your—"

"That's what you think. He found my *Scarface: The World Is Yours* video game and with his gorilla hands, snapped it in half. The last time I saw my PS3 was last night when he was carrying it out. Then he returned and started nailing up crosses on my walls. No kidding, Xavier, there is a huge Bible sitting in the place where my PS3 used to sit. Dad is out of control.

"Last night before you came home he was telling me that me and you were gonna be baptized and would join the choir or usher board at church. I'm serious, big brah, when I say that I don't know how much more of this man I can take."

Xavier's heart bled heavy for the kid, but this was a battle that the little crumb-snatcher would have to endure by himself. Right now it was every man for himself. One problem at a time. And of course Xavier's were first.

"I still wish you had your old job back. At least I would have money to buy my ice cream sandwiches again at lunchtime. Dad says there is no room in the house. No budget for 'luxury items,' " Alfonso said with a sad face.

The details about Xavier's old gig had never been shared with Alfonso. He wanted his younger brother to look at him as a provider and not some thug. But this was too much. Xavier almost cried for his brother. He missed those times, too. Moments where he'd spoiled his kid brother rotten. Got the boy anything he wanted. Alfonso's happiness meant everything in the world to Xavier. But Xavier *could* give Alfonso a little sump'n sump'n from the loot Billy gave him, to ease the kid's pain.

Xavier hadn't been able to believe his eyes as he'd sat at the back of the bus last night on his way home from

Billy's. Since there hadn't been many passengers aboard, Xavier decided to check out how much was inside, but he kept the white envelope low when he examined its contents. He hadn't realized the thickness of the thing until he'd pulled it out.

Three thousand dollars—all big-faced Benjamins.

Of course this was a mere handful of sunflower seeds compared to the grip that had once flowed through Xavier's hands. But Billy's generosity almost brought tears to his eyes.

Xavier walked over to his closet, kicked a few clothing items out of his way, and stooped down. He had stuffed the money inside the right sneaker in a box containing a pair of burgundy suede Pumas. He was careful not to pull all of it out. If his father saw the bankroll he would arrive at the logical conclusion that the money was Satan-earned and would douse his oldest son with holy water while waving a cross in front of Xavier's face.

Xavier had trust in Alfonso. He knew from past experience that the kid would manage the money properly. So he had no problem breaking his kid brother off with a hundred bucks.

Xavier warned, "Buy your ice cream sandwiches, homeboy, but don't let your dad catch you with the ends."

It was almost comical to see Alfonso trying to stuff the bill inside pants so tight that Xavier could see the imprint of the bill in his little brother's right pocket.

"Xavier, why don't you call Dad 'Dad'?" Alfonso asked.

Xavier was putting away the money when he looked

over his left shoulder. "No need to worry about that, little homie."

The truth was that he couldn't bring himself to explain it to the little dude. Xavier just left it at that, but so far he believed that Noah hadn't done enough to earn the title. Xavier had given him credit; Noah had stepped in and picked up where Ne Ne had left off, like he was supposed to. But the old dude was seriously acting like a lunatic with this religion stuff. Noah had to do more than that for Xavier to crown him "dad."

Alfonso wanted to know, "Are you wearing your suit to church?"

Until now Xavier hadn't thought about it. His devil horns and tail started to show. It would seriously piss Noah the hell off if Xavier came out to the car at the last minute dressed in jeans. But he had to hide his clothing first so that after church Noah wouldn't arrive back home on a mission to seek and destroy.

Today, Xavier was getting ready to wage a large-scale holy war against his father.

5

Xavier was at his hall locker, putting away his lab biology textbook and getting ready for lunch when his potential baby mama rolled up on him.

"What's up with you wanting a paternity test on my baby? Ninja, you know damn well that this baby is yours, so I don't want to hear none of that garbage, booboo."

Xavier was sleepy and cranky. "Don't come in my face popping off. I don't feel like hearing anything from you today, you feel me?"

Monday night, Xavier had waited until his dad went to sleep after one a.m. and spent a couple of hours hauling his clothing into the upper bedroom of a vacant bungalow four doors down. It was risky but he had no choice. Noah had gone haywire Sunday morning before church and couldn't be trusted with Xavier's clothing. He'd made sure that no one saw him. Xavier had taken extra security measures by nailing up the front and side doors. In Noah's toolbox Xavier had found a couple of huge padlocks. He used those on the bedroom and back door of the vacant bungalow. This morning Noah had asked Xavier about his missing clothes. Xavier never replied, but instead he walked out of the house.

The black ty-zillion braids, featuring red highlights, complemented Brenda Sanders's soft brown skin. "Don't try to play me, Xavier. I'll give you trouble if you don't take your responsibilities seriously, boo-boo."

Xavier shook his head and pinched the bridge of his nose in frustration. "Not right now, Brenda. I can't do this with you right now. Look at all the students looking at you."

Brenda yelled, "I can give a good damn about the students in this hallway. My baby needs a father! You better not try to pull that deadbeat dad crap on me!"

Xavier closed his locker and made an attempt to walk off.

But Brenda was all up in Xavier's stuff, playing for the crowd of students walking the hallways.

She walked behind him, saying, "Don't be actin' like you don't hear me, baby daddy. You're not gonna be like my other worthless baby daddy. Child support will straighten you out."

Xavier kept walking, trying to get away from her.

"Baby daddy, you hear me? Don't walk away from me," Brenda said at his back. "I hope it's a boy. I'm gonna name him Xavier Hunter Jr."

There was no use in saying anything to Brenda. Xavier didn't feel like throwing gasoline on an already hot fire.

Brenda got the last word. "You walk away then, fool! Do what you do best, sucka. But once it's all said and done you will be on your knees begging for my forgiveness, sucka!"

Xavier was sitting at his favorite table in the back corner of the cafeteria, but he wasn't alone. The Coleman High Wolverines' sophomore sensation, starting middle-linebacker Calvin "Bigstick" Mack, was chilling to Xavier's left. The boy rocked a baldy and was the color of toffee. At six-foot-six, weighing in at nearly three hundred pounds, Bigstick's body was a freak of nature, muscles on top of muscles.

Directly to Xavier's right—his new nerdy buddy, Simon Templeton. Xavier had felt sorry for the kid, and let him hang out so everybody could see who Simon was rolling with and wouldn't mess with him.

Students broke into laughter as Dex entered the lunchroom. His outrageous outfit was attracting lots of attention as he walked through the crowded cafeteria toward Xavier.

Xavier started in on Dexter as soon as he saw him. "Man, what the hell do you have on this time?"

Dexter didn't answer right away. He seemed to allow some time to go by, sucking up the attention. The boy stared down at his outfit like everybody around was sucking his socks. "Sweet, ain't it?" Dex bragged, pretending like his right hand was a hand broom sweeping away imaginary dust from the left sleeve of a polka-dot, double-breasted capri-pants suit. No socks. Black hard-sole shoes, trousers stopping mid-shin. The sleeves of the jacket stopping inches from the wrists.

Xavier peeped the attention Dex was getting. "Homeboy, the colorful Kanye West clothes you were sportin' last week think you're wrong for wearing stuff out of Dwayne Wade's closet."

Bigstick spoke in his deep, bass voice. "Fam, you better be glad you ain't in the penitentiary with that outfit on."

Everybody around was cracking up laughing.

Even nerdy, soft-spoken Simon got in on the clowning session. "Like I needed to see all of that while I'm grubbing." He pushed the banana pudding cup away with disgust.

Dex cracked on Simon. "Freshman, you're new to the table. You won't even have a voice until your sophomore year, so zip it, punk."

"Don't hate on Simon, Dex," Xavier said, barely able to maintain his composure. "You're the one steppin' up in here looking like the gay version of Captain Crunch."

Some dude named Andy Hudson, sitting with friends two tables away, heard Xavier's comment and responded. "So, Xavier, what are you trying to say? I'm gay and proud of it. But even I wouldn't be caught dead in that getup."

It seemed like the entire lunchroom crowd rocked the roof with laughter on that one.

The joke didn't faze Dex the least bit.

"Y'all fools just don't know what the style is these days," Dex said. "In my sophomore year I had my gangsta swag on beast mode, you feel me? This year I make my own rules, a trendsetter, you dig? This style of dress is catching on, got some of the hottest NBA players rocking it. Watch. By homecoming I'm gonna have a lot of you fools trying to dress like me."

Xavier said just five words to Dex—"Sit your happy butt down."

Dex sat across the table from Xavier. "Have any of you fools peeped this?" He struggled to get his hand into his tight pants pocket. When Dex finally pulled a folded-up flyer out of his pocket, he was winded.

Bigstick cracked on Dex. "Fam, you gotta get in shape if you gonna wear pants like those."

Dexter ignored Bigstick, and with his thumb and middle finger, he flicked the folded flyer across the table to Xavier.

Xavier unfolded and read it. "Where'd you get this from?"

"Alice Walker. Felix Hoover's cousin was passing them out in the south lobby this morning."

Bigstick said, "The flyer is advertising a memorial party for Hoover this Friday night at the State Theater, after his noon funeral service."

Xavier shook his head. "That's still messed up about Felix, man. I can't believe the homeboy is gone. Nobody knows what happened?"

Dex said, "Whoever murked out Felix is keeping it on the hush-hush."

"Which is leaving room for these clowns around here to speculate," said Bigstick. "Everybody and their mama—from Zulu, Dutch Westwood, Dylan Dallas, even some members of Hoover's own crew, on down to the janitors—are rumored to have had fam erased."

Xavier had his own theory about who was responsible. But he couldn't be sure. Living the life that Felix had chosen did come with its fair share of enemies. Could've been any number of scumbags.

Dex asked Xavier, "Let me holler at you out in the hallway, homeboy. I got something personal I want to talk to you about."

"No doubt," said Xavier.

On the way out they ran into Big Ray Taylor and Clyde McElroy, the two senior captains of the football team, and the ones who were responsible for assembling the team behind Felix Hoover's Second Street crew that had rescued Xavier from Dutch Westwood and Dylan Dallas's Straight Eight gang that day in the parking lot.

Clyde was meaner than a honey badger and shared the same physique as a muscle-bound King Kong on steroids.

Big Ray Taylor was a Goliath at left tackle. The boy also flossed a hilarious sense of humor. He burst out laughing at Dex's outfit. He said to Xavier, "X, I didn't know you rolled in the same circles as Russell Westbrook."

Clyde McElroy was laughing his butt off. "Don't pay no attention to this fool, Dex," he said.

Dex insisted, "Y'all will see—this look is gonna be popular up here at Coleman. Skip y'all lames."

Ray Taylor asked Xavier, "You going to Hoover's funeral and that thing at the State Theater they're having for him?"

"I'm there—doing both of 'em. Felix was my dude. He straight had my back, you feel me?"

Big Ray Taylor gave Xavier five. "You know I feel you. He kept it real with me too. Me and McElroy made it mandatory for the entire football team to show up in support of the homie Felix Hoover one last time."

Dex butted in, "How's that golden-boy quarterback of yours, Harvey Wellington, doing since he's been sober? I see the last two games that boy threw for more than five hundred yards."

Ray Taylor answered, "Harvey's taking it one day at a time, little homie. Thanks for asking, though."

Xavier and Dex were about to step off when Ray Taylor said, "X, like I told you in the bathroom that day when we were about to take it to Dylan Dallas and his goons: I got your back."

Xavier put his left fist up to his heart to show the love. "Thanks, big homie."

On his way out the door Xavier bumped into Heather Larkin, who sat behind him in English. She smiled at him and he politely smiled back but kept it moving. There was something about the girl. He just couldn't put a finger on it though.

Outside in the hallway, Dex put Xavier up on game.

"Y'all distracted me with jokes. But I knew it was something I forgot to tell you. Don't know how to say this, but I'm just gonna come on out with it."

"Cut the crap and bring it to me straight."

Dex looked away for a second, like he was collecting his thoughts. And then he blew Xavier's wig back. "I just saw Samantha out in the back parking lot with that kid Sean Desmond."

"Sean Desmond as in Calvary High's former all-American baseball shortstop, now a senior at the University of Michigan and the hottest thing going in the college ranks, Sean Desmond?"

"We still talking about the same cat, X."

"What is she doing with him?"

Dex shook his head. "Don't know. But from the looks of it, homeboy seemed like he was dropping her off in a brand-new Corvette."

Xavier was a master at hiding his emotions from people, but he couldn't lie to himself. The searing flames of jealousy he was feeling couldn't be contained. They swiftly spread like wildfire inside of his soul and burned with a smoldering intensity.

Before Dex knew it, Xavier stormed off down the hallway.

"Come on, X," Dex pleaded, following behind Xavier. Dexter knew damn well where this was going. He just hoped that Sean Desmond had already vacated the scene.

All the way out of the school, Dexter begged Xavier to chill out.

The temperatures outside weren't bad for a fall day. Mild. Slight breeze. Cars all over the parking lot. Some students were outside mingling, and Sean Desmond was leaning against the right front fender of a shiny red

Corvette Stingray, talking to Samantha with a smirk on his face.

Xavier walked right up and started in. "What the hell is this mess?" he asked Samantha, pointing at Sean.

Sean stood erect and tried to boss up. "First of all, check yourself, dude! My name is Sean Desmond. Soon to be one of the highest paid major league baseball players in the country." Sean was average height, but was built. Pretty-boy looks, curly hair, light skin, and carried himself in a dignified manner.

At this point words were useless. Xavier went to swing on ol' boy and would've solidly connected if Dex hadn't grabbed his arm.

Sean stood tall. Didn't even flinch. Just tauntingly laughed at Xavier.

"Xavier!" Samantha screamed, pushing her ex-boyfriend away. "Excuse me, but you should be out shopping with your little hood rat for baby clothes, shouldn't you?"

"Baby," Sean said to Samantha as he opened the door of his car. "You deal with this"—he waved disrespectfully in Xavier's direction—"and give me a call when your little *Get Rich or Die Tryin'* friend over there learns his place."

Xavier went off but Dex grabbed him up again.

"Don't make me use one of your baseball bats against you," Xavier said, trying to break loose, as Sean started up his car.

Sean mashed down on the accelerator, loudly revving the engine to drown out Xavier's voice. He powered down the passenger window of the car.

"Yeah yeah yeah." Sean mocked Xavier. He looked at

Samantha, winked, and stopped revving the engine long enough to say, "Samantha, your parents are rich and soon I will be too. When you stop slumming, call me and we can eat things and go to places that boyfriend over there couldn't begin to pronounce or afford." He then peeled backwards out of the parking space and burned rubber down the asphalt.

"Punk—" was all Xavier could get out before breaking away from Dexter, spotting and grabbing a chunk of cement and hurling it at the car, barely missing the rear end of the Corvette.

Samantha was pissed. "Do I have to get a restraining order on you?"

Xavier ignored her question by asking one of his own. "Sam, where did homeboy come from?"

"Not that it's any of your business. Sean Desmond is just a friend." She stepped right into his face. "I suggest you take care of yours and not become another deadbeat dad." Samantha headed back toward the building without saying another word.

Xavier walked off by himself in the other direction, pissed. There was no competing with Sean Desmond, and he knew it.

Where'd this fool come from all of a sudden? Xavier thought. It was just one more problem for him to deal with.

Ms. Scott was explaining the homework when the bell rang. The rustling sound of the kids collecting their belongings caused the English teacher to raise her voice.

"Remember, your first paper is an opinion paper and it

is due this Friday. And please, don't forget to bring in your copy of *The Adventures of Huckleberry Finn*. We will begin our reading this coming Monday. Until tomorrow, everybody be safe."

Xavier was still heated. Less than an hour ago he'd lost his manhood. Never before had he been pulled out of his square like that. Wanting to hurt a man over a woman. But his ego was more than bruised and he was looking for something—anything—to let him know that he was still a warrior.

Heather couldn't have timed her approach any better. She walked out behind him.

"You look like you could use a friend, Hunter," Heather said. She was carrying her English books and was all decked out in a green top, gray skirt with green square patterns, and dingy, worn-out white sandals, looking like her whole outfit came from the Salvation Army.

Xavier wasn't feeling a need for somebody being friendly right now. He looked at her like she was an irritating, pesky fly buzzing around his dinner plate. She wouldn't let up, though. She followed him right into the hallway amongst a sea of students.

"I hope I'm not being intrusive when I say you deserve better," she explained.

That line caught Xavier's attention. "How do you know what I deserve?"

"Caught the theatrics involving you and Samantha in the parking lot. Everybody knows what you've done for this school. You deserve somebody who's gonna treat you like a king."

"I guess you're the one who will, right?"

"All I'm saying is that a woman should be a little bit more understanding when it comes to human flaws. So you made a mistake and knocked up that Brenda chick."

Xavier casually said over his shoulder, "Anybody ever tell you, you talk too much?"

"Come on, Hunter. Don't act like nobody knows your business. And yes, I've been told that my mouth never closes, like Seven-Eleven, but I admire you and want to be your friend."

Surprisingly, Xavier stopped and grabbed Heather's butt in front of everybody.

Heather Larkin did not offer any resistance. "Ooo-ee, you have nice, firm hands, Hunter."

Xavier had to admit that it was disrespectful to the girl, but he didn't care. His manhood had been damaged by Samantha and her new creep. He needed this to feel empowered again.

The feeling was so good that Xavier was going in for two handfuls when down the hallway, by a door marked with an illuminated overhead exit sign, towering above the students walking around him, was Tall and Husky. The big-eared goon that Xavier had locked eyes with in the lunchroom on the first day of school.

The dude looked to still be wearing the same dark Rocawear hoodie. Anybody and their mama could see that this creep was an outsider. How the hell could he have penetrated this far inside the school? This dude was a grown man and wasn't any type of faculty member Xavier could remember. Tall and Husky smiled and pointed at

Xavier, making his fingers into a gun and pretending to take a shot at him.

It was official. There was no more guessing. The dude was after him.

Heather broke Xavier's concentration. "Hunter, I'm waiting for you to do it again. I love a man with strong hands," she begged.

When Xavier looked back up Tall and Husky had disappeared. Through the exit door, Xavier assumed. He stood out in the crowd and would've been easily spotted walking the hallways. This was the second time dude seemed to come from out of nowhere. Xavier had to do a better job of watching his back if he didn't want to get himself done up like Hoover.

Xavier didn't know who this dude was—probably contracted by Slick Eddie. Possibly Romello—hell, he didn't know. He had far too many enemies to pinpoint who'd sent this crazy-looking fool. One thing was sure: Tall and Husky had made it known that he was here for Xavier.

When Xavier arrived at the crib he found Alfonso lying on his bed, crying. He automatically jumped to the wrong conclusion.

"Noah didn't hit you, did he?"

Alfonso raised and shook his head *no* as the waterworks continued.

When he'd arrived home Xavier had noticed a distinct smell in the air, like somebody was burning something. But the neighbor next door was always out burning something or other in his backyard, so Xavier had paid it no mind.

He sat on the bed and rested a hand on his little brother's back to console him. "Dude, what's wrong with you?"

Alfonso buried his face in the pillow, bawling and pointing to the bedroom window looking out on the backyard.

The stench of something burning was becoming suffocating. Cautiously Xavier moved to the window and was hit by a very disturbing scene. He had to wipe his eyes in disbelief as he stared at Noah standing out in the yard over a pile—what Xavier could make out—of burning clothes, with a Bible underneath his left armpit and what looked to be a small can of lighter fluid in his right hand. It was one of the craziest sights Xavier had ever witnessed. There were no words.

"He caught me wearing the clothes that you bought me last semester instead of the ones he'd paid for," Alfonso explained, raising his teary face from the pillow.

Xavier just stood there. He couldn't move. His dad had taken this thing to a whole other level of insanity. Pure craziness. Xavier didn't know too much about the Bible, but he was sure that this kind of behavior didn't exist between the covers.

Xavier said to no one in particular, "Clothes—they're just clothes."

"Dad said you hid your clothes from him and when he finds them he's gonna burn them like he's doing mine," Alfonso said, dropping his face back into the pillow and bursting out crying.

Xavier was going to have to be extra careful about going in and out of the empty bungalow to change his clothes. To be truthful, Xavier didn't know how he would react if he came home and all of his designer clothing was billowing into the sky in puffs of black smoke.

As he watched his father reading from the Book and squirting fluid on a raging fire, suddenly his mother, Ne Ne, was beginning to look like a saint to him.

6

Against his father's wishes Xavier had gone to pay his last respects to his homeboy Felix Hoover. Noah tried to explain to Xavier that stuff like that happened to people like Felix because he hadn't been saved through Jesus Christ. Tried to explain that Felix was a thug and people like that belonged to Satan.

This morning, to Xavier it'd seemed like over a million people had attended Felix's home-going. And of course, Second Street had been everywhere, showing solidarity by wearing shirts with Hoover's face on them, paying tribute to a fallen soldier. With so many thugs present, nobody expected anything funky to jump off. The Detroit Police Department had made a conscious effort to show a heavy presence to discourage rivals from getting cute and trying to start anything. Almost every student from Coleman High had turned out to say their good-byes.

Now everybody was at the State Theater cutting loose and kicking back to the jams the DJ was spinning at the memorial celebration. Every place in the theater had a magnificent view of the dance floor.

Xavier had taken a few dollars of the money given by Billy and splurged. It felt good to have a new pair of kicks on his feet. He had the loot and could've gone hard at the mall, but he didn't. A crispy pair of white Nike Air Force 1s, some blue Levi's, and a nice navy blue full-zip Nautica hoodie were all Xavier had purchased. Of course he'd have to make a pit stop at his stash spot and change clothes before going home. But it was what it was.

Xavier was too hyped and paranoid to sit down. Instead he, Dex, Bigstick, the Runt—as they'd started calling Simon Templeton—and some wannabe thug named Linus Flip, who was sucking Xavier's socks every chance he got, were on the dance floor.

Flip had transferred to Coleman from Northern High yesterday. Xavier had known the dude from back in the day. He was a pretty big boy. At two hundred fifty pounds, Linus stood about six-foot-six, with a powerful upper torso and chicken legs. With skin the color of tar, a long forehead like Frankenstein's monster, and bugged-out eyes, Flip couldn't be anything else but a thug.

The boys were holding down a small area in the right far corner of the dance floor. The place was packed. Standing room only. The group stood watching guys and girls sweating hard and breathing heavy on the dance floor, getting it in to Beyoncé's "Drunk in Love" track.

And as usual Dex was getting clowned about his gear.

Xavier said, "Dex, homeboy, with all of the crotch-hugging pants you've been wearing, you can't possibly be looking to have any babies in the future."

Linus almost fell on the floor laughing.

Everybody cracked up laughing, except for Dex. He defended the sky-blue blazer, stretch pants that looked like they were camouflage, white shoes, and black man-bag.

"Skip all y'all," he said to the group. "And, X, you wouldn't know style if it threw on a set of Bigfoot monster truck tires and ran over your melon."

Runt laughed. "Now, Xavier, that was funny."

Bigstick said to Runt, "Fam, what's funny is Dex over there thinking that the women are gonna be on his shoes because of that outfit. But what fam fails to realize is that the man purse makes him look real sweet."

Xavier slapped Bigstick five. "I'm hip—all those colors, looks like a paint factory threw up on you."

Linus said, "Xavier, you're a real funny dude, a straight-up fool. Forget Kevin Hart, you should be out there making that money."

Dex was quick to call Flip out. "Damn, brah, that crap wasn't that funny. Get up off his socks."

Everybody laughed at Linus Flip. He might've been a pretty big boy, but Xavier knew he had massive self-esteem issues, which caused him to go there on Dex.

"Dude, you don't know me like that," said Linus, trying to look intimidating.

Dex was a short guy, but a punk he wasn't. "You spoke on me. Fool, if you can't take it, stay out of it."

Xavier could tell this was getting heated. And before he had to beat the brakes off Linus for trying to put his hands on Dex, Xavier broke it up. "Linus, one thing you should know if you hang with us, you will get clowned, you feel me?"

Linus shook his head super quick. He didn't want any one-on-one confrontations with Xavier. He already knew about Xavier's inner gangsta and he wasn't about to go there.

But before they could finish their convo, Brenda Sanders walked right up to them with a couple of her ghetto girlfriends, and started going in on Xavier.

Dex was the first to fire a shot. "Looks like the weave queen and stretch-mark crew is here."

"No you didn't, boo-boo," Brenda said to Dex. "I know you ain't trying to roast nobody while carrying a purse."

Brenda looked like she had gone to a Third World basement salon before the funeral. The ty-zillion braids were gone, replaced by blond and black horsehair that cascaded down her back and twisted into a fabulous ghetto ponytail. She had on a too-tight body dress which made her pregnancy look like she was trying to hide a Spalding basketball. Her shoes were scuffed big-time. Her homegirls looked horrible too—wearing dresses that were too little, and equally ruined shoes.

Xavier, Runt, Bigstick, and Linus Flip were laughing hard at Dex's silly behind.

One of the girls on Brenda's left said to Dex, "All those

colors you got on—what, you get dressed in the dark, boyfriend?"

The girl on Brenda's right chimed in, "Girl, he looks just like a pack of Starburst."

Dex came back something ferocious. "That's good, y'all able to see colors. Now if I can get you three chicks to stop skipping class and spending all seven periods in the lunchroom, you just might start looking like girls again. The rolls on the back of y'all necks look like packs of hot dogs."

Xavier could hardly catch his breath from laughing so hard.

The activity on the dance floor was hot and heavy, with the DJ spinning another one of Beyoncé's hits. The music was loud, but Brenda was much louder.

"How's my baby daddy doing?" she said to Xavier, as she rubbed her stomach. "Don't worry, little Xavier Jr., we're not going to let your dad ruin any of your Christ-mases. Because he will be paying child support."

"What do you want?" Xavier asked. "Why you al-ways up in my face?"

"Because the baby I'm carrying says I can be."

"Oooo," Xavier's boys responded.

Xavier was getting heated. Nobody ever talked to him this way. He felt completely disrespected by Brenda. He'd never put his hands on a girl and wasn't going to start now. But she was pushing him to the limit.

Heather Larkin stepped out of the crowd of dancers, strands of hair matted to her brow by perspiration, and walked over to put an arm around Xavier's neck. She smiled at the three girls like Xavier was all hers.

Heather's gear was nothing spectacular—hand-me-down city—long, flowing, solid gray skirt, a white button-down blouse, and plain black shoes. Tiny sweat droplets beaded the lenses of her glasses.

Heather's move had been done so slick it surprised everybody. Xavier didn't have time to react.

The chick on Brenda's left spoke up first. "Oh no she didn't."

With her hands on her hips, the girl on the right asked, "Who's this chick?"

Brenda finally spoke up. "Boo-boo, you better take yo' arms from around my baby daddy's neck and skip your little private school outfit outta here. Can't you see grown folks are handlin' some bidness."

Heather teased Brenda with a smug smile and said in a sultry voice, "Well, when I recognize you as being grown, I will do just that. But let me tell you a little something my mother told me: Just because a baby is carrying a baby doesn't make her grown. It exposes her for the weak and insecure girl that she really is."

"Oooo," everybody around mocked in unison.

"No she didn't," Brenda said to her girls.

Heather attacked Brenda's two girlfriends. "You two oompa loompas need to understand that your Hummer H3 bodies can't fit into clothes"—Heather slowly rubbed her hands down her curves—"made for high-performance sports cars."

Brenda and her two girlfriends had had just about enough.

They started removing their earrings and shoes in preparation for combat. To keep it one-hun'ed, they were about to whoop Heather's behind.

Xavier bossed up. "Y'all know my rep and how I get down for mine. Gonna ask you one time—ain't asking again. Get away from us. Right now!"

The fire in Xavier's eyes told the girls that he wasn't playin'. The three of them didn't waste any time putting back on their crusty shoes and moving on.

The lights had been dimmed to create the perfect atmosphere for slow dances. Recessed lighting illuminated the dance floor as couples got their cake on, slowly twirling and twisting to a slow-grinding, old-school R. Kelly tune.

Xavier put a hand around Heather's waist. "I like the way you handle yourself, ma. Real smooth, clever. The kind of chick that would hold a man down."

Heather giggled and whispered something naughty in Xavier's ear and grabbed his hand to lead him away.

Dex stepped to Heather. "This dude got plenty of honeys, girlfriend. Don't you want a man who dresses like me?" He sounded like he was player-hating.

Heather said boldly, "If I wanted a little colorful candy-stick of a man I'd go to the candy store. Now step off, twerp."

"That's what you get," Linus Flip said sarcastically.

Bigstick was next to chime in on Dex. "Damn, fam, you got dissed, son."

Runt even clowned Dex. "So far that new look of yours ain't earning you no shine time with the girlies."

Dex looked like somebody had thrown a pie in his face. Something was up with Heather, but he just couldn't figure it out. Girls loved him for his buffoonery. None of them had ever styled on him like this girl had done.

Heather was leading Xavier away when Dex shouted over the music for Xavier's attention, pointing at the dance floor.

Xavier had to keep a lid on the angry monster of jealousy inside of him as he looked out and saw Samantha and that baseball-playing punk on the dance floor getting it in to a jazzy, up-tempo track by Bruno Mars. He wanted to go out on the dance floor and pile-drive that wimp, straight snatch homeboy's spine out of his throat. Instead he chilled. After all, Samantha had walked away from him. Not really knowing if the baby was his or not.

So the way Xavier saw it, if she wanted homeboy—mo' power to her.

Heather whispered something in Xavier's ear that put a huge smile on the boy's face.

They walked out of the crowd and headed to a nice, cozy dark corner.

Linus drove his well-maintained burgundy 2001 Pontiac Grand Prix through the dark streets. The boys were now heading to an after-party at a house on the west side. LaMarcus Russell was a center for the Coleman High Wolverines basketball team, and the house on Hubbell Street, where the after-party was jumping off, a block east of the abandoned Thomas M. Cooley High School, belonged to him. His parents had saved up enough money to buy a house in Bloomfield, and as a gift for his eighteenth birthday, they'd given their only child, LaMarcus, the 950-square-foot brick colonial.

It took Linus a minute to find a parking spot. Street parking had been dominated by cars belonging to teenagers getting their groove on inside of LaMarcus's well-lit crib. Xavier, Bigstick, Dex, Runt, and Linus were joking and laughing as Linus carefully maneuvered his car into the only spot available, in front of a fire hydrant. The Detroit Police Department was on a tight budget and this area would sometimes go weeks without seeing a single squad car. Linus knew this and that's why he wasn't sweating a parking violation.

Linus had made his way out of the car and was standing on the sidewalk, as Xavier moved the front passenger seat forward to let the rest climb out of the back.

Runt was the last one getting out when out of nowhere drove a black GMC SUV with the windows rolled down on the right side. Suddenly what sounded like a shot rang out, replacing the noise of the loud rap music coming from the party. The fight-or-flight response kicked in and the boys bolted every which way. The SUV slowly rolled forward as the driver pursued the intended targets.

Xavier wasn't sure what was happening, so he hid and pinned himself down in front of a vintage red Toyota Camry in the driveway of a house. But then Linus mounted some nerve and came out from his place of concealment, spotting a brick, picking it up and throwing the thing with all of his might at the SUV, splattering the windshield, and catching the goons off guard.

As the driver panicked and punched down on the accelerator, the SUV lurched forward and took off, burning rubber up the street.

Linus called out to Xavier, "You all right?"

Xavier finally came from behind the Toyota. "Did anybody get a look?"

Dex walked out of his place of concealment. "Nah, I was too shook to leave my hiding spot."

Runt emerged from the shadow. "The windows were too tinted to see anybody inside."

"I don't think we should go to this party anymore. Let's get out of here," Linus said.

The boys weren't going to stay around and wait for the SUV guys to come back, so they jumped in the whip and bounced.

7

Even though Xavier was sitting at his desk surrounded by students in Mr. Burke's world history class, the boy's mind was a gazillion miles away. He wasn't listening to the lecture about the rise and fall of Mesopotamia.

Xavier couldn't front; Linus had saved all of their butts Friday night. It had all gone down so fast that no one was even thinking about getting a license plate number. And even if anyone at the party had witnessed the shooting, they wouldn't dare come forward with any information.

This had to be the same SUV that had been involved in Felix Hoover's murder. He had no idea why they were gunning for him.

Was this Slick Eddie's handiwork? Xavier didn't have the slightest idea.

But somehow he knew that this thing was just getting started. Those boys weren't playing. Fear had never been a factor with Xavier, but now he was starting to get a little worried. There was no place for him to hide if those boys grew brass ones and tried to creep on him in the school. The few students who belonged to Second Street had dropped out after Felix was killed. There was nobody packing the hardware. The football team was only good for Xavier if the foe wanted to go heads-up by way of a good old-fashioned, spit-flying brawl.

There was a knock at the door.

Doug popped his head in and asked, "Excuse me, Mr. Burke. Can I have a moment with Xavier Hunter, please?"

The teacher looked at Xavier. "You can go, Mr. Hunter." Mr. Burke glanced at his watch. "In any event, if you don't return for the rest of today's class, finish reading chapter five for homework."

In the hallway Xavier asked, "What I do now?"

"I just have a few questions to ask you in my office," Doug said.

Doug and Xavier were walking toward the north stairwell when a loud, piercing female scream resonated from the south stairwell.

Xavier dropped his history book and took off toward the scream like he was security. He beat Doug there and was horrified by what he discovered. Doug made it seconds later and cringed as they both stared down the staircase at Brenda Sanders's unconscious body. Girl was sprawled out and wasn't moving. Doug moved down the steps with urgency, as Xavier took out his cell and dialed 911.

Inside Doug's small, cramped office Xavier took a seat in the chair beside Doug's desk. He couldn't shake the image of Brenda lying motionless at the bottom of the stairs. When the paramedics had been rushing her out on a stretcher, Xavier swore he'd heard one of them say that she'd suffered a concussion. Xavier's heart went out to Brenda. He didn't know if she would lose her baby, but he was still 100 percent sure that it wasn't his.

Doug took his time pouring a cup of coffee. He eyed Xavier suspiciously as he placed the hot, steaming cup on the desk and sat down. It gave Xavier the feeling of being a suspect in one of those drab, white interview rooms on *The First 48*.

Doug blew away the steam rising from the liquid. "Did you hear one of those paramedics say that she'd possibly suffered a concussion? Hope the baby is all right. Word around the school is that you are the father. Her fall, was it an accident?"

"I know you ain't trying to lay her fall on me."

Doug laughed cynically. "Why are you so defensive? I wasn't about to say that, but since we're on the case, did you have anything to do with it?"

Xavier sighed. "You just plucked me out of world history. Did it look like I had anything to do with it?"

Doug carefully slurped the hot coffee. "God, I would

like to hope that it was just an accidental fall. Hope that nobody's that ruthless and cruel." He took a sip of his coffee. "Let's get serious. I heard about what happened at the after-party over at LaMarcus's house. And I'm going to tell you again: You need to go to another school."

Xavier said nothing. He just wanted to see where Doug was going with this.

"A few of the neighbors reported to the police that they couldn't see the occupants, but the assailants were driving a dark-colored GMC SUV. Why didn't y'all wait around and report the assault to the police?"

"I don't know what you're talking about."

Doug laughed and slurped some coffee. "You are a hardheaded young man."

"Even if I was there, how do you know they were after me?"

Doug reared back in his chair and put his hands behind his head. "We can play this little game all day, but we both know that the SUV was there for you. Don't know if it was the same one responsible for Felix's death."

Xavier took his time. "The last time I was in this office I snitched on Romello."

"You were caught up in a bad way and didn't have anywhere else to go. I gave you an *out*. And it's because of that *out* that you are able to sit here today as a free young man. You did what was best for you."

"That's all good in theory. But because of my snitching, Slick Eddie and Romello have probably got every wannabe hit man after me."

"Well, that's the price you pay for steppin' in my shoes and trying to provide protection for the students with the aid of Zulu. Told you when you start messing around in another man's backyard, the drama it would bring."

Xavier thought on it a minute. "You know, I've seen this outsider walking around the school."

Doug sipped a little coffee. "What does this outsider look like?"

"Big, black, satellite dishes for ears—cold eyes."

Doug scratched his head. "Nobody like that rings a bell."

Xavier looked Doug straight in the eyes. "I rest my case."

Doug was offended. "So now you're telling me that I'm not doing my job."

"This fool has shown up a few times. The last time, he pointed his fingers at me like a gun."

"So you think he's connected to Slick Eddie and Romello?"

Xavier shook his head. "Don't know. For all I know, the Hoover murder, the big-eared clown, and the shooting that happened three nights ago might be all connected—I don't know."

"I'll have my officers keep a close eye out for someone fitting the description. Meanwhile, have you told your father any of this?"

The history book lay in his lap. Xavier ran a hand over its smooth surface. What went on at the crib was none of Doug's business. Even though Doug and Noah went back quite a ways, Xavier wasn't going there with him.

Doug saw that he wasn't getting anywhere and switched gears. "So what's going on with you and Samantha? I mean—last school year, you two were booed up."

Xavier gave him a hard *Are you for real?* look. "You tell me, since you know everything," he said with a little attitude.

Doug got up from his chair to refill his cup. "Whoa, did I touch a nerve?"

Samantha was doing her thing and Xavier was most definitely getting his in.

Doug sat back down and slurped some hot coffee. "Ooo-eee, this stuff is good. Black. Just like I like it." He rubbed his hands together. "You know an old man once told me never let anything get away that was of any value. That girl loves you, but too bad you can't see it because you have your head stuck straight up your behind."

Xavier just shook his head.

"The new girl Heather seems to be taking a shine to you." Doug smiled.

Xavier stood from his chair. "You don't have anything else to do, do you? When you gonna stay out of other folks' business and get with Ms. Dowdy, the geometry teacher. She's got a thing for you. Why don't you go take her out for a night out on the town?"

Doug sipped his coffee like the taste was the best thing in the world to him. "Sean Desmond is a punk. Don't like him. Never have. Don't let that baseball-playing hotshot steal your lady."

"Are we about done?"

A look of concern wrenched Doug's face. "I still think

you should switch schools, but it's your life, Mr. Hunter. Just be careful."

Thank God he'd never deleted Brenda Sanders's number from his contacts. Outside of Doug's office he called her phone. It went to voice mail after a few rings like he knew it would. His aim was just to leave a message.

"I hope you're all right," Xavier concernedly spoke into the phone. "Call me if you need anything."

The news in the cafeteria was all about Brenda falling down the stairs. Word had gotten around Coleman. She'd sustained a concussion. But no one mentioned anything about whether or not the baby was okay. Maybe that bit of information was lost, because what everybody originally thought was an accident wasn't looking so accidental anymore. Brenda had been alert when she'd reached the ER. She'd reported being pushed down the stairs. Five-o was everywhere in the school asking questions, interviewing students. Nobody seemed to know a thing.

Xavier was hardly drinking his vanilla milkshake when Samantha appeared through the south entrance. His heart skipped a beat. Butterflies in the stomach. Damn, she looked good. Hair styled to perfection. Tight jeans showing off her booty. A thin leather biker jacket and three-quarter boots to match. He admired her from a distance, just wishing things were back to normal. Xavier thought Samantha was headed for the lunch line, but when he noticed that she was coming toward him, the butterflies in his stomach seemed like they were in a hot rush to break out through his throat and fly out.

The first thing out of her mouth—"Sorry about your baby mama, Xavier."

"You trying to be funny?"

"No. I'm just trying to say that it's messed up."

"So where's your little baseball player? I'm sure he wouldn't be all good with you slumming."

Samantha sat down beside him without waiting on an invitation. "You don't have to be nasty, Xavier. Just heard about what happened Friday night and came over here to see if you were all right."

"It's all good, you feel me?"

Samantha shook her head *no*. "I don't believe that. And it's not all good to have people after you. Do you think it's Slick Eddie?"

"What do you care?"

Samantha simply ignored his childishness and looked around the lunchroom. "Do you understand the word going around school is that standing next to you is bad for one's health? Example, look at how the other students are scattered out in here. Last semester, you were their hero. They adored you. Now look at them. They are afraid of you, thinking that any moment something is going to pop off."

He looked into Samantha's big, pretty eyes. And for a fleeting second he remembered all of the moments—the places they'd gone and had mad fun. He wanted to reach out and grab her, hug her softness, sniff her perfume—he wanted those things very badly.

"What are you going to do?" Samantha asked, laying her soft hands over his. In the past, her presence was like magic, like some kind of invisible fairy dust that had a calming effect on him. Xavier relaxed and loosened up. He turned his hands over and cupped hers from underneath.

"Sam, stop worrying. I'll be—" He couldn't finish his statement because Heather walked over carrying another vanilla milkshake.

She placed the drink in front of him. "Here, honey." Heather looked over at Samantha with the biggest of smiles and extended her hand. "You must be Samantha."

He couldn't believe it—just when he and Samantha seemed to be bonding, this chick showed up.

Samantha curled her upper lip, looking at Heather's outstretched hand like the joint was lathered in dog crap. "Yes, I am. Who might you be?"

Before Xavier could stop Heather, she put her arm around his neck and kissed him on the crown of his head. "I'm his new boo."

Samantha slowly stood up, sizing up what looked to be a bimbo Barbie doll dressed in Third World rags.

Samantha, calm and ever so ladylike, dismissed her by saying, "You might be his new boo, but you look like a hood rat wearing thrift shop rags to me." Samantha turned on Xavier. "I can't believe I came down here feeling sorry for you. Stay the hell away from me. I wouldn't want to get caught up in any of your foolishness." She stormed out.

Xavier forcefully snatched Heather's arm from around his neck. "What are you doing?"

The heated exchanges had flown underneath the radar of the others in the cafeteria. But Heather changed all of that when she yelled out, "You weren't saying all that in that dark corner at the State Theater, now were you, Hunter?!"

She had everybody's attention. The room fell silent, as if they were waiting on Xavier's reply. Before Xavier knew it, he had her by the arm, almost dragging Heather up out of there.

There was an open janitor closet next to the restroom. He shoved her in, closed the door, and clicked on the lights. It was a small room with tons of shelves of cleaning supplies. The strong smell of bleach rose up from the dirty water in a mop bucket.

"You already know what that was, ma. Just one of those things," he said, checking her.

She tried to hug him, desperately looking for some affection. "Baby, I understand that, but you understand whoever I hook up with, I expect some type of commitment."

Xavier shoved her away. "You already know what it was, like I said. We were just having fun, you feel me."

She lurched at him, grabbing him around the neck with both arms and struggling with him to force her lips on his.

"Please. Give me a kiss. I want a damn kiss from you, Hunter!"

Xavier pushed her away, which caused her long hair to fall across her smiling face. Washed over with dull light, it gave her a rather unsettling crazy look.

Then the look eased up on her face. The smile was back but not so intense.

"Don't you want what I gave you in the dark corner of the State Theater again?" she cooed softly.

Her offer was proper, even if it was in a janitor's closet. Xavier was weak because ol' girl's heat was all that. He couldn't help himself. He gave up and let her have her way. People were looking to rub him out, but at the moment, he didn't give a damn. They kissed until Xavier was able to break away, lock the door, and cut off the light.

8

Saturday evening was windy and cold. Sporadic showers came and went. Noah had asked Xavier if he could help him clean out Sister Pope's basement. Noah had volunteered because the elderly lady was a member of his church and didn't have anybody to help her wage war against a nasty mouse infestation. Sister Pope lived in a shabby colonial off of Woodward and East State Fair Street, where through the years she'd accumulated—hoarded is more like it—a lot of useless junk.

Noah and Xavier could barely get down the basement steps. It was a good thing that Noah had rented one of those gigantic residential Dumpsters. The thing sat in the driveway. This job looked like it was going to be one of those all-day affairs.

For the job Xavier wore a crunchy pair of old Levi's, a faded black Adidas hoodie, a pair of barely-clinging-to-life Adidas Top Tens, and on his hands were working gloves.

"Son, grab the headboard and take it out," Noah ordered. "Be careful on your way up the stairs."

"We just have to clean up her basement, right?" asked Xavier.

"You got somewhere to be?"

"I have an exam on a book in English class this Monday."

Noah removed the glove on his right hand and scratched his forehead. "Is that that book you've been reading around the house?"

"Yup. *The Adventures of Huckleberry Finn.*"

"You might want to start reading the Bible more. Because when Jesus comes back, Huckleberry Finn is not gonna be able to save you from burning in hell."

"Nor will Jesus be able to save me from the bad grade I'll get from Ms. Scott on my exam if I don't read that book."

Noah became irritated. "Son, that's blasphemy and I won't have you speaking like that."

"Do you realize the amount of pressure you put on me? No, you don't. I have to keep my GPA up to get a scholarship to one of the universities. No disrespect, but please back off."

Noah laughed off his son's insolence to cover his anger. "I pray for you every night that that rebellious spirit of yours leaves your body. But unless you stop wearing those clothes from them brand-name designer devils, you won't be healed. I know you hid them, son. And when I find them I'm going to burn the devil right out of 'em. That's the only way I'll be able to free you."

Xavier shook his head at his father and went back to work. He quickly shook it off and set his mind to another topic.

As he grabbed a fake brass headboard and struggled up the basement steps, Xavier was tripping on how close he and Heather had become. The girl was cuckoo but her *special skills* more than made up for it. Never one to be labeled "whipped," but he couldn't deny it. This was something that he would never tell any of his homeboys. Samantha was becoming a distant memory, though. Oftentimes he would see her in the hallway and there wasn't even a casual glimpse his way. He wondered about her relationship with that ballplayer. Was it working out? Was she talking to Sean in the back parking lot that day to get him jealous, because he'd had sex with Brenda? Had that been the end of their relationship? He knew the answer to none of these questions.

Somehow Xavier had managed to avoid confrontation with Noah by simply ignoring him. The two would sometimes go days without speaking to each other. Xavier refused to bow and accept this new way of life. He was willing to accept Jesus Christ as his personal Savior, but he wasn't buying the rest of his father's foolishness. He'd gone to church with his father over the past month. But it was on his terms. Xavier would not be bullied into it. When he'd gone, Xavier dressed like he wanted to. There were no more of those thrift-shop dress suits.

But Xavier knew that his father's hunt for his oldest

son's elusive "Satan wear" was far from being over. One night Xavier had caught the old man snooping around the bungalow where he hid his clothes. Xavier had walked out into the backyard and hid himself out of sight. It was so funny to see Noah trying to jimmy the lock on the back door. Somehow he'd caught on to Xavier's hideout. And it would only be a matter of time before his father burglarized the place and discovered where he kept his designer labels. Caught up in the drama at school, Xavier had forgotten to find a better place for his stash. He had to move them, and quickly, before his junk would be next on the old "designer label up-in-smoke tour."

The month of October had gone by without further incident. Xavier hadn't seen that dark GMC SUV or Tall and Husky again. It was like both had vanished from the face of the earth. It led Xavier to think that they'd been hired by Slick Eddie. Logically it made sense. But if so, why did they go after Felix? He'd had nothing to do with Eddie or Romello. Xavier left it alone. Out of sight, out of mind is how he chose to deal with the issue right now.

He walked down the side of the house and chucked the headboard into the Dumpster, noticing Alfonso sitting on Sister Pope's rickety wooden front-porch steps, like he was in deep thought. The kid's face was long and sad. Xavier couldn't tell if the water trickling from Alfonso's eyes was tears or raindrops, as thunder burst overhead and light raindrops started falling.

"What are you over here pouting about, rug rat?" Xavier took off the work gloves and sat down beside his little brother.

Alfonso didn't say anything. He just looked like his red eyes were about to make more water than the clouds overhead. His bottom lip was stuck out so far that it looked like the boy was wearing a turtleneck sweater.

Xavier pushed. "That lip hang any lower, I'ma wipe off the bottom of my shoe on it. Now you want to tell me what's up?"

Alfonso's voice started shaking at first but leveled out. "There's this boy who be walking a pit bull up to my school."

Xavier's protective instincts kicked in. "What'd he do?" he asked, his voice deep and serious.

Alfonso almost jumped out of his skin at his brother's tone. He put his head down in shame. "Those times when you don't pick me up and I'm waiting around in front of the school for Dad, the boy makes fun of me."

Xavier had to remember his brother's Asperger's condition, and gently put an arm around his brother's neck. "Go on."

"That boy keeps telling my classmates that I'm a wimp and my clothes are cheap. That's why I started wearing the clothes you bought me last semester, instead of the ones Dad bought. Until he found out about the clothes and that's when he burned them."

Xavier rubbed his chin. "Go on."

"He's seen you with me a few times. He says he knows you and that you're not really tough. He be up there telling people that when he sees you he's going to sic his dog on you."

Xavier was close to blowing his stack, but he kept calm.

"What's this boy's name?"

Alfonso composed himself. "I don't know. All I know is that the other kids laugh at me when he's around with his jokes. I don't know how much more I can take of the other kids laughing at me, big brother."

The kid was seriously tugging at Xavier's heartstrings. He felt so bad for Alfonso that he almost started crying. But before he would shed any tears, Xavier was going to find Dog Boy and make an example out of him.

He grabbed Alfonso up in an embrace. "Don't say anything to anybody. I'll be up there one day this week."

Noah appeared, dressed in dark coveralls, work boots, and gloves. He looked at his two sons.

"If 'God so loved the world that He gave His only begotten son'—if I don't have two of the laziest sons in all creation." He looked at his watch. "Xavier, let's get a move on before it gets dark. Wanna get this cleaned up, get home, and have some chow before I go to choir rehearsal."

Xavier put on his work gloves and followed Noah back into the basement, fuming. He didn't like it when his little brother wasn't happy. And Dog Boy was definitely not going to like it when Xavier caught up to him.

9

MONDAY, NOVEMBER 10
1:25 P.M.

The following Monday, Xavier was seated in his fifth
period English class. The students hadn't yet begun
taking the examination on *Huck Finn*. Instead the dude
who looked like Floyd "Money" Mayweather was trying
to kick some old political angle about how Mark Twain
must've been a slave owner because of his terrible love
affair with the N-word throughout the book.

"Ms. Scott, I refuse to read this trash," the Mayweather look-alike spouted. "This book is all kinds of
racist. And your boy Huck Finn needs to be wearing a
pillowcase and white sheet, is all I'm trying to say, the
way he uses the N-word."

Some dark-skinned girl from the last desk in the first

row added her two cents. "Coleman is made up almost entirely of black folks—not counting a sprinkle of white and a handful of Latinos. Why are we reading the memoirs of the KKK?"

Some light girl with a jacked-up weave, big nose, and a slight mustache was next to voice her opinion. "Ms. Scott, my mama told me to ask you why *The Autobiography of Malcolm X* can't be our recommended reading."

Before Ms. Scott had a chance to answer, Mayweather cut in.

"Girl, miss us with that," he told her. "Tell your mom to mind her business—460 pages in Malcolm X's book. Skip that. You're better off getting Netflix and rentin' the movie."

The class cut loose with laughter.

Ms. Scott stood in front of the blackboard, smiling, with her arms folded. She considered there to be nothing wrong with students engaging in healthy debate—as long as they didn't get too rowdy. She often encouraged them to freely express their opinions.

The teacher noticed that Heather and Xavier weren't paying attention. They both were looking underneath their desks and laughing. Not even concerned about the discussion.

Ms. Scott eased her way over. "Xavier Hunter and Heather Larkin, is this classroom discussion not entertaining enough for the two of you? Anything you want to add to this discussion, Mr. Hunter?"

Xavier was busted and he knew it. So he put his phone

underneath his leg, looked around the class, cut a sneaky smile, and broke 'em off with a heavy load of crap.

He began, "This book is one of the greatest American novels. Regardless of the N-word usage, the book is still a part of our history. You fools want to be safe and only read books by black authors. The 'comfortable' books. Feel-good novels. A lot of you use that word a thousand times a day.

"I hear you all through the hallways and lunchroom. So y'all need to quit frontin' and stop being scared to expand your horizons." Convinced that he had everybody's attention, Xavier sat back in his chair and confidently clasped both hands behind his head, as if to get comfortable. "And to be honest, I think that Huck Finn was a good guy, trying to do right by his partner Jim, the runaway slave. But he was just a product of the time."

The class was quiet for a minute.

That was until Mayweather said, "Yeah. What he said."

Ms. Scott smiled at Xavier. "Very well put, Mr. Hunter—very well stated, indeed. And you all can learn a thing or two from Xavier's perspective. Despite what some critics think, Mark Twain's *Adventures of Huckleberry Finn* is still an American classic." She stared sternly at Mayweather. "And yes, young man, you still have to read this book if you want to pass my class."

Heather jokingly coughed in her hand, something that sounded like she was calling Xavier a teacher's pet.

Everybody heard it and cracked up laughing.

"Ms. Larkin, do you have something you would like to share with the class?" asked Ms. Scott.

"How about if we just read some erotica books instead," Heather added, to a rousing ovation from the other students.

Ms. Scott simply shook her head. "In your dreams, Ms. Larkin."

The teacher walked back to her desk and retrieved an armful of stapled sheets containing thirty test questions. "Now, you kids clear your desks and get ready to take your examinations."

Heather surprised everybody when she said, "You can't blame a girl for trying to get rid of this dumb book by suggesting something with a little more naughty bite to the story."

Ms. Scott distributed the appropriate number of tests to the first student in each row and had them take one and pass the rest back.

"What did you say?" Ms. Scott asked Heather.

Heather had this disturbed expression on her face, like she wanted to just explode on Ms. Scott, but one look from Xavier put the girl in check. Heather backed down and didn't say another word.

"Ms. Larkin, I didn't think you had anything else to say. Any further discussion will constitute you sitting in front of Principal Skinner to explain yourself."

Although it was obvious Heather was acting wackier, Xavier couldn't walk away—Heather Larkin had him whipped.

*   *   *

The next hour in physical education class had Xavier dressed in gym shorts, a plain black T-shirt, and Nike sneakers, dribbling a basketball on the sidelines as he watched guys run up and down the basketball court trying to outdo each other. The girls were on the other side playing volleyball. Some were wearing skintight booty shorts. Xavier didn't mind that at all. But despite the gym noise Xavier found himself thinking about Samantha. At times he might not have shown it, but he really loved her. And in a way Xavier was glad that they had broken up. It was too dangerous in his life right now. Just too much going on now and he didn't want to get her caught up in his foolishness. Samantha was a good girl and deserved a better life, even if it was with a baseball-playing weasel. Sean Desmond, Xavier grudgingly admitted, would be a much better fit than himself. She would be safe.

There hadn't been any incidents the last month. Not even one single fight in the hallways. Almost too quiet. Something was up. It reminded Xavier of an Animal Planet documentary he'd watched about predators in the wild. You could tell when predators were around because the smaller prey animals kept extremely quiet. So as not to be spotted. Xavier could sense the two-legged predators around, lurking in the shadows and waiting on the perfect opportunity to carve him up. The rest of the students were merely waiting quietly and trying to stay the hell out of the way.

Xavier dribbled with his head down until a high-pitched female scream pierced the air, echoing and carry-

ing the horrifying sound out into the hallways. At first
Xavier looked to see if one of the girls was injured, but
they had stopped playing volleyball and were standing on
either side of the net, looking petrified, with their hands
over their mouths, staring at the entrance to the boys'
locker room.

Runt had barely managed to drag his body up the
stairs on hands and knees and had collapsed halfway
through the door. Xavier dropped the basketball he'd
been dribbling and bolted over to his friend. Ms. Porter
made it there at the same time. The little fella had been
worked over, all right. Left eye swollen shut, bottom lip
split. And he was struggling to breathe.

Ms. Porter yelled for someone to call 911.

"Simon," Ms. Porter said, "who did this?"

Runt's right eye popped open and closed just as quick.
The gym teacher then checked his pulse. She said it was
pretty weak.

His right leg twitched.

Xavier kneeled beside Runt's body. "Runt, stay with
us. Who did this to you?"

Rudolph Jamerson, the bully Xavier had defended
Runt from in the locker room during the beginning of the
school year, walked through the door by the health classroom, wearing street clothes.

Xavier met Rudolph's gaze.

The boy looked down at Runt and threw up his hands.
"I didn't have a damn thing to do with that," Rudolph
Jamerson shouted dramatically, backing away.

Xavier didn't attack because he knew the boy didn't have enough heart to cross him.

Moments passed as ambulance sirens could be heard pulling up.

A few minutes later the doors by the health room burst open. In rushed two EMTs—one white, the other black—with a gurney and an orange medical bag.

Xavier asked Runt one more time, "Homeboy, who did this?"

The white EMT took a stethoscope out of the bag and listened to Runt's chest. "Sounds like a collapsed lung. We have to get him to emergency, stat!"

They both worked to secure Runt's neck and placed him on a spine board before lifting the boy onto the gurney. The black EMT placed an oxygen bag over Runt's mouth to help him breathe. They were about to race off when Runt found the strength to pull the bag off.

"Don't"—he gasped for air—"they wore masks, Xavier. Said that this"—Runt huffed—"is a message—they're coming for you."

Xavier felt helpless as he watched them cart his friend away.

Doug was leaning against a wall inside of his office, and the police were back and drilling Xavier with question after question. They were in Doug's office. Two black detectives wearing dark suits and cheesy, cheap shoes took turns hammering Xavier about the incident.

Xavier was still in his gym clothes and sitting in the

seat beside Doug's desk. "I keep telling you I don't know anything."

The taller of the two stooped down, nose to nose, and yelled in Xavier's face, "You know more than you're telling us! We know that this thing has to do with you snitching on your former boss Slick Eddie and your friend Romello Anderson. So why don't you cut the crap and tell us what we need to know?"

Xavier wiped the spittle from his forehead that had found its way from the cop's juicy mouth.

These two clowns were hilarious to him. Xavier knew his rights and he wasn't saying jack.

The shorter detective with lips like bicycle pedals took his shot: "It must suck being your friend. They seem to be dropping like flies around you. We can't connect the Hoover murder with this, but we're sure that these two incidents are related, with you being the most common denominator. Now give it up and let us do our job."

It pained Xavier to know that Runt didn't have anything to do with his ongoing beef with his former boss. The boy had simply gotten caught up in the wrong place at the wrong time.

The bigger one decided to have one more run at Xavier. "You know how this is going to end, with you lying six feet under, right? What then? Maybe they don't stop with you. They'll probably go after other friends and then your family. You're willing to let all of these people pay a price for your stupidity?"

Doug was standing in the corner. They turned to him.

The shorter cop said, "This is no use. Maybe you can talk some sense into him."

The taller one added, "We're gonna be around campus all day asking questions and conducting interviews. Let you know if something comes up."

After Doug saw the officers out, he took a seat at his desk.

"First Felix, then that thing at LaMarcus's house, Brenda, now Simon Templeton—"

"Told you I didn't have anything to do with Brenda," Xavier told Doug.

"That might be true, but people are starting to have a nasty habit of coming up hurt or dead around you."

"Peep this here, fam. You want to blame somebody, take a look in the mirror. Those clowns who did that to Simon were rocking masks. Meaning they were outsiders. The school ain't as secure as you thought."

"Masks? How do you know that?"

"Simon came to and managed to blurt it out before the EMTs took him."

"And why didn't you feel a need to share that with the detectives?"

"I'm telling you, you feel me? You need to check your security."

"No, you are not going to lay this on me and my team. I told you—let me take that back—I *urged* you to go to another school."

"No disrespect, but you're crazy if you think me going to another school would stop these clowns from trying to break me off."

Doug looked him straight in the eye with a sad expression on his face.

"Snap. You're not concerned with me at all," Xavier said. "I get it though. Looking out for the other students is something I would do too. You're just doing your job and I can respect that. But I'm posting up right here at Coleman. Plan on getting my diploma here too, you feel me?"

It was frustration that made Doug pinch the bridge of his nose. "Mr. Hunter, you're going to die if you stay here. Don't know why you're not telling your father any of this. But it looks like I'm gonna have to call Noah myself."

"It's not the thing to do. The old man ain't the old man anymore."

"What do you mean by that? I mean I ran into him, but we didn't have an in-depth conversation."

"Let's just say when you holler at him, you'll find out." Xavier stood up to go. "By the way, any further news on Brenda Sanders?"

"Her mother withdrew her from Coleman. Anything beyond that, I have no idea."

"No news on the baby."

"Told you that I don't know. Her mother came up here one day after Brenda's fall and unenrolled her."

This whole thing with her pregnancy was looking kind of shady. His next thought was harsh, but he couldn't worry about Brenda right now. He was dealing with his own demons.

Xavier left the office and closed the door.

Once outside of Doug's office Xavier tried Brenda's cell phone again. He was shocked to find that her service had been terminated. The mechanical voice let him know that the number had been disconnected. *Oh well,* he thought. There wasn't much more he could do.

10

Xavier was in his bedroom reading. *The Adventures of Huckleberry Finn* wasn't actually a page-turner, but had enough colorful characters to hold his attention. Xavier couldn't imagine living back when the book had been written. He didn't really have a quick temper, but it was hard enough not to be taking it from white folks today. If he'd had to take it like the runaway slave Jim had in the story, he damn sure would've been chin-checking fools and going upside of domes back in the day.

Xavier and Dex had gone to the hospital to check on Runt after school. Simon's parents had shown the boy lots of love. Tons of flowers, balloons, and cards were everywhere from his folks. Homeboy had been resting easy. Tranquilized. Some type of sedation. He looked a lot better than he had after crawling out of the locker room. The kid hadn't really gotten a chance to give Xavier the actual number of goons who'd put it on him. But if Xavier had to judge from the butt-whipping that was put on Runt, there had to be quite a few of them.

Runt suffered a broken right arm, fractured jaw, a few broken ribs, and a collapsed lung.

Xavier was really feeling bad. The walls seemed to be closing in around him and not offering any escape routes. On the way home from the hospital, Dexter and Xavier had kicked the game around. Xavier had warned Dexter to watch his back. He couldn't understand the reason why Runt had been signaled out, but all the same he alerted Dexter to be on guard. It was the same conversation that Xavier had with Linus Flip and Bigstick. Any one of them could fall victim next. It was in their utmost interest to stay vigilant. First Felix and now Runt— Xavier didn't possess the knowledge to look behind the message. But one thing was for damn certain—somebody's wrath seemed to be focused on those around him.

Too much drama. But he was resolved to not let these fools give him a case of nerves and disrupt his studies. There was a ton of homework he had to do. Tomorrow in lab biology the class would be dissecting dead bullfrogs. There was a test in world history Friday and one in his calculus class this coming Monday. On top of everything else, his seventh-hour art appreciation class would be going on a field trip to the Detroit Institute of Arts in a few weeks.

Not wanting to be disturbed, Xavier had placed his

cell phone on vibrate. When he looked up there were ten missed calls from Heather and almost double that in text messages. All of them marked urgent. He couldn't believe he'd slipped up. She was only supposed to be a jump-off and not a full-time gig. Heather had sunk her hooks deeply in him, though. Every time he tried to walk away they'd end up somewhere smashing. Her temper was explosive and her moods swung back and forth like a child's swing. Yet there was something about her unstable behavior that had him on lock. Xavier didn't know if that was telling him something about himself.

He wasn't given any more time to analyze their strange relationship because in walked Noah.

Xavier could already tell that the old man was on that foolish tip.

"The race is not given to the strong or the weak but the one who walks with God," Noah said as he stood over Xavier.

Xavier had that *Would you get to it?* look on his face. He held up the novel. "I'm studying."

Noah was dressed in work blues and steel-toed boots.

"My hours have been cut back at the pizza parlor. Satan is always busy. But all things work together for the good and the benefit of those who trust in the Lord according to His will for them," he said.

This didn't make any sense. Xavier was under so much pressure he didn't know how much more he could take. This man was impossible to talk to. And Doug was suggesting that Xavier spill his guts to Noah. For what? To get taken to the basement, tied down, have holy water splashed on him while Noah recited scriptures from the Bible, working the whole thing with a crucifix and trying to exorcise some demon out of his oldest son?

With a finger Noah lifted the cover of the book in Xavier's hands.

"*The Adventures of Huckleberry Finn*, huh? Still not picking up the Bible, are we?"

Xavier said in frustration, "I have a test on this stuff. No disrespect, but can you leave me alone so I can study?"

"Anything outside of the King James and other godly approved materials—"

Xavier cut him off. "Let me guess: It's wasted time?! I mean, you say it all the time."

Noah stepped back, surprised by his son's aggression. "I plead the blood of Jesus over you, Xavier. Are you forgetting who the parent is? That's why you should take more time reading the Bible and less time reading Satan's work."

"I'm reading this for my English class." Xavier rubbed his temples, trying to massage away the frustration. "It's been a long day and I'm not feeling well. Can you please leave?"

Noah looked up at the ceiling like he was expecting Jesus Christ himself to come through to help him out with his wayward son. "You can't have my child, Satan. No weapon formed against me shall prosper."

"And that's just the reason why I can't talk to you. Haven't you paid attention to me? I haven't called you *Dad* one time since you've been home. I don't know who you are, you feel me?"

Noah moved on Xavier. It was done so quick that Xavier didn't have time to react.

Noah grabbed his son around the neck with one arm and with the other he tried to rip the shirt right off of Xavier's back. "I told you about wearing these clothes from the designer devils. If you won't stop wearing them I'll tear them off myself."

Xavier squirmed, dropping the book to the floor. It was almost all he could do because his father was much bigger and stronger. Noah had a good grip on Xavier's navy blue Nautica T-shirt, stretching it at the neck and trying to rip it off.

They tussled for a while until Xavier managed to wriggle free. His father was stronger, but Xavier was quicker. He fell to one knee as he sharply cut around the corner of his bedroom door and into the hallway. In a blur Xavier ran through the house toward the front door. With enough presence of mind to grab his jacket, he swung open the front door and ran out into the night.

Xavier didn't give a damn whose Ford Edge Heather was gripping. He just jumped in and told her to drive.

"Heather, you got a license?"

"I'm seventeen, and yes, I have my license."

That was all Xavier needed to know.

As they drove through the night, his temper was on bump and he had to do something before nuttin' up and losing his damn mind. But he wasn't about to go jaw-jacking with Heather. There was no way Xavier could explain to her with a straight face that his father had tried to tear the clothing off of his body because the clothes were evil. He knew he couldn't tell a far-fetched story like that and expect not to be met with an incredulous face.

So he kept it to himself. Xavier was a pretty private person anyway. Even with his mother, Ne Ne, Xavier had always kept his family matters private. His business was his business and nobody else's—bottom line.

As Heather drove, Xavier remained silent. He couldn't believe that the old man had put his hands on him. Xavier could see being physically disciplined by his father if he wasn't hitting the books and getting the grades. But trying to rip his clothes off, stating that the designer labels were responsible for Xavier's rebellious spirit, was the stuff of mental institutions.

Xavier needed somebody to talk to about everything going on in his life. But for the life of him he couldn't find one contact in his phone that could help him. He'd hollered at Billy a few days ago, but the old man was far too busy to lay that great wisdom on him. The old coot's young girlfriend finally had her baby and Billy was in the process of moving in his new family. Billy had his own troubles.

"Are you all right, Hunter?"

Xavier just kept staring out of the window.

Heather said, "I'm not just going to continue to drive you around and not know where we're going."

Again, there was no answer. Xavier continued to stare out at the bright lights from the local businesses that lined both sides of 8 Mile Road.

"Okay, I'll just take you to where I go to work out my problems," Heather announced.

Xavier was silent. Not really caring one way or the other.

Heather drove another ten minutes until she reached a crowded parking lot belonging to some rinky-dink, ghetto pool hall. It looked to be an extremely rough place that doubled as a hangout for biker gangs.

Rack 'Em poolroom sat as a standalone building in Detroit on West 8 Mile near Lahser Road. Young men stood around in groups, smoking cigarettes and trying to be on the low by sipping on forty ounces wrapped in brown paper bags.

Outside, in front of the building, six cats stood out. They were rocking red leather biker jackets trimmed in white.

In a place like this it didn't take a Cambridge scholar to realize that stepping out of line here could result in a severe beat-down.

Xavier couldn't quite understand why Heather would bring him to a place where saying "hi" the wrong way could potentially lead to gunplay and somebody being on the receiving end of violence.

Xavier pointed to the place and simply asked, "You have to be kidding, right? You actually come here to think?"

She parked and playfully laughed. "Hunter, you are so silly. Since you won't tell me about your problem I decided to bring you to a place where I work out all of my issues."

Xavier pointed again. "Once again—here? You come here, to this place, to think out your problems? Let me see how I can say this and still be respectful: You are nuttier than a bag of trail mix."

Heather glanced around the parking lot.

He said to her, "This is one of those places where murder investigations end. Missing fools are later found because somebody is pulled from in there and is interrogated by the police until the bodies are found."

She laughed. "Hunter, I just love your sense of humor."

He shook his head. "I'm not playing, and there's no way I'm going in there."

Heather turned off the ignition. "You're not afraid of a nice game of pool, are you?"

"Aye, I got a lot on my plate and I damn sure don't need any more to be worried about."

"Hunter"—she started the truck back up—"it's okay if you're afraid."

He popped his lips dismissively. "Miss me with your first-grade mind games. Too old and too tired for that. Now bounce me somewhere else."

Without word or warning, she yelled, "I want to play pool!"

"So this is not about me. It's all about you?"

In the whiny voice of a little girl, Heather said, "I wanna play pool!"

This girl was getting battier and battier. He figuratively kicked himself in the butt for slippin' on this heifer. The drama in his life had run him straight into the arms of somebody who should've been on heavy antidepressants.

When the childish tantrum didn't work she flipped the script. Heather opened the door and slid out of the truck with her backside to him and started twerking. It was ridiculous because the loose sweatpants she was wearing did little to conceal her jiggling booty, the junk in her trunk dribbling like it should've had Spalding written across it.

She seductively looked over her shoulder at Xavier while her moneymaker was going crazy and said, "You play pool with me now because if you don't"—she stopped shaking it and pulled the loose material tight to highlight her booty—"I won't love you anymore."

Xavier had forgotten about the dudes out front until they started whistling their approval at Heather's performance. The girl was setting him up for conflict but didn't seem to care.

Against his better judgment he got out of the car. Heather stopped her act and closed the driver's-side door. Her smile resembled that of a six-year-old.

"I knew I would get my way," she said to Xavier. A click of the keyless entry sounded the horn—*honk!*—made the headlights flash, and locked the doors on the Ford Edge.

She snuggled up to Xavier on their walk through the parking lot. The drama didn't start until they stepped up on the biker guys in red leather jackets. Xavier tried to keep his cool as one of them removed a knot of money out of his pocket and threw a few dollars at Heather's feet. She and Xavier kept it moving, right through a walkway where the group stood three on either side.

The fool who'd thrown the loot was a brown-skinned guy—big head and shorter than Heather, but he had his boys with him, so he was down to act a fool.

Xavier noticed that their club name, Boss Dog Biker

Boyz, was written in cursive on the back of the dude's jacket over a picture of an angry-looking bulldog riding a crotch rocket.

"When a woman like that puts on a show like that," Bighead said, "it gets a fool to thinking that she's too much for one man to handle." The rest of his guys let their disrespect for Xavier ring out in their laughter.

Heather had a look on her face like she was eating up the attention.

Xavier couldn't give a damn about Heather. It pissed him off to be disrespected by the little big head chump with all the mouth. But he was no fool. There were six of them. Didn't need a math major to calculate the outcome if Xavier stepped to them. He'd get curb-stomped.

Xavier opened the door for Heather, letting the venom in his eyes stand as a warning that he couldn't give a damn about their numbers if they came with that bull again.

Inside, there were a total of thirty pool tables. The air smelled of stale cigarette smoke and mildew. The old Arabic man behind the counter looked like a grimy old pervert, the stump of an unlit cigar dangling from the corner of his mouth. He smelled bad too, like feet and Fritos. The floors looked like they hadn't been swept in months and garbage cans were overflowing.

Xavier and Heather quickly grabbed a table in the back. The felt was dirty with God only knew what on the material. Xavier was still pissed at his dad and paid none of that any mind. In silence he racked up the balls while waiting like a gentleman on Heather to go and come from the bathroom. If this place was this dirty, he reckoned the bathrooms had to be gross.

He surveyed his surroundings. This place was a virtual refuge for ex-cons, drugged-out bikers, and murderers. What the hell was he doing here? The answer was simple. Heather's love game had him crazy and was blindly leading him around by his zipper. He definitely wasn't hanging around her because of her class. She'd shown absolutely zero in the parking lot.

After she came back, they chilled and kicked it about everything. Laughing and joking mostly about school until those six Boss Dog Biker Boyz walked in the front door with menace on their minds.

Xavier had already peeped game. The marijuana smell that rolled in on them let him know they were about to clown. Out of the corner of his eye he caught them approaching. Leaning over the table holding a pool cue, Heather was busy concentrating on her shot. She hadn't yet seen them. Beef was about to jump off and there was nothing Xavier could do but prepare to get his scrap on. While Heather ran off at the mouth Xavier stood on the opposite side, tightening his grip around the pool stick.

The boys were five tables from them when Xavier walked around and stood beside Heather, as she sank her ball in a corner pocket. He touched her.

"Touching me while I'm shooting—that's cheating," Heather said to Xavier with a smile. It wasn't until the boys were right up on her that she recognized the situation. "Oh look, Hunter, it's the Boss Puppy Biker Girls."

Bighead said to Xavier, "Your chick has a lot of mouth, partna."

Heather sized Bighead up and pointed to the enormous beer gut bulging out of his open leather jacket. "I might have a lot of mouth, but you need to learn"—she pointed at his stomach—"how to back away from the dinner table, you fat slob."

Xavier was tripping on the balls possessed by this chick. Inciting these fools wasn't exactly the smartest thing to do. Apparently the girl had some sort of death wish.

The biggest one stood eye level to Xavier and probably had him by fifty pounds. When he spoke up his voice was so deep that it seemed like the earth shook. "Yo, Problematic," he said to Bighead. "Let's show this chick how we do with big-mouths."

Problematic, Xavier thought. Based on his name alone, it didn't sound like he'd be easy to tangle with.

Xavier wasn't known for diplomacy in these types of situations. But he figured if he wanted to get out of this place in one piece he'd better try to defuse the mounting tension.

He said to the guy named Problematic, "Listen, homeboy, we're just here to play pool. Don't want any trouble."

Problematic's facial expression seemed to indicate that Xavier had gotten through to him. That was until Heather opened her big mouth again.

She blazed Problematic. "I know you don't want none of my man. That's right, fall back, chumps."

Problematic laughed it off. He said to Xavier, "My man, you better do something before I get at this gutter rat."

Heather shot back at Problematic, "You see a gutter

rat?" She looked the guy up and down. "Talking about getting at me, the first thing you better get is a ladder, with your short ass."

That was it. The red button had been pushed. Problematic reached up like a pimp and was about to give Heather his backhand when Xavier blocked him with the pool cue, splintering the stick. The move left him open and defenseless for what came next. Not able to quickly recover, Xavier was helpless as the biggest biker let his fist fly. The last thing Xavier saw was knuckles, lights, and then darkness.

Xavier seemed to be floating, with the sound of music playing somewhere in the distance. The sound kept getting closer and closer. He couldn't exactly make out the lyrics—that was probably due to the throbbing, excruciating pain and confusion going on inside of his head. He attempted to open his eyes and was met by blurriness. Then like an old television set the picture started to adjust. Blurriness, double vision, and then distorted shapes and sizes came into view, everything meshing together into one long, illuminated streak. Xavier didn't quite know where he was. His head was spinning, swimming— his brain seemed to pulse with every thought. The more he tried to remember what had happened, the harder the pounding in his head—until his eyes began to slowly focus. The bright lights from the lampposts and numerous businesses on 8 Mile lit up the street like it was an airport runway.

He was back in the passenger seat of the Ford Edge. Xavier looked over at Heather.

"Wha-what happened?" he asked her in a voice strained by grogginess.

No answer. Heather kept biting the nails of her non-driving hand and mumbling something that he couldn't quite make out. The volume of the car stereo was also turned up.

Xavier's seat had been fully reclined. Despite the pulsating pain inside of his head he made the seat adjustment so he could sit up. The time on the digital clock in the dash read 9:35.

"I said, what happened?" Xavier asked again, but louder this time. He winced from the pain.

It was like the chick was bugging out. Heather was rocking back and forth, mumbling gibberish and dining on the nails of her left hand like she had barbecue sauce on them.

Bits and pieces of the confrontation started coming back. The last thing Xavier could remember was piecing ol' boy up with the pool cue before he got his own ticket punched.

The girl was still rocking back and forth in the driver's seat. Xavier wanted to shake her but didn't want to run the risk of Heather losing control of the wheel and plowing through the showroom window of the car dealership they were just passing. He hadn't noticed before, but Heather looked like she'd been in a brawl. Her hair was all over her head. The neck of her blouse was stretched out of place and there was also a bruise underneath her right eye.

"They tried to drag me in the bathroom and rape me," she said out of nowhere.

She answered his question before he could ask—

"After you hit Problematic and knocked him unconscious, the biggest biker hit you from behind."

Well, that explains the stars and stripes I saw before blacking out, Xavier thought. It also explained why there was a knot coming out the side of his head almost the size of an Easter egg.

He said, "Go on."

Heather started to cry.

Through her tears she explained, "I hit the big one over the head with my stick. One of them hit me and I fell to the floor in front of everybody. They started trying to pull me into the men's bathroom. I was kicking and screaming until the guy behind the counter scared them off.

"He was gonna call the cops but I pleaded with him not to because I only have a driver's permit and my mother doesn't know I have her car. She's been out of town for almost a week. The man behind the counter felt sorry for me and he had a guy help me drag you to the car."

Un-freakin'-believable, Xavier thought. This had to be a sign from the Lord, Xavier figured. He was on probation and if the cops had been called out, more than likely he would've been in violation and sentenced to do a stretch in juvie. Heather had to go. He was a junior with not much longer to go before graduation. He had come too far to be stopped by a cute mental case with gorgeous hair and a banging body.

Heather was off the chain, and at the rate Xavier was going he wouldn't have to worry about Slick Eddie's hitters popping him out. He was sure to get *that* if he'd stayed around her craziness any longer.

"Would you like me to drive you to emergency?" Heather asked sadly, still sniffling.

Xavier didn't have to drop any thought into his reply. "Hell nah!" He gently touched the golf-ball-size lump on the side of his noggin. "Drop me off where you picked me up. You've done enough for—I mean to me for one day."

Heather made a right turn onto the service drive.

She instantly started apologizing. "I'm sorry for my behavior this evening."

"I don't know what is going on inside of that head of yours, baby girl. But it's too much for me. I have my own problems."

Heather successfully merged into the middle lane of the Southfield Freeway. "Please, don't leave me. You're all I have."

Yeah. This chick is bonkers, all right. "You sound crazy. Like you been smoking something. You do know that this was just a smash thing."

"*Was*—what do you mean *was*, Hunter?" She almost sounded possessed. The tears were gone but the intensity on her face was back.

"See how you can just switch back and forth like that? It's not normal."

Heather was angry now and the car behind them couldn't have found a worse time to tailgate. Looking in the rearview, she gently applied pressure on her brake pedal, forcing the tailgater to slam on his breaks to avoid rear-ending the Ford Edge. Xavier looked on in terror as the vehicle got around Heather and pulled up on Xavier's side. As if she hadn't just got him beat down back at the poolroom, she was now about to get him shot by one of these road-raging, pistol-packing motorists in Detroit. Thank God it was an elderly white man who flipped a wrinkled bird instead of pulling a gat. Heather and grandpa were riding alongside one another and flipping each other off.

"Heather, fall back. The man is old enough to be your grandfather. Chill out and drive this damn car."

He simply shook his head. The girl was loonier than any Looney Tune ever created by Warner Bros. At this point Xavier was through talking, but she wasn't.

"So you don't love me?" Heather asked in a low and creepy voice.

All he was trying to do was get home. Xavier would rather face the wrath of Noah before he dealt with any more of the insane people inside of her head.

She gradually rotated the steering wheel to the left, moving into the far left lane and across the solid yellow lines to the sound of loud honking from the motorist behind her. The loud sound of the tires running over the warning strip was horrifying. She rode the warning strip to make her point.

"Do you know I can kill us both by slamming into the median wall?"

Xavier was wearing a *What the hell did I get myself involved in?* look on his face. Homeboy had forgotten all about the pain and bump on his head. Skip crazy, this chick was berserk.

The tension eased in her face. That gorgeous smile of

hers was back. Heather straightened up the wheel and slid back into the lane.

Laughing, she said, "I was just playing. Look at how scared you look, Hunter."

To Xavier, Heather was a done deal. He had watched far too many flicks dealing with psycho, stalking lunatics not to know one when he saw one. She had gotten him knocked out tonight. Something that nobody else had ever been able to accomplish in a straight-up, one-on-one tussle with him.

Heather sat behind him in English and that was going to be a problem. There was nothing he could do about it, though. But after today, homegirl was a wrap—her and that tight body of hers.

11

After what happened to him last night there was no way Xavier was attending school today. A terrible headache was whooping on his butt and the lump on his lemon was still visibly noticeable. Xavier could've worn a baseball hat to try and cover the thing, but it would've been stupid to place a fitted cap over the tender area. Plus his pride was bleeding from several different holes of humiliation at having his teeth rattled by one of the biker goons.

When Xavier had made it back home last night he expected to go a couple more rounds with Noah. But much to his delight, the lights were out in the house and nobody was up. It happened to be a good thing the old man had been sleeping. Throughout the night Xavier was able to lick his wounds by putting cold compresses on the lump. Popped a few Motrin to kill the pain.

The drama with the bikers had given him insomnia. So he'd made it through the night lying in bed on his back with the bedroom lights out and staring into the darkness. Xavier had been tripping out, thinking about a lifetime of mistakes he'd managed to make over a couple years. Bad choices. Inability to see the big picture. No father at the crib to provide that around-the-clock leadership. The absence of his dad had left him trying to fill a man's shoes with his itty-bitty teenage feet. Yeah, he was able to get in 'em, but they were far too big for walking, resulting in slips and falls. Learn as you go—a method that had proved costly. There was a price riding on his head because of it. Samantha was gone. And now a whack job was trying her very best to drag him into an early grave.

Noah usually came to Xavier's bedroom first thing in the morning to roust him awake. Today his father hadn't bothered. Xavier had heard Noah getting Alfonso ready, but he never approached the bedroom belonging to his eldest. The old man still had an attitude.

Other than providing basic necessities, Noah had been worthless to him up to this point. Xavier was in a terrible way with some really bad people and there was not one person he could run to for help.

This was definitely not the way he had pictured a relationship with his father after the old dude had come home from prison. Xavier had had all of these fantasies in his head about their relationship being close and unbreakable. Just being able to relate to an older male other than Billy would've been tight, especially if that other male was his dad. But this was the ghetto, and dreams like that just didn't happen for people like him. It was all good, though. Xavier was a rider for his, and definitely wasn't about to waste time with the tears. The boy was sixteen going on grown and had been rudely introduced to that part of society that couldn't care less if young black men destroyed each other.

With Noah working day shift he wouldn't have any idea that Xavier had elected to post up at the crib and not have his butt in school. Xavier could just chill and think things out without having to look over his shoulder. He got his lounge on for a few hours before deciding to catch up on his studies. The lab biology book made him remember the bullfrog that he wouldn't be dissecting in class today. Can't say he was all busted up about it. Frog guts weren't working for him.

He grabbed the Huck Finn book and tried to read but it wasn't happening. Runt was heavily on his mind. Dude had gotten caught up in Xavier's beef and was laid up in the hospital with all types of injuries. Later on he would take the bus down to the hospital and see how homeboy was progressing. Maybe even take the kid some flowers.

At noon Xavier made a sandwich and had lunch in his bedroom. He wasn't just going to lie around like a bum. This time would better serve him if he ate while he performed calculus problems.

Some doubt started to creep into his mind. Was he being overly presumptuous in thinking that he would make it to graduation? The work he was now doing— was it all in vain? He was slipping and he knew it. Letting negative thinking smack him down. He'd learned a little while ago to control those things that he could and leave everything else to God, regardless of the obstacles standing in his way dressed in ski masks and wielding around bad intentions.

From his calculus book he looked at the clock. Just about time for fourth period lunch. Samantha would be there, probably eating alone at a table. At least, that's what he hoped. Even though she'd changed her phone number, Xavier had resources. He had her digits and was aching to dial them. Being with Heather had taught him a severe lesson: Samantha could be a snob at times, but after hanging around psycho Heather, Samantha was looking like the future Mrs. Hunter. He dearly missed his girl. It was why he was dialing *67 before calling her cell phone. As it rang, Xavier knew the number would show up anonymous on her caller ID screen but he didn't care. If she picked up—cool; if not, he would have the pleasure of listening to Samantha's sweet voice on her voice mail greeting.

No dice. She didn't pick up.

Instead he got voice mail action.

Xavier was one of the toughest guys he knew, but Samantha's personal voice mail greeting almost brought tears. He hung up after listening. Suddenly he wanted to find Sean Desmond and wring his neck. Just picturing baseball boy playing on the same diamond he had once had the pleasure to play on was enough to almost send Xavier through the roof. Never had he been so jealous. The junk was simply ridiculous. This was the moment that he realized how jacked up his life was. And with no muscle of his own to help him get Slick Eddie's dogs off of his back, Xavier didn't have a clue as to how he could straighten everything out.

Xavier returned to the kitchen to get something to drink. He was supposed to do something today . . . oh yeah, it hit him. While he poured himself a glass of grape soda, Xavier remembered that he'd promised Alfonso he would go up to Alex Haley Middle School today and pay Dog Boy a visit. The fat lump on the side of his noodle was telling Xavier there was no way in hell he was ready to scrap today. It would've been stupid for him to risk getting hit in that area of his head. Alfonso would have to wait because his big brother was on the injured reserve list. Noah would be there to pick him up anyway. The boy wouldn't have to endure too much teasing from that pit bull-walking punk.

Once Xavier finished the beverage it was world history time and he had every intention of studying, but when he walked by the door leading up to his father's bedroom his feet started moving up the stairs without his permission. Noah had taken the upstairs bedroom when they'd moved in. Xavier had never been anywhere near his father's lair, especially since his dad had started rolling tough with God's posse.

One step at a time he ascended into the old man's domain. The air even felt different as he climbed the stairs. As soon as Xavier cleared the last step, immediately to his right was a huge picture hanging on the wall of white Jesus. Damn near scared Xavier out of his socks. Religious artifacts were everywhere. Crosses hanging, standing, or lying around. Praying hands were centered and mounted on every wall. The wall behind the headboard of his full-size bed featured an enormous colorful banner of the Last Supper. Little crystal angel figurines sat on the dresser next to a thirteen-inch flat screen. There was a bookshelf by one of the nightstands. Four thick hardback Bibles were housed on the first shelf, the second belonging to a bunch of biblical reference books. The last held dusty CDs of vintage gospel songs.

After learning about some of the diabolical things that Noah had pulled as a kingpin on the street, Xavier couldn't be too mad at him for trying to change his life. Sometimes his father could go overboard while trying to share his relationship with God. All the crosses around the room led Xavier to believe that Noah was trying to keep away those old demons. That was probably the reason why he went so hard.

There were pictures of Xavier and Alfonso as babies on the nightstand near the window. Noah loved them, and Xavier knew that, but he just wished he could sit down and have a decent conversation with his father. It would probably never happen, though. Wishful thinking on his part.

Xavier headed back downstairs with one thing on his mind: He hoped that his father was praying for him. He would need somebody to do that for him in order to stay above ground.

12

Xavier was in class trying harder than concrete to keep his mind on his art appreciation teacher's lecture. Nathan McGillicuddy was fairly tall, slender, white, middle-aged, wore a scraggly beard, and was slightly stooped at the waist with a hump in his back. Students often made fun of him because to them it looked like his everyday outfit consisted of tan corduroys, a burgundy sweater-vest pulled over a button-up, and some cheap suede shoes. Either he was in possession of a closet filled with tan corduroys and burgundy sweater-vests or he was guilty as charged of breaking all types of hygiene laws.

McGillicuddy was animated, too, feeling whatever he lectured about. The nut was in front of the class and wildly waving his arms around explaining to his students how Vincent van Gogh was a tortured genius who sucked the paint from his paintbrushes while turning out masterpieces.

Even the part in the lecture about van Gogh's bipolar butt slicing off one of his ears and sending it to his girlfriend in a box wrapped in a pretty bow did little to keep Xavier's attention. At the moment nothing could, because the boy was lovesick over his ex. Samantha had been in the lunchroom, gorgeously stunning, looking like she was about to go and have a photo shoot done for the cover of some teen magazine. Not once had she looked in Xavier's direction. Her lips were full and beautiful, probably done up in her favorite lip gloss. Laughing and joking with her girls like her life was full of exciting new promise. While his was dark, shady, and dangerous with a questionable future. Xavier felt left behind. Falling out of touch with the one thing in his life that had made any sense.

He thought about Heather too. Since the night she'd almost gotten him bodied, Heather had fallen off the earth, resurfacing today, sweating him and blowing up his cell phone with a barrage of voice and text messages. Got so bad that he simply powered his hitter down. He wasn't trying to go there with her anymore. In his estimation, anybody who visited a rough-and-tumble, dangerous, biker-infested pool hall like Rack 'Em to get their thoughts together was a certifiable maniac.

McGillicuddy was holding some art book up in his hands, with the pages open to one of van Gogh's paintings—*Starry Night*. The teacher was explaining the technique that had gone into the piece when into the class walked a teenage guy Xavier had never seen before. He didn't strike Xavier as a threat to him. The dude moved up to McGillicuddy and handed the teacher a piece of paper. McGillicuddy took it, pulled out a pen, and closed the book so that he could use the cover to put his signature on the paper.

McGillicuddy then said something like, "Take any open seat, Mr. Kato Holloway. I'm lecturing about Vincent van Gogh. Feel free to take notes because you will be tested on the material. You've missed quite a few class assignments. Meet me after the hour and I will provide everything you will need."

The dude, Kato Holloway, was fairly dark and had sharp facial features. He was about six feet tall, 175 pounds, with a wiry, muscular frame. But his most attractive feature was his hair. His dreads were cleverly woven and interlocked in layers, freefalling and stopping at the bottom of his shoulder blades. The cat didn't spend much money on his clothes. Nothing fancy, a funny color brown Detroit Lions sweatshirt and camouflage pants. Wheat-colored Timberland boots covered his feet. But Xavier had a sharp eye when it came down to spotting a G with fat pockets. Kato didn't seem like he cared about gear that much, but his earlobes were a different story. The way that the classroom light picked up and reflected his diamond stud earrings left no doubt that the pieces were high quality. The Cartier glasses on his face gave him that young, rich rap star appearance.

The boy copped a squat in the second seat of the second row from the door, every student looking at him like he was the hip-hop version of President Barack Obama.

Xavier figured something serious had to have shaken up his world to be switching schools this late in the semester.

The rest of the hour found Xavier consistently picking up some type of thug vibe from Kato. Dude didn't seem like he walked around with a chip on his shoulder, but Xavier could tell that the boy would be about handling his business if somebody stepped to him the wrong way. Was far from soft. He couldn't be, with expensive glasses and earrings like those. Not with the predators at Coleman. The next month would be interesting. New guys got the treatment at Coleman. Those earrings and glasses, if homeboy kept on rocking 'em, would draw the wrong kind of attention. If Kato wasn't about it, those rocks and frames would be on the earlobes and face of some stick-up fool.

Right after Xavier's last hour, he was with his boys in the back parking lot. The group was chilling around Linus Flip's Pontiac Grand Prix.

Students were loitering in groups, some were walking home, and others were waiting on rides.

Bigstick asked the group, "I know y'all fools coming to the football game tomorrow. We're gonna smash those nerds from Cass Tech."

Xavier gave Bigstick some dap. "You know it, homeboy. Gotta show love to the Coleman High Wolverines, you feel me?"

Linus asked Bigstick, "What time is the game, anyways?"

"Kick-off is at eleven, so get your lazy bones up, fam. You ain't doing nothing anyway, so come"—Bigstick pointed at himself—"see this middle linebacker, the next coming of Ray Lewis, get his swerve on. We're gonna light some chumps up and break some fools off, you dig."

Xavier and Linus laughed.

Linus sat, propped against the rear left fender of his whip. "That's what's up. I'm there," he said.

The back door of the south entrance opened. Out walked Dex, a big smile on his grill, holding hands with a bad, caramel-toned breezy named Marissa Steel. The little chick was compact—no more than five-two, probably 130 pounds, and busty. Short hairstyle. Cute Asian eyes. Nice backside in her Apple Bottoms jeans. Sneakers and fitted leather jacket.

Linus Flip laughed at Dexter.

Dex stepped up and introduced her to the group. "Marissa, you might already know these characters but I'm a gentleman, so I'll introduce them anyway." Dex kissed Marissa on the cheek. "This is Xavier, Bigstick, and Linus Flip." He smiled at Marissa. "Everybody, this is my new boo, Marissa Steel."

The only thing Xavier could see was another one of his homeboy's outrageous outfits.

"You just keep getting ridiculous with your choice of threads," Xavier said to Dex, shaking his head. "Who you supposed to be today—all that orange—the great pumpkin?"

"Trick or treat." That was Linus Flip.

Everybody in the circle was laughing their behinds off.

Dex wasn't sweating it, though. He had a fine sista on his arm who validated his new look. He was rocking a bright orange body-fitting mock neck underneath the same color cardigan sweater, with darker orange skinny pants, and blue sneakers trimmed in orange. The dude was even carrying an orange man-bag.

Bigstick had to take a swing. "You got a purse to match every color of outfit, don't you, fam?"

Marissa jumped to her man's defense. "Haters. My man looks good. All of you could learn a thing or two from his style." She kissed Dex on the jaw and looped her arm around his.

Dexter looked at all his friends and smugly smiled.

Xavier said, " 'Learn a thing from his style'?—damn, man. You got her brainwashed."

Linus Flip added, "She sounds just like you."

Dex put his arm around Marissa and slowly walked off, looking backwards. "Y'all just haters. But I don't know why I expected any different; you cats ain't even on my level of fashion. Have a conversation with me when y'all get up outta sneakers and jeans—you know, little boy stuff. I'm a grown man, dog."

It took Xavier to bring his homeboy's big ol' helium head back to earth. "Last year you wanted to be a thug. This year you don't know if you wanna dress like Dwayne Wade or Kanye West. Next year you probably gonna be wearing a blouse, skirt, and stilettos—punk!"

With his arm draped around his chick, Dexter threw a dismissive gesture at Xavier with his free hand and continued walking.

As they watched him walk away, the new dude, Kato Holloway, walked out of the south entrance by himself, like a true boss. Still flexin' those nice, glittery stones in his ears and confidently looking out at the world through Cartier frames.

Linus Flip looked at Kato and questioned, "Who dat dude?"

"Kato Holloway," Xavier answered. "All I can tell you is that blood's in my art appreciation class, a latecomer."

Bigstick said, "Those earrings have to be two karats apiece, and those glasses ain't no joke, fam. They had to set a brotha back a few Gs."

"Does the fool know exactly what kind of school this is?" Flip wanted to know.

Kato walked right by them and acknowledged them with a nod as he kept it funky. The cat walked like he hadn't a care in the world and with his keyless entry, popped the locks on an out-cold black Chevy TrailBlazer SS sitting on twenty-inch chrome. He jumped in, started up, and skirted out, a powerful bass beat thumping from the speakers of his car stereo system when he reached the parking lot driveway. Way after Kato turned and disappeared down the street, his volcano-like bass could still be heard rumbling in the distance.

Linus Flip just shook his head. "I'm not the sharpest knife in the drawer but, X, didn't you tell us this dude just enrolled?"

Xavier scratched his head. "Yep. There's something about this cat I just can't put a finger on."

"Skip putting a finger on, but if fam get caught slipping at Coleman styling like that, man, some stick-up kid is gonna push his wig back," Bigstick said. "I'm just saying."

"I don't know about that, B," Xavier replied. "Something is telling me that this kid is no joke. Unless he's been living under a rock, the cat is familiar with Coleman's reputation. He just walked out of the building without backup and jumped into a sweet sled with no fear whatsoever. I hope these fools up here don't take Mr. Holloway lightly."

Kato was a mystery wearing Timberland boots and driving a freaky TrailBlazer SS. You just didn't do those kinds of things at Coleman and think that you weren't going to be touched. In time the truth would be revealed. This movie had yet to play out. But this dude's gangsta was legitimate. Every drop was advertised in Kato's swagger.

Nothing got past Xavier. He understood it because he was it, a true beast in his own right. So it took one to know one. Xavier already knew what Kato was about. The only thing that could be said about this situation was that game recognized game.

13

There were five minutes to go in the third quarter of the high school football game. The Coleman High Wolverines were whipping up on the Cass Tech Falcons, 40 to 16, and the Wolverines had just scored off a Falcon fumble caused by the tackle put on their running back by Coleman's own super-sensation middle linebacker, Calvin "Bigstick" Mack. Coleman High students in the stands went berserk, yelling and screaming. The roar was even more deafening after the Wolverines kicked the extra point through the uprights. The stands, filled to maximum capacity, emptied as spectators swarmed over every square inch of the football field.

Xavier, Dex, and Linus Flip had enjoyed the game. They remained in the stands, enjoying the spectacle, when

Xavier excused himself to use the restroom. Linus offered to escort Xavier to the lavatory by the boys' locker room. Xavier declined and made his way out of the stands. Once he was on the ground, he spotted Samantha and Sean Desmond way up at the top of the bleachers, surrounded by scores of people. Mr. Shortstop was making her laugh by whispering something in her ear.

And she said they were only friends. Looks like more than that to me, Xavier thought. He turned quickly and walked away. Once, she used to laugh and look at him like that.

People were all over the back parking lot. Standing in groups. Talking and laughing with one another. Having a great time. Xavier had to weave his way through the crowds to get back to the locker room.

Samantha was on his mind. He'd lost her forever. Xavier wasn't in her league when it came down to money, and despite how bad it hurt to recognize this, he had to keep it one-hun'ed with himself. There was no way he could compete with Sean Desmond's future multimillion-dollar contract. The only thing he could do right now was try to stay alive and hope to finish his junior year outside of a body bag.

Xavier was through the side door and around a corner, headed down a corridor to the boys' lavatory near the gymnasium when he thought he heard the same door he'd come through open and close behind him. He paid no mind and proceeded to the restroom. But it was locked. The one by the cafeteria was always open, so he headed that way.

Xavier didn't get it. As he freely roamed the hallways,

there were no signs of security anywhere. In the past when he'd gotten the urge to take a leak during a game it was nothing to spot Doug and his team walking through the building. By the cafeteria he entered the restroom. As he did his business he hadn't meant to think about Heather and all of her foolishness. He hadn't responded to any of her text messages, so she had stopped. She must have gotten the message. He hadn't seen the lunatic around school either. Not even in English. And that was okay. Xavier had never told the fellas that he'd gotten his bell rung at the pool hall that night. It wasn't their business. Matter of fact, nobody needed to know that. The secret would die with him.

He finished up, washed his hands, and dried them on a paper towel. He walked out of the lavatory and right into a blood-chilling scene eerily reminiscent of some high school horror movie. Tall and Husky with the charcoal skin and big ears was back and standing to Xavier's left, blocking off the intersection to the hallway. The thug was still wearing the same dark Rocawear hoodie Xavier had seen him in when they first locked eyes in the cafeteria.

This wasn't the time for his sense of humor to kick in, but Xavier couldn't help it. Either this moron was a rabid Jay-Z fan or the hooded sweatshirt was his favorite to wear when he felt that occasional impulse to try and hurt somebody.

Xavier thought about getting cute and walking up to Tall and Husky. That was until the fool went underneath the hooded sweatshirt. It was on. The dude had to have been sent by Slick Eddie. But Xavier wasn't sticking around to find out, or see what type of weapon he'd pulled. Tall and Husky didn't look like the type to bluff. Going underneath the hoodie was all it took. Now Xavier's initial reaction was to get ghost. And that he did. The boy could hear nothing but the sound of his feet pounding the hallway as he broke to his right and ran like his feet were on fire.

Despite bullets not being fired, Xavier knew that the hit man was behind him. He could hear the soles of homeboy's sneakers squeak against the surface, as he tried to keep up. But Xavier kept his head down, leaning forward too much and almost taking a tumble, as he ran for his life. It would've been foolish to look back. The dude behind him was packing and that's all he needed to know. Xavier kept his head down and ran toward the stairwell on his left.

The adrenaline was flowing and he was moving faster than he'd ever run before. Xavier was up the first flight when Tall and Husky started talking to him.

"You can only run so far, boy," he said in a low and creepy voice.

Xavier leapt forward, taking three steps at a time until he managed to run through the doors leading to the fourth floor. Halfway down the hallway, Xavier looked back to see if the hit man was still behind him when— *BAM!*—he ran smack into Doug. They both hit the floor hard.

Doug yelled, "What the hell is wrong with you, boy?!"

Xavier wasn't saying anything. He was trying to get up and move out but Doug had him around the waist.

"Xavier!" Doug screamed, trying to calm him down.

Two more security guards had heard their boss scream and came running. Xavier was a handful and appeared to have lost his mind. He was in fight-or-flight mode, tussling with all three men, still trying to run. A few seconds later the guards managed to restrain the teen.

Xavier was able to calm down and relay his harrowing experience with the hit man.

"There is no hit man behind you," Doug said to Xavier.

None of them really believed Xavier's story because no one heard any shots or saw anyone chasing after Xavier.

"Boy, get a hold of yourself," said Doug. "Show us where the so-called hit man went off to." Xavier couldn't show any proof that he'd been chased.

"I swear," said Xavier. "There was somebody behind me."

Doug used his cell phone to call the police. After the phone call, he wearily shook his head. "I still think it was your imagination, Mr. Hunter. But all the same, when are you going to seriously consider switching schools?"

It was Monday, November 24th—five o'clock sharp. Xavier was sitting in front of the desk belonging to his hairy-forearmed parole officer, Oliver Meyer.

"Do you have any weapons on you?" Oliver asked Xavier in the same old uninterested, flat tone—his face buried behind stacks of paperwork.

"No, sir," Xavier answered back with the same tone.

"Have you participated in the use or sale of illegal narcotics?"

"No, sir."

"Do you understand if I give you a drug test right now and you fail it, you would be in violation and would be forced to serve out the remainder of your time in juvie?"

"Yes, sir."

"Keep your nose clean, Mr. Hunter, and you have no problems. Your next meeting with me will be"—he finally lifted his face out of the paperwork to flip the pages on his desk calendar—"Monday, February 25th. At five o'clock. If you miss this appointment for whatever reasons, you, Mr. Hunter, will be in violation of your probation and will be forced to serve out the remainder of your time in a juvenile facility." Oliver sternly looked at Xavier. "Do you understand everything that we've gone over?"

"Yes, sir."

14

The last day of school before Christmas break found Xavier sitting quietly at his desk in Ms. Scott's English class. It had been a little over a month since Xavier's harrowing experience with the hit man wearing the Rocawear hoodie. To avoid mass panic at Coleman, the police, along with Doug's security force, had managed to keep the incident involving Xavier on the hush-hush because there hadn't been any other staff or students present in the building at the time. And for his own safety, the police had advised Xavier to keep his mouth closed. At least until the hit man had been apprehended.

All of Xavier's pleading with Doug to not involve Noah had paid off. Xavier had persuaded Doug to call Billy instead.

Doug understood that not contacting the boy's father was wrong, but something was seriously going on in Xavier's household. Until he could figure it out, Doug got in touch with Billy. Billy's instinct was to come up to the school, find whoever was trying to off his little protégé and go all Vietnam on him. It had been hard to restrain Billy, but somehow Xavier had convinced the old man that he had things under control.

The last thirty minutes of class had been devoted to a short pop quiz on *Huck Finn*. Xavier was trying hard to focus, but Heather was aggravating him by lightly kicking the right back leg of his desk. Though the two hadn't spoken since their last encounter, the tension around them was escalating.

"Can you please stop tapping my desk with your foot?" Xavier was straight up with it.

Heather disregarded his question and got personal. "I don't care about this test, Hunter. Why did you stop talking to me?"

Xavier looked around. His fellow classmates were looking and now Ms. Scott was staring in their direction.

But Xavier still tried to whisper. "This classroom ain't big enough for this personal crap."

"Is there a problem, Heather and Xavier?" Ms. Scott asked, rising from her desk. She began walking toward them. "Because if there is one, you two can discuss it with the principal."

Heather ignored the teacher as if Ms. Scott were invisible. "I'm not good enough for you anymore—is that it, Hunter?"

A dark girl sitting in the first desk of the last row said,

"Yeah. Go ahead, Xavier. Heather wants to know why she is not good enough for you anymore."

"Sherry Wilson," Ms. Scott said to the dark-skinned girl, "I can also send you to Principal Skinner as well."

"Nah, Ms. Scott, you can keep that action," Sherry said.

Ms. Scott said, "Ms. Larkin, please close your mouth and finish the quiz. Being that it's almost Christmas, take my generous offer as an early Christmas gift. I have a no-tolerance policy for students talking while taking an exam."

Heather turned on her teacher. "You can take your policy and stuff that ish. I think you know where." She turned back to Xavier. "What did I do that was so foul that you had to stop talking to me?"

Ms. Scott had had enough. "Ms. Larkin, get your things and leave this minute. Tell the principal that I will be down after class is over."

Some type of switch flipped inside Heather's head. With her right forearm the chick violently cleared her desktop of its contents, sending ink pen and the quiz paper flying through the air. She popped up from her desk like toast from a toaster.

"Do you think I'm afraid of that old fool?" Heather growled at the teacher.

Xavier told Heather, "You need to calm yourself down!"

She screamed and stuck an index finger in his face. "I don't remember your name being on my birth certificate! Did I tell you what would happen if you ever tried to play me?!"

It just got real.

Xavier slapped her finger out of his face and rose from his seat. "I wish you would." He looked at Ms. Scott. "You better get this girl before I do something I might regret!"

The size difference between Heather and Xavier was ridiculous. The girl wouldn't have a chance.

Ms. Scott yelled, "Heather Larkin, get out, right now!"

Tears started to flow as Heather looked around like she was helpless. "I told you what would happen."

"Now, Ms. Larkin!" yelled Ms. Scott.

Heather was at the door and looked at Xavier with angry eyes. "I told you what would happen," she repeated in a flat tone. "Seriously, I told you what would happen." She ran out of the classroom.

Xavier was at his hall locker after his seventh-period art appreciation class, putting up his books. With what he had going on at school, he was looking forward to the holiday vacation, even if it meant putting up with Noah for two weeks. He had to keep it real: Noah was a little over-the-top with the Holy Bible, but his father wasn't the one chasing him around the school, trying to kill him.

Xavier was still tripping out on Heather, though. She was nuts and there was no figuring her out. But he came to the conclusion that he wasn't a psychiatrist. Heather was mentally out there on a planet that hadn't been discovered. The girl was nuts and that was all there was to it.

"Ho, ho, ho," Dex said, doing his very best Santa impression. He and Marissa walked up to Xavier. Both were wearing Santa hats and decked out in festive Christmasy colors. And as usual, everything fit Dex like a glove.

Xavier asked, "Who in the hell are y'all supposed to be, the broke edition of Jay-Z and Beyoncé Claus?"

Dex said, "I knew there was a reason why I love you, my brotha from another mother. It's the way jealousy oozes from your mouth when you see somebody else shining." With his hands held high over his head, Dexter turned to the students in the hallway and shouted in a joking fashion, "I'm the best-dressed dude walking the hallways of this infernal high school, you dig?"

"Fool, you gotta be crazy," said some fat boy six lockers down, standing around with a few of his buddies. "Running around here like a colorful clown dressed in booty-hugging spandex." Almost everybody in the hallway gave Dex a good laugh. But Fats wasn't finished. "Those pants you got on now are so tight, when you and Marissa walked by us a few seconds ago me and the fellas were having trouble trying to tell her booty from yours."

Students roared with laughter.

Xavier said, laughing, "I know you ain't gonna let fat boy style on you like that."

Dex cracked back, "Now see, you done got your mother in trouble. I was gonna let her go to the prom with me, but thanks to her big-mouth son, that hairy-back gorilla gotta take her prom dress back."

The students let go with the chorus of ohhhs and ahhhs.

The fat dude said, "You got me. I give up."

Kato Holloway walked out of the stairwell and through

the hallway doors. The diamond studs in his ears looked to be bigger than the first pair he'd worn. And he had on a different pair of Cartier glasses.

Xavier and Dex looked on as one of the fat boy's home-boys wasn't watching what he was doing and backed up, bumping into Kato. It was as if life stopped in the hallway with everybody wanting to see what type of juice the new dude was flexing with. Kato stared the guy down but didn't choke homie up. Just let the warning in his eyes speak for him.

"Did you see that?" Dex asked Xavier.

"I'm standing next to you with a pair of eyeballs. How could I not see it?"

"What do you make of it?" Dex queried.

"I think we have a new playa on the block," Xavier replied.

They both nodded their heads.

"Anyway," Dex said. "Man, you have more drama floating around in the gossip going through this school than anybody else."

Marissa added, "Rumor has it that you and Heather are getting y'all freak on."

Xavier ignored her and said to Dex, "Don't y'all go anywhere without each other? Jesus. It's like y'all joined at the hip like some Siamese twins."

Dex cracked up laughing. "Don't try and change the subject, X. You hooked up with strange Heather and didn't tell me."

Xavier closed his locker. "One, it's nothing to tell— two, it's nothing to tell."

Xavier felt bad lying to his homeboy. Dex was the one

person outside of Billy who he could rely on. Through no fault of his own, Dex sometimes had loose lips and loved to gossip.

Dex dapped Xavier. "You holdin' out, but that's cool. Word has it that that chick's unstable, so watch your zipper, you feel me? Don't want to end up"—he made his fingers like a pair of scissors—"in emergency with the surgeons trying to sew it back on, you dig."

Xavier asked Marissa, "What is this cheap-imitation sucka buying you for Christmas?"

Dex stepped in and answered, "She already got a guy like myself." He popped his collar. "Anything else can't measure up to the kid."

"Great, Marissa," Xavier said, trying not to laugh. "I guess you'll be taking the wrappings off super sucka Christmas morning."

"Just for that crack, you are not invited to my New Year's Eve party," said Dex.

"No, your parents are not letting a lame like you have a New Year's Eve party," Xavier teased.

Marissa said proudly, "Yes, they are letting my baby host his own party."

Xavier analyzed Dex's outfit. "Let me guess who's going to be there: all the different colors from the Crayola box, right?"

"Guess what sucka is not going to be there: you, tough guy," Dex joked.

"I wouldn't want to hang out at some New Year's Eve party for squares, anyway."

Dexter and Marissa walked away.

Xavier asked, laughing, "What time should I be there?"

Dex hollered over his shoulder, "Starts at nine, sucka."

Linus Flip was waiting on Xavier in the student parking lot to give him a ride home. Since the GMC SUV boys rode down on them that night, Flip had been trying to stick extra close to Xavier.

The calendar was swiftly coming to the end of the year. The New Year, Xavier hoped, would come bearing peace, tranquility, and a solution to end all of the madness popping off around him.

15

THURSDAY, DECEMBER 25
9:00 A.M.
CHRISTMAS MORNING

Despite the absence of a Christmas tree and holiday decorations throughout the Hunter household, Xavier thought that Noah would at least get Alfonso a few gifts.

No dice.

Alfonso was in his room, lying across his bed crying, when Xavier walked past on his way to the bathroom. There was no need to ask him why, when Xavier already knew the score. It'd been a very bad mistake a few days ago to ask Noah about the missing Christmas decorations. Noah had jumped all over Xavier. Spouting off some crap about the true meaning of the season. He said that Christmas trees and video games didn't have anything to do with the birth of Jesus Christ. The devil was behind the commercialization of the holiday. Noah had also said that Satan wouldn't get a penny of his bread. He'd rather go to the soup lines and give it away.

Xavier closed the door behind him and sat on the bed beside his kid brother. "Don't cry, Alfonso. I'll make this right for us, you'll see."

Alfonso had his head smothered in his pillow, so his voice was muffled. "I guess it wouldn't be so bad if I weren't a good kid."

One look around Alfonso's bedroom left Xavier speechless. The joint looked to be a mini-version of Noah's bedroom. Crosses and the praying hands were affixed to the wall over the headboard, and a Bible lay on top of the dresser, opened to Psalms 23.

"Big brother, I used to pray for dad to get out of jail and take us from Ne Ne," Alfonso said, sniffling. "Now I kind of wish that we were back with Ne Ne. At least I could play my Scarface game on PlayStation." Alfonso wiped his eyes. "Why is he doing this to me? Doesn't he think I'm a good kid?"

Xavier rubbed his brother's back to console him. "You have been a good kid—a great kid. No matter what, your big brother is going to always be there for you. I promise, Alfonso, I'll make up for this Christmas. You'll get what you want, okay?"

The kid looked innocently at Xavier. "The boy with the pit bull is still talking about me every day after school. Tellin' everybody that you are a coward because you won't come up there and stop him."

As soon as it came out of Alfonso's mouth it smacked

Xavier in the face like a huge, powerful backhand. Dealing with his own issues he'd completely forgotten all about his brother's needs. Xavier was going through hell, but there was no need for Alfonso to be doing the same. Yeah. Xavier couldn't do anything about his brother wearing crunchy gear, but he could sure change the attitudes of the students at Alex Haley Middle School about bullying, especially picking on his little brother.

Xavier wasn't given a chance to comment. There was a knock on the door and Noah barged in, dressed in a colorful bathrobe and carrying a few plain white boxes. He noticed Alfonso's tears.

"Son, why are you crying?"

Alfonso didn't answer.

Noah placed the boxes down at the foot of the bed. "These are for you," he said to his youngest.

Alfonso slowly wiped his eyes and sat up, halfheartedly trying to smile. He timidly grabbed the boxes. When the boy popped the first lid Xavier wanted to grab his father around the throat and strangle him. There was no toy. No electronic game. No cell phone. Not even a board game—nothing fun and adventurous. Instead, there was a dark blue thrift-shop outfit.

Noah proudly said to Alfonso, "I want you to look sharp this evening. There's a Christmas program going on and I want us to attend as a family."

The look on Alfonso's face was priceless.

Noah was feeling himself. Smiling from ear to ear. "Aren't you going to go ahead and open the last gift?" he pressed Alfonso.

Alfonso looked sadly at Xavier and burst into tears. He leapt from the bed and ran out of the room and into the bathroom, slamming the door behind him.

The awkward moment didn't last long. Xavier wasn't holding 'em up anymore. "You couldn't even give Alfonso his little moment. Instead you spoiled everything."

Noah was putting the lid back on the box. "You are forgetting who the parent is again. Remember: 'Honor thy father and thy mother and the days—' "

"That's all good, but you remember this: We both have made adjustments for you. You haven't made one bit for us. That boy has worked his tail off in school and the least you could've done was give him something he wanted."

"Who do you think you're talking to like that?" Noah checked Xavier. "I was away from my family far too long. I've made a lot of mistakes in my life until I found salvation. You two are not going down that road. Jesus Christ is your salvation."

Xavier didn't back down. "Those were your mistakes. We have a right to make ours without you slapping us over the head with Scripture when we do. Can't you see it's only pushing us away from you?"

"In prison—"

"You're not in prison anymore. And I *think* I understand why you go so hard with this religious thang. Too scared you'll fall off and become what you used to be. But your fear is tearing this family apart and you're too blind to see it."

Noah hadn't seen that one coming. Knocked off balance by his son's accurate perception of him.

It was as if Noah had lost all holiness in the face of this low blow. "And your mother was better at raising kids, right?"

"Hypocrite," Xavier spat. "I read a few lines in that Bible about judging others when I was locked up in juvenile detention. I know you think that I probably heard this from my man Tupac, but 'only God can judge me.' "

Noah had this stupid look on his face.

Xavier laughed sarcastically. "Not as Scripture-illiterate as you thought?"

"You're a rebellious child. You don't want to listen to me and you don't go to church. Satan has become your master and this world your playground, but I will guide you back into the light, Xavier. Best believe that."

As Noah picked up the boxes and was about to exit the room, Xavier said, "I'll be waiting, sinner."

Noah couldn't say anything. He just shook his head and walked out.

16

WEDNESDAY, DECEMBER 31
8:00 P.M.

New Year's Eve found Xavier and his father at each other's throats. Noah was trying to force the boy into going to the watch night service at the church to usher in the New Year. Xavier wasn't buying it. He had plans to wild out at Dex's New Year's Eve party. At one point in the heated exchange, Noah looked like he was going to lay hands on his son but then he thought about it.

Before Xavier stormed out of the house, Noah threatened him that he'd be sorry. Xavier looked at his father like he would be a perfect candidate to win the worst-father-of-the-year award, shook his head at his old man, and bounced.

* * *

Dexter's parents are cool as hell, Xavier thought as he got off the bus and began walking toward his street after the party. Laid-back. They'd let the teens have their fun, as long as things didn't get too crazy. Dex's father was hip for a man in his mid-forties. Spoke the lingo with his son's guests and was a joy to be around and kick it with. Dexter had had a lot of Coleman High students in attendance, way more than Xavier thought would come. Everybody had a dope time. No liquor. No fights. No arguments. Just a fun time. They danced and got it in to good music. It was just what Xavier needed. Some serious stress relief.

It was thirty degrees out. Pretty cold. Xavier was dressed for it, though. There was no snow on the ground, so it was all good.

It was a little after midnight and the streets were dark and vacant. An occasional lamppost beamed down pockets of light onto the street. Xavier was floating on cloud nine as he crossed Warren Avenue, thinking about Dexter's mom. She was one fine lady. Real easy on the eyes for an older chick. Dex's father was lucky to have her.

In the distance Xavier could hear gunshots. People in the D had this crazy ritual of bringing in the New Year by shooting guns, and some fools would bust caps way into the a.m. hours. Before he'd left to get his groove on, Xavier had been concerned about coming back home after midnight. This was one of the worst times for being out and about. Occasionally bystanders had been struck and killed by stray bullets once the clock struck midnight.

Why can't every day be like this? Xavier thought. So

far, not counting the occasional differences he'd had with Noah, his holiday vacation was pretty peaceful. Now, how his old man would choose to handle Xavier coming home after midnight would be a different story. But Xavier wasn't sweating it. He'd just had a ball. Never once thought about the drama in his life. At no time had he been concerned with Tall and Husky, the GMC SUV boys, Heather, or whining like a sucka over Samantha. Yes sir, he'd had himself a good time.

Xavier was about seven houses from the crib when he smelled smoke. Nothing to trip out about. Just smelled like some inconsiderate butthole out back burning garbage.

I wonder, Xavier thought. *Nah, he couldn't be.* He dismissed the notion.

Xavier didn't get alarmed until he actually saw dark smoke rising over the top of his house, highlighted by the light of the lamppost out front. And that's when it hit him.

No he wasn't! he yelled inside of his head. Xavier ran between the houses, screaming, "Aye, stop!"

The figure saw him coming and started feeding the fire like crazy, pushing the flames higher, spreading the light and devouring the darkness.

This couldn't be happening to him, Xavier thought, jumping the fence that separated his house from the neighbor's. His heart was racing as he ran to the fire just in time to see Noah feed the last pair of True Religion jeans into the raging inferno.

Xavier bent over at the waist and put his hands on his knees, tears sliding down his face. He just couldn't take it anymore. His father was trying to break him and he knew it.

Noah was dressed in a topcoat, open, showing off a secondhand suit and crinkled black leather shoes. The Bible lay on the ground next to his feet.

"The Lord led me to the house where you kept your designer devils," Noah said, the light from the fire ghoulishly framing his face.

It was like the last of Xavier's strength went away at witnessing the fire ravage his last pair of Air Force 1s. His tears were for the rest of the money that Billy had given him. He'd stuffed the loot inside of the shoe a while ago. Not only was he now without clothes, but he was flat broke.

The blaze snapped and crackled as if to urge Noah to feed it more.

Xavier fell to the ground on his knees and cried like his world was coming to an end. He wasn't really shedding tears over the loss of his clothing. It was the fact that his father was so cold and cruel. Xavier had been like Alfonso—couldn't wait until one day he would get a chance to somehow meet his father and they would have the great father-son relationship that he'd always dreamt about. This wasn't what Xavier had had in mind.

His mother Ne Ne would've been a welcome sight right now. She might have done some foul things to him, but burning his designer clothing wasn't one of them. This was a new level of craziness that he was being forced to deal with.

His chest heaved and he slipped to the cold ground,

coming to rest in a fetal position. Death would be a welcome comfort. The pressure on his shoulders had become too much. And now this—the only clothes he had left in this world were on his back and he had no money left.

Noah tried to stoop down and console his son. "Now that we've gotten rid of those designer devils, you can come to God."

Xavier came to life and slapped away his father's hand. "Don't touch me. Get your damn hands off." He stood up, dusting off dirt and dry grass from his pants. "You just don't get it. You will never get it." Xavier broke and ran between the houses, out to the front and disappeared into the darkness.

Here he was, in the last place he'd ever wanted to be, but Xavier had nowhere else to go. Nobody to turn to at this hour of the morning. Of course he could've called Billy. But he didn't want to get the old guy in trouble with his young baby mama. She was on Billy's head every time he turned around.

"Do you know why I love you so much, Hunter?" Heather asked Xavier. They were sitting across from each other on beanbags.

Xavier could care less. All he wanted was to go to sleep and deal with all of his troubles in the morning.

She sipped the drink from the red plastic cup. "It's just me and my mom. Just the two of us—all the family I've ever had in this world. Don't know about my father. My mother never married him. She said that one day he woke up and decided that he didn't want to be a father anymore, so he stepped. Moms didn't have much luck when it came down to choosing the right man. One was so bad that he would drink and then beat on the both of us.

"I always wanted my daddy to come and save us. The bum never showed, though. It was all good. Girls want to feel protected, safe, you know, like nobody can hurt them. Hunter, you make me feel that way. You make me feel like I'm safe from harm." Heather's eyes became misty. "Do you understand what I'm telling you?"

Xavier wasn't trying to understand. The only gear he'd owned in this world was now polluting the Detroit skies. This conversation was way too deep for him. Too many things going on inside of his head to even try to understand what had happened to her.

"I knew you still loved me, Hunter," Heather said, sitting across from him drinking something out of a red plastic cup. She offered the cup to Xavier. "Since you won't tell me what's going on with you, why don't you drink some of this? It'll make you feel better."

Xavier was sitting on a colorful beanbag chair, still in disbelief at what his father had done to him.

"I'm good," said Xavier. "The last thing I need is to be out of control."

There was a brown paper bag over the bottle that Heather refreshed her drink with. She took a few sips from the cup. "Come on, Hunter. I don't like to drink by myself."

Xavier kept looking around. "I can't believe you're squatting in this abandoned house. Who turned on the utilities for you?"

The vacant house was nice and toasty inside. Xavier could even hear the furnace kick on every once in a while.

Heather took a few more sips. "That's not important. Besides, I only come here from time to time. Just to get away from my overbearing mother." Heather set the plastic cup down on the floor and reached inside a navy blue book bag at her feet and grabbed some bottled water. "Can't you see how much I love you, Hunter?"

Xavier craned his neck to look around the room. "Yeah. By bringing me to a vacant house. How can I not feel the love? It is almost as bad as taking me to a rowdy pool hall"—he used air quotes—"*to think.*"

She cracked open the bottled water and poured a little into her red cup. She slowly swirled the drink around. "Hunter, you are so silly. It's kinda hard for me to do, but I'll have to admit the poolroom was a bad idea. We're absolutely safe here, though."

The only light in the room came from burning candles. There were fancy-colored comforters covering two full-size mattresses. Xavier and Heather were sitting on nice, fluffy beanbag chairs across from each other. Heather had quite a few personal items in the space and Xavier could tell that this place meant something to her.

She picked the cup up and refilled it. As she offered the drink to Xavier, she said, "I can tell you have some deep stuff on your mind. A little of this will help you relax . . . and we could probably have some fun."

"How many times do I have to tell you that I don't drink?"

"I know, honey, but you look worried and I want to

make you happy." Heather wobbled as she stood and placed herself in his lap, almost falling over. "Oops," she said, trying to balance herself to keep from spilling the liquid. Heather studied the cup. "This stuff has quite a kick. You should try some."

Xavier wasn't feeling Heather like that. He was only in her company because he had nowhere else to go tonight—to keep it one-hun'ed. But the sight of her left him nauseated. The plan was just to spend the night here and bounce early in the morning, but she was so annoying Xavier didn't know if he would be able to survive to sunrise.

"I gotta take a leak. Does the water work in this joint?"

"Yup. Down the hall on the left."

Xavier stood, shedding Heather from his lap like she was just trash, spilling most of her drink onto the carpet.

Heather balanced herself to stand. "You are upset and I can see it. I'm gonna make you feel good when you get back. I promise you, Hunter."

Xavier looked at her with total disgust. He left her fumbling around in the book bag. He returned to see her shaking up the water in the bottle.

If she thinks it's going down tonight, this chick has another think coming, Xavier thought as he went and dropped onto one of the mattresses, removing his boots. So much had happened to him in a few short hours, Xavier just wanted to go to sleep. Deal with his problems in the morning.

But Xavier knew Heather wasn't going to make it easy because she stumbled over to him, still trying to force him to drink from the cup. "Hunter, baby, don't you want to join me in having a good time? Drink this"—she gestured with the cup—"and let's escape this madness together, please," she begged.

Xavier was strong-willed. Stood firm on his principles and alcohol was an absolute no-no. The monkey oil always led to poor decision-making. He was already in a wide-open abandoned house, with a liquored-up psycho chick. There were crazy fools that were armed and a tall and husky hit man all trying to smoke him, and the last thing he needed was his judgment impaired by alcohol. Xavier needed to stay loose and have his wits about him.

Heather remained persistent. "Hunter, if you're not gonna have any of my drink"—she placed the bottled water at his feet—"I don't want to drink alone. The least you can do is drink the water and keep me company, you know, pretend like we're sitting at a bar, enjoying tasty conversation."

Maybe she had a point. Plus he hadn't had any liquids since leaving Dexter's New Year's Eve party. His mouth was dry and his thirst was slowly building.

"This drink is really kicking in," said Heather. There was a dumb-looking smile on her grill and her eyes were small and red. "I know I shouldn't get like this in front of male company. Don't want you trying to take advantage of me, Hunter."

Xavier had been there and done that and had no desire to go there anymore. Every last one of the girl's fifty different personalities was a complete turnoff. He didn't want anything from her except to be left alone with his thoughts.

Heather was wearing jeans and some kind of old-fashioned, grandma-looking floral print blouse. She slowly peeled out of the top and sensually dropped the garment to the floor. "Phew, it's getting hot in here. Have to go and check the thermostat." Heather retrieved one of the burning candles and was about to step from the room.

Xavier asked, "What's with the candles? Thought you had electricity."

Heather answered, slurring some of her words. "Hunter, sweetie, you have a lot to learn about living ghetto-fabulous. If you don't legally have power then the worst thing you can do at night is to turn on the lights. That's how you get busted. Besides, there's nothing wrong with a little candlelight to see where you're going. Our ancestors used it back in the day." She steadied herself to hold the candle out in front. "Be back in a minute." She giggled as she stumbled out the door.

Xavier watched as Heather disappeared into the darkness. If she wanted to drink herself into a coma it was all right by him. Matter of fact, he might try to encourage her to consume more alcohol when she returned. Knock her out for the rest of the night.

Xavier looked at the bottled water and licked his lips. He cracked open the cap and took a swig. Heather was a complex piece of human confusion. But once the night was over, Xavier would never talk to the chick again. The thought was cruel, but she only existed right now to provide him with warm shelter and a nice, dry place to lay his head.

Xavier chugged the water again. His life was upside-down and drama haunted him from every corner. As of now he could add homelessness to his growing list of problems. The urge was strong to go back home tomorrow and find a way to pay his father back for his cruelty when—

Whoa! What the hell? Did the floor just move? A few seconds later it moved again. Then the bottom seemed to completely fall out from underneath him and he felt like he was dropping, free-falling through darkness.

He shook his head and rubbed his eyes. He was lying flat on his back on the mattress and was looking up at the ceiling through blurred vision.

No this trick didn't, he thought, as he held up the bottle of water. How could he be so stupid, so gullible? His arm suddenly fell lifelessly to the mattress and the bottle bounced to the carpet, spilling the remainder of the contents.

Although he couldn't move, Xavier could hear Heather reenter the room.

"I thought you were never gonna drink the water. But lady luck seems to be on my side. Now I'm about to make you love me, Hunter."

With all of his energy he tried to get up, but it was useless. Xavier stopped struggling and allowed darkness to take him.

The next morning Xavier woke, groggily opening his eyes to the dull sunshine filtering in through the clear plastic that covered the bedroom window. His head was throbbing and he had no memory of the night before.

The dryness of his tongue gave him that cottonmouth sensation. He went to move, but Heather's head was lying on his chest and all her weight was bearing down on his right side.

Alarmed, Xavier instinctively raised the covers with his free hand—and damn! The two of them were completely naked underneath. He sat up and Heather's head slid off his chest.

"The hell!" he yelled.

Defensive and wide-eyed, Heather slid off the mattress and backed into the nearest corner, quickly bringing the comforter with her and wrapping it around her naked body. The devious smile on her face spoke volumes.

Xavier stood up, pissed! "What the hell did you put in that water?"

Heather said nothing. Just kept on smiling sinisterly, like she'd set Xavier up to be miserable for the rest of his life.

Xavier ran around the room, gathering up his clothes. "I tell you, Heather, stay the hell away from me."

Xavier threw on his clothes in a hurry. He wanted to get as far away from this lunatic chick as he could. Xavier put his baseball cap on and held his jacket.

He pointed and threatened, "Don't you ever come around me again! I ain't playing, you little crazy trick! If you do, I won't be responsible for what I might do!"

Xavier was halfway down the stairs when he heard Heather cry out, "You're never getting rid of me, Hunter! I'm gonna be with you until the day we both die . . . together."

Her statement chilled him to the bone. Xavier didn't want to think about what had just happened. He didn't want to think about anything. His troubled mind ordered him to run. And that's what he did. Xavier ran down the block and clear out of the neighborhood.

17

Xavier was lying around the crib listening to music on the Pandora app on his cell phone. He'd had one stressful week and music was what he needed right now to relax. Xavier hadn't been to school since the start of the year. And judging by the cruddy way he was feeling, he didn't know when he would return.

The morning he'd left that little psychotic witch, Heather, Xavier was forced to make a hard decision. He chose to swallow his pride and knock on Billy's door. There hadn't been anywhere left for him to turn. Billy took him right in with no hesitation. Regardless of what his baby mama, Brandy James, was spitting in his ear. The old man ignored her request to make Xavier pay rent, and gave the boy the keys to the rental property.

Billy even set Xavier up with a few dollars to put in his pocket—one-hundred-fifty dollars wasn't much, but it was sure better than nothing. Took him shopping to cop toiletries, food for the fridge, household cleaning supplies, socks, underwear, and T-shirts. He even called the boy's father and somehow convinced Noah to let things simmer down between the two of them. Meanwhile, Xavier was welcome to stay in the rental property for as long as he wanted.

Noah agreed.

And Xavier had been there ever since. Billy's generosity had boundaries, though. The old man had a brand-new family to support and left it up to Xavier to figure out how he would replace the wardrobe Noah had sacrificed as a burnt offering to the crazy gods inside of his twisted mind. To say that Xavier was depressed would be a gross understatement. Homeboy was so far gone that the thought of taking his life had flirted with him a few times. But that weak, pathetic coward's way out was shot down every time. Xavier was a true warrior, with the strength to make pebbles out of mountains of trouble, a feat that he'd thoroughly demonstrated over the last couple years. There was no way he was going to lose in this epic clash with life.

Living in the old house that he'd shared with Ne Ne and Alfonso had come with a few reservations. He damn sure didn't want it to seem like he had come crawling back to the old neighborhood because he couldn't cut it in the new place. But it was what it was. Until he could do better, this place was home. And he was grateful.

The house didn't really have much by way of luxurious

amenities. Two stacked mattresses on the floor of his old bedroom were as good as it got. Three huge throw pillows lay in a corner of the front room so he would be comfortable while studying.

Xavier had left his schoolbooks in the locker over the holidays, and without them there wasn't much to occupy his mind and keep it off what that deranged mental patient had done to him early New Year's morning. He could twist and turn it however he wanted, but the fact remained that Heather had date-raped him. Snuck something into his water and had had her way with him, like he was some helpless punk.

Xavier kept on telling himself that he was tough, a straight-up, head-cracking G. His attempt to rally his inner gangster failed miserably. At this point Xavier was thinking that he might have to go out and choke a fool out just to prove that his manhood wasn't dressed in a skirt and wearing high heel shoes.

On Pandora, 50 Cent's "In da Club" started bumping and seemed to be speaking to the beast that lived inside of Xavier's soul. The boy jumped off the mattresses and got down on all fours. As the beat banged, Xavier caught the rhythm and started doing push-ups. Heather couldn't have his manhood. It was his and he'd worked hard to be the man that he was becoming. He didn't know what the chick was up to, but he didn't care. This episode would be swept underneath the rug like Xavier had done the night when that big biker put a two piece on him and made him go night-night at the pool hall.

As he pushed the floor, Xavier had to figure out a way to get into the school and grab his books tomorrow without being spotted. The money Billy had given him just wasn't enough to buy a complete outfit. The old man had done enough for him. It was all up to Xavier to find a way to cop some new clothes. The ones on his body were the only pieces he had left in the world. And that wasn't going to fly. But the longer he stayed out of school, the worse his grades would suffer. The dude had to think of something quick before he'd fall too far behind to catch up.

18

Xavier had been extremely stealthy in creeping into the school to grab what he needed before he was spotted by anybody that mattered. He'd waited until after school, when aside from a few hallway drifters, most of the students had gone home.

Doug and his security team would be busy at this time, policing the parking lots and making sure students were safe. Yeah. There were a few guards on the inside, but Xavier managed to stay clear of those high-traffic areas, sticking to the shadows.

An arctic front had the temperature outside in single digits. Strong gusts were blowing folks around and tossing about trash and dead leaves.

Now toting a backpack loaded down with books, Xavier was walking toward the main street to catch the bus back to the crib when a horn blew. The traffic was heavy on the four-lane street beside him, and he couldn't tell which car had honked. He stopped at a corner with a traffic light, his head darting back and forth, looking for a place to run, just in case.

To make matters worse, snow had started to descend in huge, fluffy flakes.

Xavier realized he'd set himself up to be sprayed with bullets by walking down this busy street, but he was sick of hiding. The horn blew again and this time Xavier made the car. A silver Lexus LX 570 sat idling at the red light, surrounded by other vehicles. One thing was for certain: It wasn't the boys from the black GMC SUV cause something would have been popping off already. His nerves were on edge as the factory-tinted front passenger window slowly wound down.

Aw, shoot, Xavier thought, nervously exhaling. It was Ms. Scott.

She beckoned to him with her hand. "Mr. Hunter, get in."

Xavier was reluctant.

"Boy, get your butt in here before the light turns green," she ordered, smiling warmly.

It was nice and toasty inside the luxury SUV. The interior was all black with heated leather seats. Based on its elegance and style, Xavier slapped a guesstimated eighty-thousand-dollar price tag on the whip. If this was true he was now rolling around in a vehicle that cost more than the crib he was presently living in.

Ms. Scott slowly accelerated at the green light. Xavier looked around the vehicle. It definitely was her style. He knew his English teacher was paid from the first moment he'd stepped into her classroom. And there was no doubt Ms. Scott was the best dressed teacher at Coleman. The black expensive-looking trench coat, nice solid black dress, and pricey leather riding boots she was wearing gave her the flamboyant look of those reality TV *Basketball Wives* starlets.

She made a right onto Grand River Avenue. "It's been almost two weeks, young man. Why haven't you set foot in my classroom?"

Xavier sat staring out of the window watching cars go by and people stroll down the sidewalks. Snowflakes were now falling with a fury, blowing and swirling around in the strong wind. For some reason Xavier felt like he could trust her.

"You are a promising student with a real bright future. Something's wrong. It's not like you to miss my class. You've missed out on a few exams, not to mention loads of classroom work. You want to tell me what seems to be the problem?"

Xavier had nowhere else to go with it. He said straight out, "My father burned up my clothes."

Ms. Scott was floored. In her entire teaching career she'd never heard anything like this. Which prompted her question. "Why? Did he hurt you?"

Xavier looked at her like she was crazy.

She smiled softly. "I have to ask those questions be-cause—"

Xavier cut her off. "You wouldn't understand. You also can't tell anybody."

Ms. Scott came to a red light. "It's my job to protect you students if you're being harmed."

"Since it's your job, pull over and let me out."

She hit a button on the console and the doors locked. "You haven't been in my class for almost two weeks. I pick you up off the street and you accuse your father of child abuse. Excuse me, young man, why wouldn't it concern me?"

"You know I've never been able to trust anybody in my life and here I am telling you something that nobody outside my family knows about. You gonna blow the whistle on me? This is what I get for listening to the voice inside my head telling me that I could confide in you."

Ms. Scott accelerated at the green light. "Mr. Hunter, what would you have me do then?"

"I need you to listen to me and don't judge."

The teacher agreed and for the next fifteen minutes, Xavier thoroughly explained his situation, pouring out his heart about everything, but careful to leave out the seedy details about his former gang affiliations with Zulu and the price now riding on his head because of it. He also neglected to tell her about Heather's unstable be-hind. Nobody needed to know that his weakness for her had led to a few embarrassing firsts for him. Telling her about his busted relationship with Samantha was pretty hard.

Ms. Scott drove while processing the information. "Well, we can't have you flunking out of school because you don't have clothes to wear. Let me ask you this: Have you and your dad tried to get counseling?"

Again Xavier looked at her like she'd grown an extra nose. "I can't even talk to the man without him slinging some type of Scripture my way."

"Would you like me to speak with him?"

Xavier was quick to say, "Uh-uh, don't do that. It'll only make matters worse. I'm living with my godfather right now. Don't need you stirring up any foolishness with my father. My only focus right now is trying to figure out how I can come up with the money to buy some clothes so I can get back in school."

Ms. Scott took the Tireman Street on-ramp and headed west on the Jeffries Freeway. "Okay. Since there are no issues of physical abuse in your household, I won't get in trouble for not reporting this—I'm going to leave this up to you."

Xavier looked around the sophisticated interior again. "What, you hit the Powerball or something? Teachers at Coleman barely making it and you—let's just say they ain't flossin' like you."

Ms. Scott smiled. "Mr. Hunter, are you trying to get into my business?"

Xavier laughed. "No, ma'am. I'm just saying, some of the teachers at school be hating on you, that's all. Got all of these wild theories floating around. The most original one is about your husband or boyfriend being a dope dealer."

"Typical. From my experience in dealing with you, I would say that you're pretty private with your personal business. Is this assessment accurate?"

"Ms. Scott, that's not fair, because I just told you about what's been going on in my house. You're right about privacy, but only to a certain extent. I've just learned that letting somebody in is a good thing."

Ms. Scott laughed. "Mr. Hunter, you are quite something, and you are right." She adjusted her rearview mirror. "But I won't be letting you in on my finances. Good try, buddy."

Xavier hunched his shoulders. "Can't blame a man for trying."

"My colleagues speculate because I don't freely divulge my business. Regarding my financial matters, let's just say I've invested my money very well and I can afford certain luxuries other folks can't."

Ms. Scott was pretty cool—a little bougie, but cool. Xavier didn't really understand why he trusted her with his business, but it sure felt good to unload.

The teacher was now headed south on the interchange for the Jeffries and Southfield freeways. Xavier was clueless as to where she was going. He wasn't tripping, though. Chatting openly with someone like Ms. Scott was tight. She was smart, beautiful, and in his estimation, financially well-off. Somebody he could aspire to be like.

Ms. Scott smiled. "I just might be able to give you some advice on your ex-girlfriend."

Xavier took his hands and fanned out both ears. "I'm all ears."

Ms. Scott laughed as she maneuvered her SUV around a shabby rust-bucket of a Dodge Neon. "Mr. Hunter, you're funny, no doubt about it. Charming and smart.

Now you take all of those attributes and pour them into the truth and tell Samantha who you really are."

"I don't know if that's a good idea. You're trying to get me killed." Xavier cracked a smile of uncertainty.

Ms. Scott came up at the Michigan Avenue exit and took it west. "There is nothing a woman values more than the truth, Mr. Hunter. Don't ever forget that."

Xavier was about to comment but was wondering why they were pulling into the Fairlane Town Center shopping mall. She navigated the SUV down the narrow aisle and parked in the Macy's lot.

The teacher reached in the backseat and grabbed a sweet Gucci bag. She opened it and pulled out her checkbook. "I don't have all day. Take out that cell phone of yours and call Samantha and tell her that you have something important to say. And that it's too important to discuss on the phone. Politely ask if she can meet you out here at the food court for a bite to eat."

Xavier didn't know what to make of her forwardness. So he did what he was told while she wrote in her checkbook with an expensive-looking pen.

Xavier conveyed to Samantha all that he'd been directed. And to his surprise she agreed to meet him.

"I told you," Ms. Scott said, rubbing it in. She ripped out a check and handed it to him. "Now you have no excuses. Be back in school next week."

He wasn't sure if he should be accepting money from his English teacher. These days, many an inappropriate student-teacher relationship had led to jail time. Xavier just looked at the piece of paper like she was holding a snake.

Ms. Scott sensed his battle. "Call it a loan. You can pay me back when you graduate from college."

Taking money from Billy was bad enough, but taking loot from his teacher made him feel some kind of way.

"I belong to the bank across the street. Hurry up and stop being so prideful. Samantha will be here in a few. Go cash the check and buy what you need."

It was hard, but Xavier slowly took the check. He made an attempt to gather his things—

"Leave your book bag here. I picked you up and I'll drop you off at home." She wrote down her cell phone number on the back of an index card. "Once you take care of all your business, call me and I'll be back to pick you up." She handed it to him. "Oh, Mr. Hunter. Nobody needs to know about this conversation and our little currency exchange. It's strictly between you and me."

"Don't worry about it. I'm tight-lipped." Xavier opened the door. Just before he jumped out, he asked, "Why are you doing this again?"

Ms. Scott's eyes glazed over, like she was trying hard not to tear up. "Because nobody did it for me."

There was pain in his teacher's eyes. It was almost like looking inside of them and seeing his own suffering.

"Thank you."

"Don't keep the young lady waiting," she said, dabbing at the corner of her eyes with a Kleenex. "Oh, by the way, I don't know what you have going with Heather Larkin, but stop it. You're trying to win back somebody special and you don't need Ms. Larkin's crazy drama— What did happen between you and her, anyway?"

Xavier smiled pleasantly at his teacher and used her line. "I'm pretty private and I don't divulge that information freely to people."

Ms. Scott laughed. "Touché."

Xavier closed the door and walked off. The bank was across the street. It was cold out but the warmth his teacher had shared was insulation enough.

Xavier sat at the far end of the food court. He wanted to see people coming and going, so no one would be able to creep on him. While he waited on Samantha, Ms. Scott's gesture was still fresh in his mind. Though confused, Xavier had gone and cashed the five-hundred-dollar check at the bank. The mere thought of someone outside of his circle doing something for him like this surpassed all understanding.

Forty-five minutes had gone by without Samantha showing up, calling, or texting.

He was about to bounce when he spotted her driver, the black Lurch, coming around a corner with Samantha, like he was Secret Service leading in Michelle Obama or somebody.

It was evening, and the food court was beginning to get busy, people looking to have a quick meal. Samantha was styling in her waist-length black leather jacket, jeans, and thigh-high black suede boots. As usual, Lurch sat five tables away. The man pulled out his cell phone and busied himself.

Xavier didn't know what to expect. Samantha's facial expression was stoic. Now that he thought about it, there hadn't been a shred of friendliness in her voice when she agreed to meet him. Samantha walked up to the table and reluctantly took a seat in front of him.

The silence was awkward at first. Too much had transpired between them to make her believe his greeting was sincere.

Xavier took a stab at it. "You look nice, Sam."

"Thank you, but you told me you wanted to talk, so let's get to it, Xavier."

Xavier almost shivered from Samantha's coldness. "No pleasantries?"

Samantha rolled her eyes at him and was about to get up to leave until he gently reached out for her shoulder to keep her seated.

"Keep your hands to yourself."

Black Lurch heard her and began to rise from his seat. She waved her hand and he sat back.

Xavier didn't miss a beat. "You know I wasn't putting my hands on you like that, but as for Lurch over there"— he pointed at Samantha's driver—"I ain't sweatin' him."

"This is what you wanted to tell me, that you're not a punk, Xavier?"

"No, Sam, I'm sorry. Didn't mean any harm. Just been going through a lot."

Samantha eased up a bit and folded her arms. "Talk."

It was hard for Xavier to open up to her. But he pushed himself and re-created the night he'd made one of the biggest mistakes of his life: smashing with Brenda.

Samantha said, "I have one word: Why?"

There was no stopping his flow now. "Dumb."

"Do you know how I felt that day Brenda openly admitted to carrying your child?"

Xavier took a minute to rethink it. "What I did was irresponsible. And I hurt you. Sam, the last thing I wanted to do was bring pain into your world."

Samantha tried to fight off the single tear that was now effortlessly leaving a wet, salty trail down her right cheek.

Xavier ran a hand down his face. "I've missed you so much it's ridiculous. So much has happened. I'm sorry for everything. I feel all alone right now. Not a friend in the world. Sam, I'm not asking you to take me back, but please don't banish me from your world. It's hard not talking to you, you feel me?"

A smile appeared on her face.

"What's so funny?"

Samantha confessed, still smiling, "I've missed you saying that."

"What? 'You feel me'?" Xavier said, laughing.

Samantha's smile suddenly disappeared. "What are you going to do, Xavier? You still have those people after you."

Xavier shook his head in frustration. "Not sure."

"We have to do something before you get yourself killed."

Xavier perked up when he heard the word *we*—and the girl wasn't speaking French either. "Sam, *we* ain't doing anything. This is way too dangerous for you to be involved. I could be putting you at risk right now. Don't need for anything to happen to you. I love you."

Samantha said with a smile, "You have a funny way of showing it. Running around with thugs and sexing crazy jump-offs and everything."

"You got jokes," Xavier said. "Well, you're the one running around with Derek Jeter—you're not still with that base-running clown, are you?"

Samantha laughed. "No. Derek Jeter—see what you have me doing?—I mean Sean, has gone back to school. I told you, we're just friends."

Xavier was trying his best to fight off jealousy. "Where'd you meet that jerk at?"

Samantha giggled. "We grew up together. His family knows mine very well. I guess I should be asking you, where's your little girlfriend Heather?"

Xavier almost choked. "That dizzy chick was far from being my girlfriend—you need to quit it."

"Her mother sure dropped her on her head. If she keeps staring at me around the building like she's crazy, I'm going to snatch the heffa out of those rags and beat her down. You sure you're not still with her?"

Xavier shivered at the thought. "No, Sam."

"Good, because I don't want to have to push her wig back."

Xavier cracked up laughing. " 'Push her wig back'? Go ahead, you old suburban gangster."

"You don't think I could? I'm more than just dance moves, you know?"

"So are we cool, Sam?"

Samantha didn't say anything at first. Doing her best to sweat him and not make it easy.

Xavier smirked like he was up to no good. "So what I

gotta do, get down on one knee in front of all these people and beg you?" He spontaneously slid out of his chair and kneeled on the floor in front of her. He said real loud, "I'm sorry for cheating on you with that two-ton woman who wears a beard like Rick Ross and dances around on that popular YouTube clip dressed in a thong and combat boots. Pretty please, with sugar on top—come back to me. I'll even try to get help for my phone-sex addiction—if you just take me back as your friend. *Please!*"

While folks around were cracking up, Samantha was shrinking with embarrassment.

"*Okay!*" she said in a muffled tone, turning red. "Get off your knees and stop humiliating me, please!"

Lurch even seemed like he was cracking a smile at Xavier's antics.

Xavier was trying hard not to laugh. "So, Ms. Fox, I'm asking you to hold me down. Get a brother's back. Can you do that? Because I can't live without you in my life. You're my best friend and I can't go any farther without you."

Samantha was straight up. "Just a friend."

Xavier made it seem like he had to think about it, and then he said, laughing, "Ouch, but I think I can do it."

Samantha smiled. "Well . . . yes. I can hold you down then."

Xavier joked, "Look at you, trying to sound gangsta again."

"Whatever."

They talked for a few minutes, with Xavier catching her up on the current events in his life, especially his dad barbecuing his clothes. That was examined in detail, accompanied by a little laughter. They discussed almost everything, except for what happened at Heather's that night. That little tidbit would remain one of the many skeletons hanging around in his closet.

"And you're calling me a gangster. Your dad, now he's a real gangster. Only a gangster for the Lord would roll the way he did, burning up your clothes to get the devil out. Why not use Tide washing powder?"

"Why you trying to clown me? I ain't gonna say nothin' about when my mother almost slid across the dinner table at that Italian restaurant to kick your father's hairpiece off. 'Member that?"

Samantha was laughing so hard she almost started choking. "Stop it. My daddy doesn't wear a hairpiece." She giggled like she had a joke of her own to deliver. "Are you sure you weren't confusing my dad's so-called hairpiece with your mother's mustache?"

"Ooh. You want to go there."

"Yep. That thing was so hairy I kept looking at it expecting it to grow eight legs and crawl from underneath her nose."

"You got me," Xavier admitted, shaking his head. "Your jokes are a lot better. I've trained you well."

"But in all seriousness, Xavier, is that why you haven't been coming to school?"

"Yep."

"Well, I can't approve of what your father did. But I can say that those clothes were better off in the fire because you bought them with dirty money. What are you going to do about school clothes?"

He hadn't looked at it like that before.

"Yeah, you're probably right—matter of fact, I know you are." Xavier looked down at the gear he'd been wearing since New Year's Eve. "I will probably get my money game on to buy some more by running some illegal guns to Nicaragua."

"Will you get serious?"

Xavier sighed. "I'll find some way to get them." Oh yeah, like he was going to tell her about Ms. Scott tightening him up with a five-hundred-dollar check.

Samantha looked at Xavier and rolled her eyes.

"What I meant to say was that legally, *legally* I will find a way to buy more," he corrected. "There, are you satisfied, heffa?"

"To be in my future you have to graduate from high school so that we can attend college together." With that said she reached inside of her wallet and pulled out her MasterCard. Samantha stood up and held the card out. "Let's get you back in school."

No matter what was going on in his life at the moment, it sure felt good to be back in Samantha's good graces.

19

Xavier returned to school just as he'd promised Ms. Scott. Before he went to his first-hour calculus class, he made a stop. It was to see her. Xavier handed her a white business envelope containing the money—five hundred in crisp, one-hundred-dollar bills. And he told her that her advice on "keeping it real" helped him out tremendously. Of course, Ms. Scott had questions when he gave back the money while styling in a nice leather jacket, fresh jeans, and sweet sneakers. But she knew the rule about private business. So she didn't ask. Just was happy to see him back. Xavier had one request, though. To avoid anything from jumping off in her classroom, Xavier asked that his seat be reassigned. Things would probably get real ugly when Heather found out that

Samantha and Xavier were back together as friends. And it wouldn't be in his best interests to be sitting in front of the berserk chick, with his back exposed, when she mentally melted down.

Ms. Scott laughed, stating that she understood and it would be done.

After missing quite a few days of school, Xavier hadn't realized how far behind the other students he was, until he had attended his first three classes. The extra work those teachers had dropped on him was bananas. A lot of his free time would be devoted to catching up.

Fourth-period lunch was a welcome break. He sat at a table in the cafeteria, posted up with his back to a wall, where he had a decent view of every part of the room as he watched students come and go. Everybody and their mamas were in the cafeteria today. Subzero temperatures outside accounted for the place being so packed.

Xavier's head darted back and forth, observing every movement. He didn't trust anybody, especially after Tall and Husky had chased him through the school and tried to turn him into a chalk outline. Even the fact that Doug had beefed up security, and uniformed officers occasionally walked the hallways, did little to comfort him. It wasn't gonna be the first time nor the last that the hitters would come for his head.

Xavier was drinking a milkshake and looking paranoid when his boys rolled up on him. Linus Flip and Dex sat down with glum faces.

Xavier asked them, "What are you fools looking so sad about? Y'all look like y'all just came from a funeral or something."

Dex mumbled, "You don't know how close you came to being right."

"Stall me out with the riddles, homeboy, and kick it to me straight with no chaser," Xavier said.

Linus was about to open his mouth and start explaining until Bigstick walked up with the same look on his grill.

Xavier knew something was up. He was anxious to find out. So he asked, "Bigstick, what's the deal, dog?"

Bigstick came out with it. "Our two defensive captains, Ray Taylor and Clyde McElroy, were shot this morning coming to school, fam. Same MO too—a black GMC SUV drove up and started cappin'."

The news blew Xavier's wig back. First it was the homie Felix Hoover, then Runt, and now Ray and Clyde. It definitely didn't make any sense to him. These three people hadn't had anything to do with rolling on Romello or Slick Eddie. So why in the hell were they targeted? The more Xavier thought about it, the more it was looking like the GMC SUV boys and Tall and Husky were working individually. But why Felix Hoover and Runt and Ray Taylor and Clyde McElroy? Junk just wasn't adding up.

"Those gotta be the same fools that came gunnin' for us the night of LaMarcus's party," Linus Flip added.

"Had to be," Dex agreed.

Xavier was dreading asking Bigstick his next question, but he had to know. "Did they make it?"

Bigstick didn't sit down. "Ray was hit twice—once in the back and once in the leg, but he's stable. Clyde is in critical condition. He took one in the stomach."

Xavier asked, "Why am I just now hearing about this?"

Bigstick answered, "Just happened about a half hour ago, fam. I don't think anybody up here knows yet. Both boys were taken to Detroit Receiving Hospital. Just stopping by to let y'all know. I gotta go and put the rest of the football team up on game. Probably gonna go down to the hospital after school." Bigstick walked away before the tears could fall.

"Damn!" Xavier slammed his right fist against the table. "Something is going to have to be done about those SUV boys."

Dex said, "Right about now I wouldn't mind transferring to another school. Preferably somewhere where the body count ain't that high."

"Is it just me," Linus asked, "or do it seem like these cats are trying to pick us off one at a time?"

Dex said, "The way kids are dropping up here at Coleman, they're gonna have to change the name from Coleman High to Murder High. I can see it now, a sign out front in the lobby during registration that reads Graduate At Your Own Risk."

"Ray and Clyde were two of the squarest dudes at Coleman," Xavier stated. "They definitely didn't deserve what they got, you feel me?"

Xavier was trying not to look shook but he was—they all were. It was the first month of the New Year, but drama from the old one wouldn't die. The hitters seemed to be as persistent as Pac-Man, and they weren't gonna stop munchin' until the board was finished and there were no more dots left.

Xavier mentally got himself together. "From now on, nobody gets caught alone in the school or around it."

Linus Flip said, "Since I got the ride, I'll swing by y'all's cribs and swoop y'all in the morning for school."

Dex was only keeping it real when he said, "The way these fools are letting people have it, what you're talking about might not even matter. Those GMC SUV nuts seem to be on a mission. Remember what happened to Runt?"

"Dex, homeboy, that probably was random," explained Linus. "Xavier said Runt told him that the goons responsible for stomping him out were wearing ski masks."

Dex argued, "And right before he blacked out, Runt also said they told him to tell Xavier that they were coming for him."

Linus said, "What's your point?"

"The only point we need to know is that these boys are all business," Xavier interjected. "And we have to stay tight until this thing is over, watch each other's backs. Hold each other down."

"Poor Runt," Dex solemnly said. "Heard that his parents took him out of Coleman."

Xavier just shook his head.

Linus added, "This damn school—you have to really watch your back to go to this school."

At that moment a loud bang went off inside of the cafeteria. Some of the students in the lunchroom gasped. Linus and Dex hit the floor in dramatic fashion, but Xavier stayed composed and kept his seat. Something inside him just wouldn't let him dive for cover. And if he had, Xavier wouldn't have known that the sound of a gun going off had stemmed from some goofy, nerdy kid accidentally dropping his lunch tray flat against the floor. The nerd with the big glasses, with the navy blue Dockers kicked all up in his crack, and a checkered button-down shirt, was stooping and shoveling the spilled food back onto his tray.

A huge sigh of relief could be heard throughout the lunchroom.

Xavier was cracking up at his boys. Linus and Dex got up from the floor, brushing themselves off and looking kind of embarrassed.

"And y'all wannabe gangsters can't tell the sound of a real pistol from some goofball dropping his tray," Xavier joked, smirking.

"That junk ain't even funny," said Dex, trying not to laugh himself.

"Linus," Xavier said, "I'm surprise you didn't pull your gat and start letting off up in here." Xavier couldn't stop laughing. This junk was too funny. "Somebody should've been recording with a cell phone. Y'all floor dives would go viral on YouTube."

Linus took his seat. "Very funny, homeboy. Nah—it was actually funny. Almost broke my damn knee trying to dive up under the table."

Even though the boys were laughing, the threat was very real. Nobody wanted to admit to being frightened, but in some way they all were. Tons of energy went into hiding their fears. In order to survive in the ghetto many young boys couldn't afford to wear their feelings on their sleeves. Cold stares and mean mugs were standard issue in a world where soft punks meant fresh meat for predators.

Through the south door entered Samantha with her girlfriends, Jennifer Haywood and Tracy McIntyre. They followed Samantha over to Xavier's table.

Linus Flip was the first to act up. "Damn, Tracy! That booty is fat."

All three girls were dressed nice, but the way Samantha and Tracy's backsides were popping in their jeans, they looked like they should've been models for some clothing catalog. And since Flip wasn't going to disrespect Xavier by commenting on Samantha, he went hard on Tracy.

Tracy was about to respond but was cut off by Jennifer: "Is that all you cavemen think about? Somebody's booty?"

Dex butted in. "Do I smell a hater? Now, Jennifer *Haywood*, since nobody was talking to you, why don't you take your flat back over there, far over there, and have a seat."

Linus Flip burst out laughing. He analyzed Jennifer's jeans. The girl was flatter than hot bottled beer. "Jennifer, you should tell your parents to get you some of those booty injections next Christmas."

Dexter almost fell out of his chair laughing.

Tracy came to her girl's defense. "Linus, you gonna have to get off my girl like that. Ain't you legal drinking age in the club? You're supposed to be in twelfth grade but I hear that you're carrying sophomore credits. Dummy."

Linus abruptly stopped laughing. "Girl, that ain't funny. I'll be graduating this year."

Jennifer scolded, "I hope none of these teachers graduate you, not saying grammatically incorrect things like 'That ain't funny.'"

Jennifer and Tracy high-fived each other.

Samantha finally stopped laughing to say to her girls, "Y'all take it over there so that I can have a conversation with my new best friend." She stooped and kissed Xavier on the cheek.

Dex said with a look of disgust on his face, "There y'all go. Get a room."

As Tracy was walking away, she cracked on Dex. "You get some Clearasil, you acne-havin' varmint."

Xavier asked Dex, "I know you are not trying to go there, homeboy. When every time I see you and Marissa y'all got tongues down each other's throats."

Linus started laughing.

Xavier told both of them, "Y'all go over there and keep the ladies company."

Samantha sat down in a chair next to Xavier.

He asked her, "Have you heard about Clyde and Ray?"

"That's why I was coming over here, Xavier. Heard it five minutes ago. Plus it's on the news."

Xavier put his head down, simply frustrated.

"You okay?" Samantha put a hand on his right forearm.

He slowly shook his head. "I don't know what to do. Seem like these goons are taking it out on my friends. I don't get it. All of this from me trying to do the right thing."

"It'll all work out, Xavier. You just have to have faith."

He patted Samantha's soft hand. "I know you're right."

"This is some real Romeo-and-Juliet type stuff," Heather said, approaching the table.

Samantha let her actions show Heather who the original queen bee was by getting out of her chair and sliding into Xavier's lap.

Heather backed away from the table. "Oh, it's like that, Hunter."

Samantha and Xavier tenderly looked at each other and then back to her, dismissing the girl through one unified voice: "YUP!"

Heather didn't make a scene. "I told you what would happen," she threatened him. But she hadn't seen Linus creeping up from behind. Linus Flip snatched Heather up with the quickness, and escorted her out of the cafeteria.

"What are we going to do about her?" Samantha asked Xavier.

"Sam, one problem at a time. She ain't the one I'm worried about, you feel me?"

Doug walked through the east entry and was headed in Xavier's direction.

Xavier pinched the bridge of his nose and let out an exasperated sigh. He kissed Samantha on the cheek and they both stood.

Doug went to say something but Xavier cut him off. "Don't even waste your energy," Xavier said. "Just lead the way to your office."

Xavier was beginning to lose count of how many times he'd been pulled into Doug's office this school year to be questioned about violent acts of crime. Times were getting so ridiculous that if a student sneezed himself into a bloody nose, it would lead to Xavier being questioned. Now he was on his way to Doug's office to be grilled about big Ray Taylor and Clyde McElroy. The results would be the same as always: He didn't know anything.

20

It'd been three weeks since Heather had pulled her little stunt in the cafeteria. Since then, homegirl was nowhere to be found. Hadn't shown in English class or been seen anywhere around campus.

She'd up and vanished like a wisp of smoke.

If Bipolar Betty doesn't show her face ever again at Coleman, I'll be straight, Xavier told himself as he got off the bus and was walking to his place at Billy's.

He was supposed to be riding home from school with Linus, but Flip hadn't attended school today—car trouble. Xavier had been after Flip for two weeks about how the Pontiac sounded like it had a slight engine knock. Linus was on that ol' "I know my car better than you" ego trip and paid no attention to Xavier's warnings. Now he was probably somewhere looking stupid, as his ride sat in the driveway of his mother's crib with the engine locked up.

This had to be the coldest winter Xavier had ever experienced. Temperatures were below zero and the wind chill factor left him feeling that his layers of clothing weren't enough. As he walked north on Schoolcraft Avenue, his mind was on his homeboys. Ray Taylor was coming along as well. Clyde McElroy was still in the hospital. The boy had long since been upgraded from critical to guarded condition. He still wasn't out of the woods. Several stomach operations and a nasty staph infection had left the All State offensive guard in one of the toughest fights of his young teenage life.

The traffic on Schoolcraft Avenue was heavy but flowing smoothly, except for some jerk driving an ancient metallic-blue Honda Accord with a crumpled rear end. The idiot decided to run through a red light and almost caused a major collision with a school bus. Car horns blared as the Honda-driving maniac had the accelerator to the floor and was burning rubber down the crowded street, coming dangerously close to sideswiping a few other vehicles.

Somewhere, someplace in a faraway laboratory, scientists had to be working on a cure for stupidity, Xavier thought as he continued, not breaking stride.

He'd gone down to the hospital to visit with Clyde after school yesterday. The boy was heavily sedated. And Xavier couldn't stay too long because of the twisted condition his homeboy was in. Tubes, wires, and beeping machines surrounded his bed. Even though he was intense on the football field, Clyde was a lively guy with jokes for days. That boy lying in the hospital bed looked close to death and bore little resemblance to the comical one Xavier knew.

Xavier was near his street and moving toward a vacant lot where a corner store used to stand. The pity party he was having had completely hindered the focus needed to be observant of his surroundings.

Xavier had cut through the vacant lot to get to his street when he heard it, a screeching noise. Almost like the sound made by car tires striking and jumping the curb at a high rate of speed. Xavier looked back at the Ford Edge barreling toward him, could see the demented look on Heather's face through the windshield. Her determined, grim look was peppered with the heinous intent of giving him a half-ton "Built Ford Tough" makeover. Talking about his bad decisions—one of them was now behind him and trying to take him out by using the American-made as a potential murder weapon. Out of pure desperation, Xavier hurled his backpack at the windshield and dove out of the way just in time.

With no time to waste, Xavier dug his heels into the frozen dirt and launched himself forward. He was running in the opposite direction when he heard what sounded like her braking, cutting the wheel sharply and skidding around on the cold ground, the tires spinning, trying to get traction. The sound was terrifying.

But stealing a glance over his shoulder to see her coming at him was worse than any nightmare. There was no way he could outrun the vehicle. There was an alley off to the left. He took the corner, slipping and sliding, almost losing his footing. But Xavier dug down deep and managed to stay on his feet.

He had made it three houses down when he heard the powerful engine as Heather drove into the alley, the Ford Edge's undercarriage bumping and scraping over the dips in the concrete. She was intent on carrying out her threat. Xavier hadn't taken her seriously at first, but only now, as he was running for his life, did he realize that the crazy girl hadn't been just mouthing off. She was for real with hers and was now closing the gap between them. Xavier's heart was pumping so fast that he thought his ticker would break through his rib cage in an attempt to outrun him to safety.

With Heather now two houses back and closing fast, Xavier started searching for fences to jump. The private fence to his right was too damn tall to scale. The chain-link to his left held a pit bull and an enormous Rottweiler, showing their razor-edged canines, growling, snarling, and barking as they tried to get at him through the fence. The house two down from the dogs had what was left of a dying vegetable garden on the other side of a wrought-iron gate. Operating on pure adrenaline, Xavier grabbed the top of the gate, jumped, and with his arms propelled himself over and landed in dead, brownish-looking tomato plants. Not a minute too soon because Heather rolled by and sideswiped the fence on her way past.

He got to his feet and looked in the SUV's direction. Heather gunned her ride, made it to the end of the alley, and slid onto a side street. She burned rubber getting up out of there.

Xavier jumped back over the fence, past the dogs, and

ran toward the vacant lot. He retrieved his backpack, which still had everything in it. Xavier took off down the street with one thing on his mind—skip reporting her to the police. And he wasn't gonna be responsible for his actions if she showed her face at school tomorrow.

The first person he called when he got to the crib was Samantha, to give her the scoop on Heather's homicidal behavior. Samantha had her driver bring her right over. After Xavier introduced Billy to Samantha, both teens were chilling in his bedroom, sitting on the mattresses. Samantha's driver sat in the black Cadillac Escalade parked outside at the curb in front of Xavier's house, drinking coffee. As well as being her driver, the black Lurch doubled as her bodyguard.

"Are you sure you're all right, Xavier?" Samantha asked.

Xavier took his time answering. "Yeah, I'm straight." But he was obviously furious.

"You have to report this to the police," Samantha advised. "It wouldn't be a good look to take the law in your own hands, especially with a girl."

Xavier shook his head. "Ain't no *girl*—that's Satan dressed up like one."

"Be that as it may, you remember the last time you took the law into your own hands, and now you have people trying to kill you. Let the police do their jobs, Xavier."

"With all due respect, Sam, look around you. This is not Birmingham, Michigan, where you live. Detroit police have their hands full with triple murders, idiots shooting up income tax stores, busting drug houses, and violent rapes. They couldn't be bothered with just another stalker case."

"Don't remind me of where I stay, please. I know Detroit is dangerous. As if I don't hear that enough from my father. I told you last year why I attend Coleman High and the reason hasn't changed: the dance program. The program here is better than any other high school I know."

"I wasn't trying to be disrespectful, Samantha."

Samantha argued, "This is not just another stalker case, Xavier. Jesus—the girl tried to run you over with—of all cars—a Ford Edge."

"Can we stick to the script? I almost got run over by a maniac driving a *Ford Edge*, for Christ's sake. Show me some respect."

Samantha started laughing and shaking her head at how silly he could be.

"Can you be serious?" Samantha asked, still laughing a bit. "I've never met a guy like you before. How do you manage to get yourself into trouble like this? You have killers, and now a car-wielding, crazy psycho chick on your butt. I mean—how does all this happen?"

Xavier stared Samantha directly in the eyes. "I don't know. Do you know I have to be the only guy in the world with killers and a girl stalker trying to whack him?"

Samantha thought about it for a second. "Yeah, I know, right."

Xavier detected the slight change of tone in her voice. "Sam, I'm not the safest dude in the world to be hanging out with right now. I wouldn't hold it against you if you bust up and never look back. I would die if anything happened to you because of me, you feel me?"

Samantha looked tenderly at Xavier. "So what did you get on your report card today?"

Xavier put a hand over his mouth and ran his fingers over his jaw. As long as he lived he'd never understand women. His backpack was pretty dirty after he'd used it as a weapon. He retrieved it from the far corner of the bedroom, dusted the thing off, and looked through it. He found the report card and handed it to her.

"I'm not surprised by your grades, Xavier. But I am surprised by how you managed six As with all the drama you got going on."

"It damn sure wasn't easy, I'll tell you that right now."

She examined his report card closely. "I see you have Nathan McGillicuddy as your art history teacher."

"I've never seen a white man with a nappy beard before." He laughed.

"You're so silly, but you're right. I have him for art history also. He's funny to me. I can't seem to figure out his wardrobe. I swear, either the man wears the same clothes every day or has a closet filled with tan corduroys and burgundy sweater-vests."

"Look who's being silly now. People think that his class is hard because the old buzzard drops a ton of notes on us before the test. The trick is to memorize all the notes. It'll be pretty easy to ace the test."

Samantha arched her left eyebrow in admiration of her ex. "My friend, you have to be the first nerdy bad boy I've ever laid eyes on. And you wonder why you're having trouble with the girls at Coleman. Those heifers love what you are."

Xavier blurted out, "Will there ever be a chance we get back together?"

Samantha looked off. "You were about to have a baby on me, Xavier. How can I forget about that and try to have anything with you?"

"We didn't know if that was my baby or not."

"I guess we'll never know because Brenda doesn't go to school anymore—unless she shows up on the *Maury* show later, claiming you as the baby's father later on in life."

"Will you get serious?"

"I suggest you put your mind on other things. You have more important stuff to worry about."

Xavier softly smiled. "I guess I'm pushing my luck. I should consider myself fortunate that you still want to be my friend. But you sitting there looking all good, I couldn't do anything but give it a shot, you feel me?"

Samantha cracked up. "Yeah, I feel you."

Xavier laughed a little and stuck out his chest. "Don't mess up a brotha's line."

Samantha confessed, "I still love you, my gangsta-nerd . . . but just as friends. Okay?"

Xavier already knew what time it was with her. He cracked a smile. "I can dig it. *Just as a friend.* It all sounds good to me." He scooted closer to Samantha. "Can a friend get a kiss? Because with everybody out to get me, I don't know if I'll get another chance to kiss a beautiful lady like you."

Samantha gestured *talk to the hand*. "Cut your crap.

You are indeed a smooth talker, but friends don't kiss each other on the lips. So here." She leaned in and gave him a peck on the cheek.

His face wrinkled up. "What's up with the grandma kiss?"

She smiled at him and wagged her index finger. "Just friends, remember?"

"So you expect me never to feel your lips again—is that how it's laying?"

"I'm afraid so, just-a-friend," Samantha teased. "Have patience."

Xavier rubbed a frustrated hand over his head. "But if I get bumped off tomorrow . . ."

Samantha laughed. "Then I'd lean over in your casket and give you a final kiss."

"Not funny at all."

Samantha couldn't stop laughing.

"Okay. Since you wanna go there, I hope my corpse rises up, pulls you in, closes and locks the lid, and shows how us zombies get busy." Xavier devilishly smiled. "In all the zombie movies, has that ever been done before, a corpse getting busy with a live woman?"

Samantha was wearing a look of disgust. "You're gross."

"You started it, talking about kissing me while I'm not there. I hope my dead body does come back and take you. It'll be just what you get for trying to play with me."

The two of them went on like that, laughing and joking, until Samantha had to go home.

After she left, Xavier took a minute to relax and think about the day. He kept going back to Samantha's question as to how he'd gotten himself involved in a world filled with this much drama. Before Samantha arrived, Xavier had been thinking about multiple ways of getting rid of Heather. But thank God, Samantha's presence had a calming effect. Xavier loved her, and if he ever made it out of his dangerous situation, he planned on making everything up to her.

It was nine o'clock at night.

Time to hit the books! He said to himself.

But first he needed to freshen up. Xavier peeled out of his clothes and took a fifteen-minute hot shower. Out and dripping wet, feeling refreshed, he heard his cell phone ringing. He wrapped a towel around his waist and went to answer it. When he saw whose number appeared on the caller ID screen, Xavier had a good mind to send the caller straight to voice mail. After almost being squished like roadkill today, he wasn't in any mood for no religious mumbo-jumbo from Noah. Xavier hadn't talked to the old man in weeks, and as far as he was concerned, he didn't care if he ever communicated with his father again.

But Xavier quickly thought better and answered. As soon as he did he was glad that he hadn't ignored the call. There was sniffling on the other end of the phone and he knew who the noise belonged to.

"What's the matter with you, Alfonso?"

The kid didn't have a cell phone anymore, so he had to sometimes sneak Noah's. And this was one of those times, but if Noah had heard him sniffling he would've intruded on their conversation.

Alfonso still didn't say anything. Just kept on sniffling.

"Alfonso, did Noah hit you?"

The boy finally responded. "No."

"Alfonso, let's try this again. What's wrong?"

The next line out of the kid's mouth would envelop Xavier's body in pure rage.

"Dog Boy at school hit me."

Damn. He had been so consumed with his own issues he'd forgotten about the bully that was terrorizing his little brother after school. Again.

He felt like a bad brother for having forgotten about something so important.

Xavier wanted to find the tallest building and fling himself off for forgetting his first priority, which was the health and welfare of his baby brother. To go up to that school and handle his business with that pit-bull-walking punk. Xavier not showing up at the school had given Dog Boy the balls to take his taunts and teasing to the next level by getting physical with Alfonso. But it was about to change. Nobody put their hands on his brother.

Xavier had a question. "Did you tell Noah?"

The tears started flowing and Alfonso choked up. "Yes."

"What did he say? Did he do anything?"

"He made it worse. He went up to the school and talked to the principal. Now kids are calling me a snitch. The principal said he would look into it. But since Dog Boy doesn't go to our school, I don't think the principal can do anything."

Xavier knew how his brother was feeling about being labeled a snitch. The only difference was that the epithet had been spray-painted on Xavier's lockers. Nobody at

Coleman had a big enough set to approach Xavier and pop that junk to his face like they were doing to his younger brother.

"Don't worry, little brother. I gotcha back. I'll be up there tomorrow."

"I haven't seen you in a while. When are you coming home?" The boy's small voice sounded desperate.

The question stopped Xavier dead in his tracks. The truth was that he never wanted to come back again. Noah was a religious psycho and the two of them would never see eye to eye.

"Don't worry about that right now. Let's see what we can do about your little situation first. Relax your mind. Don't worry about anything. Big brother's got this. Now take your butt to bed."

"I love you, big brother."

"I love you too, baby brother."

After he hung up, Xavier bit down on his bottom lip to suppress the angry urge to throw his cell phone against the wall. He was pissed at himself for letting this happen. Too busy dealing with his own demons to check on Alfonso.

He removed the towel and wiped himself off. He slid into his boxers and had his head through the neck of a wifebeater when his cell phone went off again. No name or number registered on the caller ID—just "private." It hadn't been his practice to answer those kinds of calls, but this time, for some reason, he pressed the Answer key.

"Hello, Hunter," Heather said in a playful voice. "I'm not bothering you, am I?"

Xavier wanted to go the hell off, but he played it cool. "I haven't seen you around school lately. Where have you been keeping yourself these days—a mental institution, I hope?"

Heather giggled like a teenage sociopath. "I see you still tripping 'bout me slipping you that roofie?"

Xavier ignored her. "Girl, you are testing my patience."

"Have you gone to the police yet?"

"I'm not a punk. I can handle my own. Don't need five-o in my business, you dig?"

She laughed, and it sounded creepy to Xavier.

"Good," she said. "Real good, Hunter. I plan on painfully loving you the hard way. You're the best thing that ever happened to me and I want to personally show you my appreciation."

"Yeah. I can tell. You almost *appreciated* me to death today."

Heather laughed so hard that she started snorting. "Hunter, I love your sense of humor. The way you make me laugh is heartwarming. Nobody has ever been able to do that for me before."

"Sorry, but I guess you've been hanging out in all the wrong mental hospitals. The next one they put you in, I'm sure you'll be able to find Mr. Right."

Heather laughed again, but stopped abruptly. "I told you that I would make you sorry for leaving me, didn't I? You messed over the wrong one this time. And don't think I've forgotten about that prissy bimbo. Samantha will have her day too, and I hope I get to see the stupid look on her face before I run her over."

Xavier went off. "You better pray that that crazy mind

of yours tells you not to harm one hair on that girl's head. You think you're crazy now? Homegirl, you ain't seen no parts of crazy. What I do to you will be the stuff of nightmares. Leave Samantha out of our beef. This thing is between me and you."

Heather mocked him. "Did I hurt him's itty-bitty feelings? So sorry, Hunter, but it's too late. You put her in this—remember in the lunchroom that day? Now she has a debt to pay also. Oh, darling, it's going to be so fun— all of us in this thing together. I promise you that we're going to have great times."

"You're sick and need help."

"I'm going to make you wish you were dead."

"Stand in line. I got others wanting the same thing."

"My dear Hunter," she said, laughing. "I'm a lady and we're always first, remember that!"

The line went dead. It seemed like everything was falling out of the sky at once and landing right on top of his head. At this point Xavier didn't know who would be responsible for bodying him first—Tall and Husky, the GMC SUV boys . . . or Heather.

21

Xavier and Dexter stood in front of their lockers before third period class, kicking it.

The hallway was alive with bustling students en route to their next class.

Xavier brought Dexter up to speed on Heather.

"Yo, dog," Dex said, "I really think you should tell somebody about Heather's craziness."

Xavier explained in a low voice, "That's why I'm telling you not to say anything. I got this handled, guy."

"Got it handled? Man, the crazy piece almost ran you down yesterday. What you mean, you got it handled?"

"I'm not about to be punked out by no girl," said Xavier. "This junk gets out about this trick trying to run me over, next thing you know every cat in the school will grow a pair and try to step to me, thinking I'm soft."

Dexter made some stupid-looking face. "Dude, you already have problems with cats trying to mow you down. Doesn't matter, though. I still think you need to tell somebody. Have you told Samantha about Heather threatening her?"

"Nah. Didn't have a chance to yet. Heather called after Samantha left my crib last night. Haven't spoken to her since. I'll holler at Samantha during lunch."

"Have you seen Linus?"

Xavier shook his head. "Haven't seen him. He might be out hustling up to get his engine rebuilt." Xavier removed his lab biology book from the locker.

"Did you hear that Ray Taylor is out of the hospital and at home?"

"Nope. That one got by me. When did he get out?"

"Ran into Bigstick earlier and he told me that Ray hit him up on the cell a little after eight this morning and said he'd been released from the hospital. His mother picked him up."

"What about Clyde?"

"Ray said that Clyde was doing good. Said homeboy has to wear one of those colostomy bags for a while."

"Boy, those two were pretty lucky."

"*Lucky?* How you figure that? The boy has to wear a doo-doo bag. Don't see anything lucky about that."

"Fool. Surviving that attack. Getting hit like that ain't no joke."

Dexter examined Xavier's face. The dark rings underneath his eyes were probably from lack of sleep. Stress. Worry. Pressure. "Homeboy, are you all right? I mean it looks like you gonna face-plant the floor any moment. I'm starting to think that you should transfer to another school. Just get away from it all."

"Now you're starting to sound like Doug. I'm cool, mother. Thanks for your concern."

Dexter shook his head. "Maybe you should listen. Look, I understand about your pride, and your reputation for being hard. But, dude, you're up against it. Slick Eddie is never going to stop sending cats after you until you're out of this piece. Now you've gone and gotten yourself mixed up with a psychotic female. I think you should cut your losses, man, and go to another school."

Xavier's reply was simple. "Nope."

"Why?"

"I plan on graduating from Coleman High, you feel me?"

Dexter scratched his head. "I feel you, but if all those cats that are trying to body you get their way, you'll be graduating all right—just not in a cap and gown from Coleman High, though. Instead you'll be dressed in a pair of wings, a white gown, a harp, and a halo."

Xavier laughed at Dex. "You got jokes, chump. Get to class, fool. I'll holler at you at lunch, homeboy."

Dexter also laughed. "My moms be watching how psycho stalkers be chopping up people on that Investigation Discovery channel. I hope I don't see your story on there, player."

As he walked away, Xavier couldn't help but acknowledge that Dexter was right. Xavier was completely exhausted–both mentally and physically. He couldn't front any longer. The stress was wearing on his young body. Didn't know how much more he could take. Between trying to keep his grades up and his head from being blown off, sleep was rare. And then there was that thing of Billy supporting him. The old man had gone out of his way to put Xavier up at his rental property until he and his father could come to some type of understanding.

Xavier had started to feel guilty about throwing an extra burden on Billy's wallet. The old man had a young girlfriend and a baby to think about. Xavier didn't want to come between Billy and his family responsibilities. But for right now he would have to postpone the talk with his father. Xavier had too much on his plate and needed a chunk of time to figure things out.

Linus Flip had finally shown up to school and was sitting at the lunch table with Xavier, Dex, and Bigstick. The boys were clowning him about having to take the city bus to school.

"Say, man," Dex joked, looking at his watch. "You're about three hours late. I know you know this is fourth period, right?"

"Very funny," Linus said. "This coming from a dude who looks like a paint plant threw up on his clothes."

Dexter was looking pretty colorful in his bright yellow blazer covered with different colored circles, and deep red pants. And of course frames without lenses.

Bigstick said, "I'm with Dex on this one, fam. What? You jump on the wrong bus or something? Took your ratchet butt at least three hours to get here."

"You fools gonna learn to get up outta my business,"

Linus retorted, smiling. "Not that I have to explain my-self to you chumps. I finally found a mechanic who wouldn't try and bend me over to rebuild my engine. Lee's Automotive Repair. Mr. Lee came through this morning and scooped up the ride on his flatbed."

Dex said, "That's what's up. So how long until we're back on the road, big homie?"

Linus laughed. "We? Since when did you start speaking French, Dex? If *we* gonna help me pay Mr. Lee five hun'ed snaps for the rebuild, then I wouldn't care if *we* rode that joker till the tires fall off. But if *we* ain't going in *we* pockets, then *we* becomes me. And *I'll* be back on the road real soon, sucka."

Xavier wasn't saying much. Too busy paying attention to his surroundings. To him the bogeyman underneath his bed was real and on the loose in broad daylight. Xavier figured it was better to be on guard than caught slippin'.

He watched as the dude Kato Holloway—and his sig-nature Cartier frames and sparkly diamond studs—walked into the cafeteria and sat at a table of cruddy characters. Lately Xavier had been observing that Kato was starting to mix in and become real chummy with the superstar lowlifes of the game. Those criminal figures who had moved back into Coleman and set up shop im-mediately after Xavier had been stripped of his command as Zulu's top lieutenant. There was something about this dude that wasn't vibing right with Xavier. He couldn't quite put his finger on it, though.

While the other two talked to each other, kicking it

about Clyde and Ray's recoveries, Linus leaned over to Xavier and broke his train of thought.

"Yo, X, you in there?" Linus said, almost whispering.

"Yeah, homeboy," Xavier said. "Just have a lot on my mind. I'm glad that Mr. Lee character is gonna tighten up your ride for you."

"Me too. But that's not what I'm talking about. Talk to me, dog. I think I know you good enough by now to realize when something is eating you up inside." Linus let his gaze settle on the floor for a second. Then he looked back up. "Is it those GMC SUV clowns, or the situation with that chicken, Heather, who I put outta here some weeks back—is that it? You know all you have to do is give me the word and I got some hard pipe-hitting chicks that wouldn't mind plucking ol' girl's feathers."

Xavier put a fist to his chest. "I appreciate the love, homeboy. Ain't no question. If I need that kind of muscle I got you on speed dial. But everything's all good in the hood, you feel me?"

Samantha entered the cafeteria amongst the backdrop of movement and noisy chatter. She was a delightful girl and everybody loved her. One could tell by the warm reception given to her by the students she passed on her way over to Xavier's table.

Dex was the first to greet her. "And if it ain't the lovely Ms. Fox."

"Hi, Dexter," Samantha said, smiling. She addressed the table. "Hi, everybody. Listen, on February twenty-seventh my girlfriends and I are getting together a gang of students and we're going to check out the new romantic comedy *Ratchet Chicks* at the MJR Marketplace Digital Cinema 20 out in Sterling Heights. We want to know if you guys are interested in joining us."

Bigstick said, "Count me out. Me and the rest of the football team will be taking Ray Taylor to Dave and Buster's that night, have a little celebration for him."

Linus Flip said, "If it means getting next to yo' fine partna Tracy McIntyre, I'll buy the popcorn—oh, and tell her I'll even let her get butter on it."

Samantha laughed. "Okay now, Mr. Big Spender. I'll give her the message."

Xavier asked, "February twenty-seven? Is that on a Friday?"

Bigstick pulled out his Android phone and scrolled through screens until he arrived at the calendar app. "Yup, X, it's a Friday, all right."

Dexter said, "*Ratchet Chicks.* I heard the critics were shooting that film down."

Samantha said, "Wouldn't surprise me. They're always hating on black films. But it's supposed to be funny."

"Is Kevin Hart going to be in it?" Linus asked, trying to be funny.

Samantha smiled. "Boy, don't run my nerves. You know Kevin Hart is not in this movie. But can I pencil you guys in?"

"Hell, I ain't got nothing popping off that Friday," Linus said. "I'm wit' it."

Dex added, "Me and my ride-or-die chick, Marissa, will be there."

"Homeboy," Xavier said, pointing at Dexter's jacket,

"please remember to turn down the volume on the colorful jacket you plan on wearing that night."

Everybody at the table cracked up laughing. Linus almost fell out of his chair. Tears were streaming from Bigstick's eyes.

Samantha was quick to defend her boy. "I'm not going to allow any roasting of Dexter on our little trip. Is that clear?"

Dexter said, "Samantha, I appreciate the love, baby girl, but I don't need your help. I got this. Mr. Gangsta over there"—he pointed at Xavier—"knows he don't want any of this—skin so black that when he was standing next to a blackboard, the teacher wrote on his face by accident."

The table erupted into laughter again.

Xavier said to Samantha, still laughing, "Pencil me in, Sam. You're paying for big daddy?"

Samantha stooped and kissed Xavier on the forehead. "Don't I always pay for big daddy?"

"I'm not sure, X," Linus said. "But is she trying to call you a deadbeat?"

Samantha was quick with the snap. "Don't go there, Mr. Engine Trouble. I heard that every time your car leaves the driveway, tow trucks follow you like vultures circling over a dead animal."

This time laughter along with oohs and aahs rang out at the table.

Dexter stood from his chair and dapped Samantha, smirking.

Linus couldn't do anything but shake his head. "Damn,

Sam, why you go hard on a brotha's ride so cold like that?"

Bigstick said, "Samantha, fam, I didn't know you had it like that." He looked at Xavier. "She can hold her own, huh, X."

Xavier hunched his shoulders. "What can I say? I taught her well."

Samantha playfully slapped Xavier on the head.

Fifth-hour English saw Xavier struggling to pay attention in class.

Ms. Scott was going on and on about how to write a successful research paper. She had lost Xavier somewhere around the research process and plagiarism. He was bothered by his own issues. All sorts of wild thoughts were swimming around behind his eyebrows. He had yet to have alone time with Samantha to tell her about Heather's threat. It was funny. There were goons on his head, trying to make him a memory, but here he was sweating Heather. Homegirl had tried to use her vehicle as a weapon to bring about his demise. So she had to be considered a legitimate threat. Xavier was not too worried about himself. It was Samantha he was most concerned about.

"Mr. Hunter," Ms. Scott said. "Is my explaining the criteria needed to complete your research paper boring you?"

Xavier sat up at his desk. "Umm, no."

"Then can you point out some of the facts in the research process?"

Xavier looked around the class. Everybody was waiting for an answer.

He said, "I gonna keep it one-hun'ed with you, Ms. Scott. Right about now, if you asked me my name I couldn't tell you."

"You people will have three months to compose a stellar research paper," Ms. Scott explained to the class. "This paper will comprise 50 percent of your grade on your last report card." She looked at Xavier. "Young man, is there something you need to talk to me about?"

There were quite a few things he needed to get off of his chest. The truth of the matter was that if he didn't vent soon, the pressure from his issues would cause him to go nuclear on the next person who looked at him the wrong way. He had his pride, but he didn't want pride to get Samantha hurt. An adult had to know about Heather's crazy threats.

"Mr. Hunter, I'll see you outside in the hall."

The hallways were empty. Xavier stood with his back against a set of lockers. The boy was mentally spent and there was no way he could continue without talking to somebody about his problems.

"Okay, Mr. Hunter," Ms. Scott said, stepping out and closing the door behind her. "Out with it."

Inside of three minutes Xavier managed to explain everything about his situation with Heather. The teacher winced at the part when Heather tried to turn him into a hood ornament. Ms. Scott feared for Samantha and Xavier's safety.

After Xavier was finished, Ms. Scott said, "We'll go see Doug once class is over."

She kept her promise and they were now discussing a solution in Doug's office. Doug stood with his arms across his chest and his back to the door. The place was small and had only two chairs—Doug's desk chair, which he'd given up for Ms. Scott, and the one Xavier sat in.

"So let me get this straight," Doug said to no one in particular. "You mean to tell me that cute little Heather Larkin almost ran you down in a vehicle? She also threatened Samantha Fox, right?"

Xavier said with an attitude, "Why is that hard to believe?"

Doug simply shook his head. "Mr. Hunter, you manage to get into more trouble than anybody at this school. You have a 4.0 GPA, but your decision-making ability stinks." Doug looked at Ms. Scott. "Ms. Scott, I want to thank you for bringing this to my attention. Lord knows we don't need any more violent incidents going on at this school. Do you mind if me and Xavier talk a bit?"

Ms. Scott excused herself and walked out.

"Xavier, why didn't you call the police and report this?" Doug asked.

"Because I thought it was just gonna be me and her. Didn't know she was gonna involve Sam."

"That's not the point. If what you tell me is the truth, you could've been killed."

Xavier hung his head.

"Has she been around school?"

"I haven't seen her in school since we had that little dustup in the cafeteria a few weeks ago."

"Did anyone witness it?"

"Linus Flip."

Doug wrote something down on a small piece of paper, mumbling to himself. "Okay. I'm going to try to get in touch with Heather's parents. See if she's there, so we can bring her into the office and get her side of the story."

"Doug, there isn't another side—the girl is straight up whacko, period, point-blank."

"Okay. While I'm checking on her, try not to get yourself into any more trouble. By the way, we haven't been able to come up with any information about the tall and husky guy who chased you."

"Is that it? Can I go now?" Xavier said, almost cutting Doug off.

Doug looked Xavier straight in the eye. "I can't believe you. You get into all this trouble and you got the nerve to give me attitude. It's kids like you who make my job difficult. Do me a favor, Mr. Hunter. Try not to get into more trouble."

"Oh yeah. She took me to one of her hangouts, some abandoned home."

"Where is this house?"

Xavier gave up the location and directions to it.

Sixth and seventh periods had been one big blur to Xavier. He'd been too anxious to dress in gym class and hadn't heard a single word spoken by his art appreciation teacher, Nathan McGillicuddy. Xavier had been too busy counting down the minutes until he met Dog Boy, the creep who had been physically bullying Alfonso. The terrible part about it was that the lame didn't even attend the school. Xavier could just about tolerate all scumbags except for bullies. They were nothing but pathetic punks who'd been picked on themselves. Somewhere along the line—after a growth spurt, hitting the gym and packing on muscle, they set out to prove their toughness by exploiting the weak. But this wasn't gonna fly with Xavier. Simply put, the jerk had stepped to the wrong little brother.

Xavier was lugging his books back to the locker when he heard his name called. He turned around and was surprised to see that it was Kato Holloway, Mr. Expensive Cartier Glasses, the dude from Xavier's seventh-hour class.

Xavier didn't know what to expect, so he shifted his books to his left hand, freeing up his right. Just in case some wild junk jumped off and he had to swing on a fool.

Kato walked up, holding out his hand. "My name's Kato Holloway and I hear tell that you're the man up in the school. That you're a good person to know."

Xavier was hesitant to shake Kato's hand. He had been sitting in the classroom with the dude since Kato had arrived the first week of December, but homeboy hadn't spoken to him one time.

Xavier was suspicious that the boy might have some motives. He shook Kato's hand and said, "Don't be misled by a bunch of gossip around here. I'm just Xavier Hunter."

"I can dig it. Aye, man, what you cats do for kicks around here?"

"Try to survive the madness here at Coleman, my brotha. Sometimes just making it through the day is enough adventure and drama for me."

"I heard that," Kato said, smiling. "I see you have your own little crew up in the lunchroom. You seem like a cool guy to kick it with. Maybe we can chop it up together at lunch one of these days."

"Yeah, maybe, one day," Xavier said without a smile. He wasn't friendly nor was he for any foolishness. "Nice to meet you, Kato."

Kato said, "Same here." And then he stepped off.

Xavier didn't know what that was about. Nobody he'd talked to knew anything about Kato or where he'd come from. It was like dude had appeared out of thin air one day. For all Xavier knew, Kato could've been secretly employed by Slick Eddie or Romello to keep tabs on him. It didn't matter though. The boy had better step lightly. These days Xavier was a loose cannon and it wouldn't take too much to set him off. And it didn't matter who was in front of him.

But Kato was the least of Xavier's worries right now. He put his books up in the locker and headed out of the school to the bus stop. Dog Boy needed to be taught a lesson. It was time to give that lame bully a taste of his own medicine.

Xavier got off the bus three blocks from Alfonso's school. There was a hardware store on the corner, one block east of the bus stop. Before he executed the handling of his business with that dog-walking troll, Xavier stopped off in the store and made a purchase. Something he would need to protect himself from the pit bull while teaching the owner a thing or two about picking on somebody his own size.

He walked out of the store and made the three-block trek to the school. It was thirty degrees out, but the jacket he was wearing was light, wasn't restricting, like the material had been made for combat.

When he finally arrived at the school grounds there were ten minutes to go before the students would come spilling out of the building like ants from cracks in the ground. A crowd stood around the main entrance in the cold, anxiously waiting for the bell to ring so they could pick up loved ones. This wasn't going to be one of Xavier's proudest moments. Never did he want Alfonso to be saddled with a reputation for having a crazy older brother. Instead he wanted Alfonso to be known for his work ethic and academic achievements. But in order for Alfonso to have the opportunity, the boy couldn't be stressed out by some rat, looking to make a name for himself. There was nothing Xavier could do. No other solutions. This thing had to be done.

A careful scan of the crowd in front of the school revealed nothing. Dog Boy had not shown yet. Xavier stood across the street, so as not to be on school property when he put the beat down on the bully. Therefore, when word got back to school security, there would be nothing that they could do to Alfonso. It would be strictly a matter for the police.

As he waited, Xavier started thinking about Kato and

what his reason was for approaching him. In the danger-ous world Xavier now lived in, he couldn't afford to overlook anything. Every detail had to be weighed and carefully examined to assure Xavier's survival.

The traffic was starting to get thick, with folks pulling up in cars and lining the streets to wait on kids. Xavier had both hands in his pockets when he heard a dog bark-ing in the distance. Dog Boy was walking up the same side of the street Xavier was standing on. Like Alfonso had reported, the dog was lunging and viciously barking at everything with a heartbeat. Not to bring attention to himself, Xavier reached up with both hands and pulled the jacket's hood over his head. His heartbeat picked up, the testosterone-fueled anticipation to make an example out of the bully coursing through his veins.

With his right hand, Xavier readied the small canister in his right pocket. The clerk behind the counter at the hardware store had sworn to Xavier that the product was the real deal. It had better be. Everything was riding on it. The moment the kids started running out of the school doors, Xavier looked to his right. The punk and the mutt were about to cross the street. Xavier couldn't have that, so he immediately started walking toward them with his head down. The dog must've picked up the scent of Xavier's intent and started aggressively barking, lunging for him.

Dog Boy laughed wickedly and leaned back with both hands on the chain leash to restrain the dog, like he was proud to have a killer pooch. He warned Xavier, "My dude, you better stop where you are. Not my fault what the dog does to you if you keep getting closer."

Xavier realized that the bully's heart wasn't fully invested in the warning. The smug smirk on his grill suggested he'd enjoy seeing his dog tear into human flesh.

But the laughter died in his throat and horror etched into the clown's dark-skinned mug, as Xavier raised his head, whipped off the hood, and pulled out the small canister.

"You," the boy said, fear in his voice as he recognized Xavier.

He let go of the chain and the dog lunged at Xavier. This time the mutt got a face full of pepper spray. The pit gagged, snorted, and made other funny noises as it dropped its massive head to the ground and began helplessly pawing at its eyes. It bounced up quickly and shot off down the street, yelping.

Dog Boy lost it and charged at Xavier. He got a face full of pepper spray too, followed by a vicious right haymaker to the left temple that dropped him. Xavier bent down and for the first time noticed the audience. Spectators were on the other side of the street at a safe distance watching the action, some even applauding. It was pathetic that this jerk and his dog had been terrorizing folks at this school to the point that these people were cheering and clapping their approval.

The dude was on the ground, paralyzed by the punch. He was out of his head and groggy. Xavier grabbed the boy up by his collar and smacked him across the face for good measure.

"From now on, homeboy, if you see my little brother walking up the block, you better cross the street. Don't have me come back up here again. The next time I smash you, your own mama won't recognize you."

Xavier stood up and spotted Alfonso. Noah was just pulling up when Xavier nodded his head at his little brother, as if to say that everything was going to be all right now. Alfonso smiled and Xavier could immediately see the relief in his little brother's face.

Not wanting to be spotted by his father, Xavier bounced.

22

Ms. Scott had her entire fifth-hour class in the library doing research. Xavier was sitting behind a computer terminal, tapping away. It was an odd topic, but Xavier had chosen to do his research paper on a few of the world's deadliest snakes. There was no obsession or anything like that; a mild fascination at best. Truth be told, when the teacher had asked him to declare his research subject, it was the only thing he could think of off the top of his noggin. After all, having to watch his back was a full-time gig. Left him with very little room for concentration. But given what different kinds of snake venom could do to the human body, the gory detail would almost assure Xavier's complete and undivided attention. He needed to ace this thing. The boy still held

out hope of crossing the stage at the end of his senior
year, regardless of the goons lurking in the shadows with
itchy trigger fingers.

Xavier yawned and stretched his limbs. He'd been kept
up last night listening to Billy argue with his baby mama,
Brandy James. From the way the two were getting after
it, Xavier concluded that they'd argued before. But this
time the confrontation had spilled outside, where Xavier
could hear every word. The chick was mad ghetto,
cussing and yelling. A lot of the stuff Xavier had ignored,
except when his name had come flying out of her mouth.

"Xavier ain't yo' damn son!" he'd heard Brandy yell
last night. "Send his freeloading behind home. Get him
outta that house so we can rent it. Worry about home
and less about a kid who ain't yours!" Of course Billy
had defended him, but the only words that stuck in
Xavier's head were hers. In his opinion the chick was too
young for Billy, and too stupid. But in her own ghetto
way, she was right. Xavier had become a burden and the
financial strain was starting to wear on the couple's relationship. He had to bounce. It would be good for Billy's
family.

There was a light tap on his shoulder. Xavier turned
around and saw Ms. Scott staring squeamishly at the pictures on his computer screen.

Her brow was wrinkled and her lips were pulled in.
"Mr. Hunter, you are an interesting piece of humanity. I
never knew that you liked snakes. And, oh my gosh, look
at the head on that one. And are those small horns on its
nose?" She pointed to the snake on the computer screen.

Xavier smiled. "I kinda got hooked a few years ago.

Was watching Animal Planet and they had this documentary on dangerous snakes." He gestured at the picture on the screen. "It's a Gaboon viper. Has the longest fangs in the world and the venom is what they call hemotoxic. Means it destroys tissue."

"I have to admit that the dark, yellow-edged pattern is pretty, but I wouldn't want to run into it," Ms. Scott said, wrapping both arms around her body and shivering.

"I wouldn't worry about you walking up on one of these bad boys, unless you plan on visiting Africa. It lives in the bush."

"I expect a thoroughly enlightening and entertaining paper from you, Mr. Hunter."

"No doubt. My paper will be tight."

"By the way, has Doug contacted you?"

Before Xavier could respond, Doug walked into the library. He spoke to Ms. Scott and asked for a little time with Xavier. The two walked out into the hallway.

Xavier asked, "So have the white coats from the mental hospital nabbed that insane girl yet?"

There was an intense look on Doug's face. "Mr. Hunter, I'm afraid this is no joke. We did some looking into the matter. Found out that Heather was adopted by a lady named Mickey Larkin. We got in touch with Ms. Larkin and she reported Heather hasn't been home in three weeks. Said she went to sleep one night and when she woke up next morning, Heather was gone, and so was Ms. Larkin's Ford Edge."

"The police?"

Doug said, "I'm getting to it. Because Heather has a history of staying away from home for long stretches,

Ms. Larkin thought this was just another one of those times. And as for the vehicle, Ms. Larkin didn't want to get Heather in any trouble with the police. So she never reported it missing."

"So you're telling me that nobody knows where this Bipolar Betty is?"

Doug scratched his head. "I know you're referring to her as Bipolar Betty as a joke. But, son, this is no joke. Her mother says that she does have bipolar disorder. She stopped taking her meds about a month ago."

This didn't happen to Xavier much, but goose bumps crawled over his flesh. The silence around him was creepy, almost reminiscent of a swimmer treading in the ocean while watching a shark fin break the surface and then chillingly dip back down, out of sight.

Doug reminded Xavier, "You have a lot of enemies for somebody so young. You are stretching my security team thin, you know that? The police are investigating and looking for Heather. In the meantime, Mr. Hunter, you better watch your back."

"That's the understatement of the year," said Xavier.

"Oh by the way. That abandoned house lead turned up empty."

Xavier said to Doug, "Why am I not surprised?"

The very next day Xavier was chilling in the lunch-room. He was surrounded by the usual suspects. This time the cast had been joined by Samantha. On the phone last night Xavier had gotten a chance to put Samantha up on game. Heather was out of her head and off her meds. And even though Samantha had said that she wasn't worried about the threat, Xavier knew better. She had that same fear in her voice that she'd had during the time of those prank calls last year.

Dexter asked Linus Flip, "Will your ride be ready when we mob to the MJR Cinema 20 on the twenty-seventh to see *Ratchet Chicks*, my dude?"

"You know it, but I'm taxing the fools rolling with me."

Samantha smiled. "You have to make that engine money back some kind of way."

Linus laughed at Samantha. "You back on my ride again." He looked at Xavier. "Man, why don't you get your girl up off my car. Everybody can't be rich like her and have a driver."

Xavier was sitting right next to Samantha. "Homeboy, better you than me."

Dexter asked, "Where is the jock?"

Xavier said, "Bigstick said he was skipping today to chill at home with Ray Taylor. The two of them are gonna breeze down to the hospital and check out Clyde."

They started discussing Clyde's improvement when Kato Holloway walked over. He was flamboyantly dressed, of course—high-profile Cartier frames, a sweet Gucci hooded sweatshirt, big-money diamond studs, expensive jeans, and high-top signature black Gucci sneakers. His dreadlocks flowed smoothly down his back.

"Xavier, what up doe?" asked Kato.

This dude is up to something, Xavier thought. But he played it off by saying, "You got it all day, homeboy. Let me introduce you to a few of the homies." Xavier introduced Kato to Dexter and Linus. "And this lovely lady sitting next to me is my girl—I mean my friend—Samantha

Fox." Introducing her as just a friend—Xavier had never stopped to realize how hurtful it felt.

Kato complimented, "And yes, you're all kinds of foxy, mama."

Samantha blushed and said, "Why, thank you, Kato. That was sweet."

Xavier didn't think it was sweet. He wasn't trying to show it, but he was jealous.

"Kato?" Dexter asked. "Is that like Bruce Lee in *The Green Hornet* Kato?"

Linus said, "Man, I heard of Bruce Lee, but what the hell is *The Green Hornet*?"

"Don't you know anything, Mr. Engine Trouble?" Dexter said, laughing. "*The Green Hornet* was a TV series back in the Stone Age when Bruce Lee got his start on television. It just so happens to be one of my father's favorites."

"Okay, *Mr. Engine Trouble*," Linus said to Dex. "Samantha got a ride to the movies. Don't let her get you in trouble by using her jokes."

Kato stood there laughing. "You cats are funny. But to answer your question, Dexter—"

"Call me Dex."

"No doubt, homie. Much like your dad, my old man watched the show back in the day and he also loved Bruce Lee. Pops named me after his favorite action star."

Xavier didn't have the complete facts as to why Kato was starting to get so friendly. He'd learned recently that potential enemies should always be kept in front. Couldn't see what they were doing behind. If this guy wanted to play the game, then Xavier could too.

Xavier waved his hand. "Why don't you cop a squat, homeboy. Kick it wit' us. We're all family around these parts."

Kato said, "Thank you. Don't mind if I do."

"Look, Kato," Xavier said. "February twenty-seventh we're all going over to the MJR Cinema 20 to the movies. Why don't you come kick it with us?"

Linus and Dexter looked at Xavier like he had completely flipped his wig. Since Kato's arrival, all three had been trying to figure dude out.

"Yes, Kato," Samantha said joyfully. "It's on a Friday. Bring a girlfriend, friends—whoever. We're going to have a great time."

Kato smiled. "That's what's up. I'm there."

Xavier was determined to keep this dude by his side. No matter what. At least until he found out what Kato had up his sleeve.

23

Death might've been riding on his coattails, but Xavier wasn't going to be deterred by his enemies. He was driven to think positive thoughts, and having an opportunity to flex at his prom and walk across the stage to receive his diploma were two of them. The boy was so committed that he'd passed on an invitation to kick it with Dexter and Linus Flip tonight. And despite the teasing he'd received from Dex and Linus about being a bookworm, Xavier had put his foot down. This research paper would be 50 percent of his grade on the last report card of the school year. So Dex and Flip could kick hot rocks wearing open-toed sandals. He had to stay focused. And though Slick Eddie's henchmen were out there somewhere and probably waiting on Xavier to make a wrong move, that was no excuse for him to fall behind in his grades.

Xavier was working in the front room, using his cell phone to look up the deadly black mamba, as he sat snugly in the corner on the throw pillows, his back against the wall. The serpent he was researching was super aggressive, with lightning strikes, a drop of his venom was able to take out ten to fifteen adults. Highly distinguishable by the black color inside the mouth, it lived in Africa and had been recorded as being the fastest land snake on the planet. Xavier was finding out some pretty interesting facts about the serpent world. Like the deadliest snake in the world didn't live on land but slithered in the sea—the Belcher's sea snake. It was tiny, not as big as its land cousins, but a few milligrams of venom would be enough to wipe out a thousand people.

Yes, the research was interesting enough but failed to capture his total attention. The dark recesses of his mind were in command and taking his thoughts down a pathway to the troubles that were disturbing his world. Dude seemed to be wanted by everybody. It was a wonder that he was still alive. Tall and Husky had no doubt made an attempt on his life, but had missed the opportunity and came up busted. And after they'd done Clyde and Ray Taylor, the GMC SUV boys seemed like they had completely vanished. Even Heather's ratchet self hadn't been spotted creeping. Xavier took no comfort in this. At any given time he could step out of his front door and become a victim. He wasn't going to let down his guard or bank on his enemy giving up the chase.

And poor Samantha had been nothing but a trooper

behind all this madness. For the life of him he couldn't understand why she still was willing to be his friend—all the crap he'd taken her through. Any other girl would've been in the wind by now, especially after being threatened by some demented chick who possessed a dark fetish for wanting to leave tire tracks over her victim's mangled body.

Xavier had kicked it with Samantha about an hour ago. Just before she, Tracy, and Jennifer had stepped out for an evening of shopping and probably dinner. This was the only time that Xavier wasn't worried about Samantha. Her driver, the black Lurch, wasn't quite as tall as Shaquille O'Neal but just as thick. He'd also been given strict orders by her parents to protect their daughter at all costs. Smash whoever might jump in Samantha's face, popping junk.

Kato Holloway continued to be quite friendly. The boy sometimes went out of his way to have a conversation with Xavier in school. Had the nerve to ask him a few times if Xavier wanted to be dropped off at the crib. Even before Linus had his ride back, Xavier had declined. Didn't know Kato like that, and there was no way he was going to show homeboy the location in which he laid his head.

On his phone Xavier had pulled up a picture of a Philippine cobra, when there was a knock on the front door. Instinct forced him to click off the living room lights. He crept toward the windows to peek through the vertical blinds. No way on God's green earth was he gonna place himself in harm's way by standing directly in front of the door and staring out the peephole. Cats had been blasted out of their shoes and socks in the past for such a careless action. The front window gave direct access to the porch. It was Billy standing there in the shadows.

Xavier opened the door. "Old man, you were about to get your head blown off."

Billy moseyed on in, bringing with him the cold air from outside. "With what, your cell phone? Because I know you don't have any illegal firearms up in here—not my rental property, you young punk."

Xavier closed the door. "You can't tell me what to do in this house—I'm paying—oh, wait a second. I'm not paying rent. But I do live here."

"For free, you little parasite," Billy joked. The old guy had on a thick winter jacket, his regular hospital scrub pants, and tightly laced old-school black combat boots. He paid attention to Xavier's notepads and thick textbooks scattered around his work area. "You in here getting your lesson, I see."

Xavier walked back over to the throw pillows and sat down. "I would offer you a seat, old geezer, but somewhere I heard that standing up for a guy your age is healthy for circulation." He pointed to the pillows. "Besides, this is the only chair I have to sit on in here."

Billy looked at the picture of the Philippine cobra on Xavier's cell phone screen. "What are you doing in here looking at snakes?"

"Research for my paper. Writing about some of the deadliest snakes in the world."

"Aw shoot, young'un. You could've saved your research on the Internet and come to talk to me. Do you know when I was over in the jungles of Vietnam we had to be very careful? If it wasn't the red ants, it was those pesky tiger leeches. But in the field you had to be alert because they had some stuff over there nobody wanted to tangle with. We used to be over there, knee-deep in heavy bamboo or elephant grass. The spitting cobra, bamboo pit viper, Malayan pit viper, and the Malayan krait—a bite from any one of those would've gotten a grunt shipped back to the United States in a metal coffin."

Xavier asked, "You ever see some?"

Billy popped his lips. "Shoot, yeah. Especially at night, when we were lying around on our air mattresses. Suckers would slither right on by."

"I guess I should've come over to pick your brain."

Billy walked over to the window and peeled back the blinds and looked out.

Xavier could tell something was heavy on his mind.

"Youngster, I'm not gonna beat around the bush. I know you heard us fighting the other night. Brandy and I are butting heads—the woman is like a wildcat. And I went and got her knocked up like a darn blasted fool, should've had my head examined. But anyway—"

Xavier said, "You don't have to say it, Billy. I'm coming between y'all. You've been nothing but good to me. It's time for me to go back home."

Billy put a hand up. "Listen, take your time. If you feel you need another month to get yourself together, then you take it. You are a good kid and I want to see you do well. One thing the heffa is not gonna do is bully me into doing anything." Billy pulled up his coat and removed a thick business envelope from his right scrub pocket.

The envelope was like the one Billy had given him before, but a little thicker.

He handed it to Xavier. "When you leave here, this ought to get you through the rest of the school year. Don't go tricking—"

Billy's words were cut off by the explosion of the middle window. Xavier and Billy hit the deck, as jagged glass flew through the air. Xavier looked over at Billy. The old man had pulled his pistol out but stayed down. Outside, a car door closed quickly and tires squealed as the vehicle sped away.

Billy said, "You okay, youngster?"

"Yeah . . . I'm good."

Billy told Xavier to stay down as he slithered over to the window on his belly. One peek over the windowsill— nobody!

They hadn't seen it before, but a brick lay in the middle of the floor, a piece of paper affixed to it with duct tape. Xavier gathered it up, removed the note, and read it.

Billy asked, "That crazy heffa you been telling me about?"

Xavier just shook his head. "Can't tell. All the note says is 'I keep my promises.' "

"You sure know how to pick 'em." Holding his pistol with his right hand, Billy opened the door with his left, and slowly stepped out into the night air. Once he was sure that everything was clear, he said, "Perimeter secure."

He put his pistol up, still looking around.

Xavier walked out wearing a heavy coat. "The head of security at my school has already reported this to the police. He has friends on the force. Guess Monday I'll be taking this to him." Xavier held up the brick.

The door to Billy's house opened and Brandy came storming out.

"I didn't see who it was, but it was some type of Ford crossover," she yelled, cold vapor escaping her mouth. "Busting windows out—you get him the hell out of here, right now!"

Billy looked at Xavier and then back to Brandy. To Xavier's surprise, the old dude calmly walked over to the hysterical young woman and whispered something in her ear. Whatever it was, Brandy scooted back inside the house without offering any more lip.

"Excuse my language, but what the hell did you say to her?"

Billy wiggled his eyebrows up and down in a mischievous fashion. "You didn't know the old man's game was tight like that. Never let it be said that Billy Rupert Hawkins can't handle his women, you feel me?"

Xavier just shook his head. "I feel you, Rupert." He laughed. "I feel you, big dog."

24

MONDAY, FEBRUARY 23
9:00 A.M.

Two days later Xavier was back in Doug's office. The police had been there to question him about the incident, then left. Their hands were totally tied, they said. Since nobody had actually witnessed Heather committing the offense, the police couldn't do a damn thing. As far as they were concerned, the note wasn't signed by Heather, and the fact that it had been computer-generated made it extremely difficult to trace back to her. The chick might've been insane but she was clever. Had covered her tracks like a seasoned pro.

Xavier asked Doug, "So what—I guess the lunatic has to kill me before the police can actually get up from the doughnut counter to arrest her?"

"Mr. Hunter, you've made so many wrong decisions

and now you are paying the consequences. You know how this works: There isn't anything we can do because as far as the police are concerned, there is no proof of a crime. And you reporting that she almost ran you over? Show me some proof—did anybody see her chase you with the vehicle? I know how you kids are with these cell phones nowadays. Did you even try to take a picture of the license plate of the car that chased you? And you didn't bother to report it when it happened."

Xavier was growing angry and it was showing. "This is straight busted, you feel me? I'd be wrong if I took the law into my own hands and found her and ran her over with her own car. And speaking of cars: hers is stolen. You mean to tell me five-o can't run it down?"

"Doesn't work like that here in Detroit. You stole cars for a living one time. You of all people should know how it works. There is no way with the amount of stolen cars on the streets of Detroit that our overworked police department would be able to find it just like that. Unless she does something stupid and they pull her over."

Xavier paced around the small office.

Doug said, "You do know Heather is the least of your concerns, right? The police still haven't caught up with those boys in that GMC SUV who are responsible for killing Felix Hoover and wounding Clyde McElroy and Ray Taylor. Word around the building is that they are targeting what's left of your crew for some reason. Not to mention the guy that you said chased you in this very building. Ain't no telling who threw that brick through your window—hell, take your pick."

"You trying to be funny?"

"Of course not. I told you that you should've transferred—"

"Here we go with this transfer nonsense. Miss me with that. I'm trying to graduate from this piece."

Doug ran a hand over his face in frustration. "Well, I hope you get that diploma and don't end up getting it before you get it."

Xavier walked out on Doug by dismissing him with the slam of the office door.

25

MONDAY, FEBRUARY 23
12:00 P.M.

Samantha was on her way to fourth-hour lunch. She'd had to stay behind to discuss some things with her calculus teacher. Now armed with a pass, she was racing through the deserted hallways to her locker to put her things away. She couldn't believe how crazy her world had become. There was so much drama going on in her life right now, enough to keep her confused until graduation. Her father was still refusing to let her have peace at the crib because of her friendship with Xavier. Her mother just wanted things to get better between Sam and her father. Stress in the household was starting to take its toll on the family.

Samantha put her calculus textbook into the locker.

Junk was all over the place, crap that belonged to her locker buddies and best friends, Jennifer and Tracy. There was a small square vanity mirror affixed to the inside of the locker door. Samantha slid the purse straps from her shoulder and removed some lip gloss from the expensive vintage Louis Vuitton Monogram handbag. In the mirror, the Shiny Kiss lip gloss slid on perfectly. She popped her lips and then put everything away.

Her love for Xavier was incredible, but she hated the trouble that seemed to follow him around like a shadow. Samantha really couldn't believe the thoughts running through her head—thoughts of a life without him. He was charming, possessed a great personality, was funny, tough, and brilliant—all adorable qualities. The question was could he make it in her highly sophisticated world, a place where poor folks were an entertaining topic of discussion and debate over brunch by the rich and snooty. Samantha had plans to live a fascinating life after college. To pursue her dreams of becoming a professional dancer, getting married, and eventually having a family. But at the rate Xavier was going, she doubted if he'd even be alive to graduate from high school. Right at this moment, there were people out there who wanted to harm him. Maybe there was some truth to what her father was preaching. She knew the old man meant well and was just being protective.

Samantha entered the stairwell, distracted by a mind full of sensitive issues and teenage angst. The college baseball sensation, shortstop Sean Desmond, would be in town next week, and had asked her to go out with him.

She was so confused. On one hand she loved Xavier, but on the other, her father expected her to be with somebody like Desmond, an accomplished thoroughbred who had professional scouts clamoring every time he stepped up to bat.

Caught up in her feelings, Samantha hadn't paid any attention to the stairwell door opening and closing behind her until it was too late. She was halfway down the second flight of stairs when she felt a blow to the small of her back. The force almost launched her from the stairs but instinct kicked in, and she threw her purse and reached out to grab hold of the railing. The move was the only thing that broke her fall and saved her from going airborne and dropping to the landing below. Though she'd smacked her head hard against the wall under the railing, Samantha held on for dear life, trying not to slide down any farther.

"I can't believe you're the weak little tramp Hunter wants." Heather's eyes blazed as she walked down the stairs behind Samantha. The psycho chick had her cell phone out in front of her and looked to be recording her handiwork.

Samantha was dazed from banging her head. She couldn't do anything but lie on the stairs, trying to get her bearings.

"I told Hunter that I would make him pay, and I keep my promises," Heather said calmly. She was right on top of Samantha and had raised her foot to strike her in the head when two huge arms bear-hugged Heather from behind.

"What the—" was all Heather could shout as she struggled.

Xavier was sitting alone at his favorite cafeteria table, going over some research. After the brick had smashed through his window last night and the circus Billy's baby mama created, Xavier had called it quits and stopped working on his research paper. Although he'd been tripping over the amount of money Billy had given him to hold him down for the rest of the school year—thirty-five hundred dollars. The old man was forever looking out.

Xavier was now trying to make up for lost time. Rarely did he work on assignments in this loud, rowdy atmosphere. This paper would count for half of his grade. Somehow he had to find a way to stay focused. Linus and Dexter respected his wishes and had left him alone to work. The two weren't far. Just on the other side of the cafeteria and gettin' their clown on with a table full of girls.

Xavier was poring over a printout. The death adder was a species of snake native to Australia and New Guinea. This particular serpent fascinated him because it hunted down and killed other snakes. With its triangular-shaped head and short body, the death adder is a fierce competitor and has the fastest strike in the world.

Xavier was jotting down some notes when he looked up and saw Doug, followed by Kato, walk in through the south entrance. When Doug sat down at the table Xavier knew that this had to be serious. He'd never seen the head security guard sitting in the lunchroom before. Kato sat down beside Doug.

Xavier was so wiped out from trouble, all he could say was, "What now?"

Doug looked at Kato for a moment before returning his gaze back to Xavier. "Samantha—"

"*What's wrong with Sam?*"

Doug said, "Calm down. Samantha is fine. We have Heather. The police just took her into custody."

"But what does Sam have to do with it?"

"She tried to kick Samantha down the stairs," Doug said.

Kato interjected, "And she was recording the whole thing with her cell phone."

"Is Samantha all right?"

"Yes, she's fine." Doug patted Kato on the back. "And thanks to Mr. Holloway here, Heather didn't get a chance to carry out her threat. He's the real hero."

Xavier nodded his head at Kato, then asked, "Doug, where's Sam?"

"She's in the office being interviewed by the police. But, here's the thing: We were going through Heather's cell phone and found footage of her kicking Brenda Sanders down the stairs."

"So Brenda was telling the truth," Xavier said. "Heather is a freakin' sick, psycho bunny."

Doug explained further, "We have enough video evidence to charge Heather with assault with intent to do bodily harm to Brenda."

"Can I go and see Samantha?"

"Not yet. After the investigation is over I'll come find you. But what you need to do is thank Mr. Holloway here."

"Okay. Am I missing something? Wasn't Brenda carrying a baby? The charges should've been attempted murder, right?"

"Oh, that's what I forgot to tell you," Doug said, scratching his head. "With all the drama going on with you I forgot to tell you that Brenda wasn't pregnant."

"And how did you find this out? The last time I called Brenda, her cell had been disconnected."

Doug explained, "She called me on my office phone a few days ago. She confessed to lying about the whole thing. Said she made the whole thing up because she wanted to see you sweat. I believe 'have some fun' was the way she put it."

Doug got up from the table and walked away.

Kato could do nothing but shake his head. "The games that some people play."

To Xavier, it didn't matter. The only thing that did was that he wasn't nobody's baby daddy.

Xavier and Kato kicked it for the rest of the lunch hour. Kato had gone from suspected enemy . . . to ally.

Later that day, Xavier was sitting across from his probation officer Oliver Meyer, being asked the same dry questions the officer usually asked during their sessions.

And then at the end of the session Oliver raised his head up from the pile of paperwork on his desk long enough to say, "Mr. Hunter, May twenty-fifth will be our last meeting. If you should make it through to that date without getting yourself in trouble, it would conclude these meetings and you will have satisfied the terms of your probation. I wish you well."

Xavier said, "Thank you, sir." That was the kind of news he needed to hear.

26

Everybody was out and having a great time. The MJR Cinema 20 had been off the hook with people packed in to see *Ratchet Chicks*. And the movie was all that too. So many students from Coleman had shown up that the line of cars on the trip over looked like a caravan of student drivers. And of course, Samantha, Xavier, and the black Lurch led the way. Her girls Jennifer and Tracy also rode in the car with Samantha. There was so much love directed at Samantha and her two BFFs for assembling the event that somebody suggested that they should pull outings like this one until the end of the school year.

After the flick, the posse had invaded the Dave & Buster's in Utica, Michigan. They had eaten at the restaurant and were now spread out throughout the arcade, playing games. A diverse crowd of people were standing around and enjoying the atmosphere.

Samantha and Xavier were challenging each other, one-on-one, to a basketball arcade game. The buzz of laughter and fun was a little loud inside the game room, but it was all good. Samantha was winning, and she had a fat stack of game tickets to back her up.

Compared to the time she'd been assaulted in the auditorium by two outsiders in her sophomore year, the thing with Heather was relatively mild. Aside from having a headache afterwards, Samantha hadn't sweated the incident. And she had practically pleaded with Principal Skinner not to involve her parents. She explained that it was just a minor offense and that her father had threatened to remove her from the school if anything like that auditorium thing happened again. It was a judgment call, but Skinner had ended up contacting her folks anyway. Samantha's mother had saved her. Mr. Fox had threatened to take his little girl out of Coleman, but her mother wasn't buying it. The dance program at Coleman was excellent, and too important to Samantha to just pull her out of school. After a lot of bickering between her mother and father, Samantha, her parents decided to let her remain at Coleman.

This was one of too many bad situations Xavier had placed her in. And mentally Samantha was exhausted. She didn't want to keep pushing her luck because one day it would eventually run out. Samantha had seen far too many innocent bystanders killed for being in the wrong place at the wrong time. She couldn't put her family through such heartbreak.

After the last game of shootout she looked at Xavier. "We need to talk."

Xavier shot the loose balls into the cylinder, then he turned to her. "Sam, what's the matter? This whole thing was your idea. Everybody's having a blast. You should be happy."

Samantha toyed with the tickets in her hand. "I know, but so much has gone on, Xavier."

"What? Is it that Heather thing? The police have her for assault. She won't be bothering us any time soon."

Samantha didn't know how to verbally express her thoughts. So she came right out with it. "You remember when I told you that the slightest little scandal could affect my father's status in the community?"

"Yeah, I remember."

"Xavier, you're all over the place. You're staying in Billy's rental property because your father is a tad touched by his faith, people are out to kill you—your own mother tried to kidnap me to do God knows what. Not to mention that you got Brenda pregnant on me—"

"She wasn't really pregnant. Brenda was faking it."

"—It doesn't really matter anymore. I'm tired, Xavier. I don't want to be caught in the middle of your issues."

Xavier's face tightened. "So what you're trying to tell me is that you don't want to be my friend anymore."

Confusion was all over Samantha's face. "This is not a friendship. It's like we're still together as boyfriend and girlfriend. And it's draining."

Xavier saw something in her eyes that led him to ask, "This doesn't have anything to do with that base-runnin', steroid-juicing fool Sean, does it?"

"How can you say that I'm basing my feelings toward you around another guy?"

Xavier folded his arms over his chest. "Look me in my eyes and tell me that it has nothing to do with that fool Sean."

Samantha looked away.

"You see, I told you. What he do? Tell you that you're gonna get married after you finish high school? Live in some thirty-million-dollar crib after he makes it to the majors?"

"You know that I'm not impressed by material things."

"Oh, I get it. Your parents expect you to be with somebody like him because he's class and I'm not, right? Because he has a bright future and I'm a kid from the ghetto with hopes and pipe dreams, right?"

"You're ridiculous," Samantha said. "I'm confused. Can you please not contact me? I really need some time to think."

"Go ahead then. Do you. I ain't sweatin' it. Get back with that home-run-hitting creep."

Samantha walked off.

Kato walked up. "Aye, man, you and your girl all right?"

Xavier shook his head, still looking in Samantha's direction. "Yeah, we cool. But what's with you, though? You having a good time, or what?" Xavier looked at a beautiful, shapely girl playing a video game. "Homeboy, your girl is a stunner."

Kato bragged, "She aight. Just a dime with no attachment—that's how we do around these parts, see what I'm sayin'."

Xavier allowed his gaze to drift to Dex and Marissa. The two looked like they were going head-to-head on some NASCAR circuit video game.

Xavier and Kato started walking through the arcade.

Xavier said, "Good lookin' on that Heather madness, homeboy."

"It was nothing. It was just coincidental that I was coming from hollerin' at my guidance counselor. When I saw the babe getting ready to stomp Samantha, I grabbed her up in a bear hug to stop it. I kind of felt sorry for Heather."

"How so?"

"All the way to the office she kept on trying to explain that she was sorry, that she didn't mean to harm Samantha, but you weren't paying her any attention anymore."

Xavier said, "So trying to kick my girlfriend—I mean Samantha—down the steps was her way of crying out for my attention?"

"I'm just telling you what she told me."

The two talked for about ten minutes, getting to know one another, and wound up sitting in a booth, sipping on sodas.

Kato said, "I haven't let anybody know this about me. But, Xavier, you seem like a cool brotha."

Xavier took a swig of his soda.

Kato continued, "You know Felix Hoover?"

Xavier's stare was one of curiosity.

"Felix was my dog. After they killed him, I made up

my mind to transfer over here to see who was behind the trigger, see what I'm sayin'?"

There it was in black and white. The reason this dude was here. Xavier always knew that there was another level to Kato.

Kato said, "I've been working the homies in the school for info."

"I'm surprise those morons even talked to you. Nobody at Coleman trusts outsiders."

"Oh, that junk didn't come cheap. Had to lay down a few big faces for it."

"Why are you telling me this?"

Kato stared intensely at Xavier. "I heard that you and Felix were close. I can use somebody else to pull off this caper I got planned for those cats behind the trigger."

"Who are these fools?"

Kato smiled and sat back. "Those guys that drive the GMC SUV?—I don't know 'em."

"You don't know or you can't tell me?"

"Can't tell you that . . . yet. Are you in?"

"Homeboy, when you get back at me with some names . . . then I'll let you know."

Kato removed a pen from his jacket and scribbled down his cell phone number on a napkin. "Here's the number to my hitter once you make up your mind."

Xavier grabbed it and got up from the table and walked toward Samantha.

27

SATURDAY, FEBRUARY 28
4:00 A.M.

Xavier's cell phone rang and almost scared the be-jeezus outta him. He rolled over and snatched the phone. He sat up in bed and tried to wipe away the blurriness, thinking, *Who in the hell could be calling at this time of morning?* He had just gotten in a couple hours ago after leaving Dave & Buster's. His eyes had yet to focus but the phone kept on ringing. The caller couldn't be Samantha because she was steamed at him. And she had a right to be. He'd given her a few choice words in the parking lot before jumping into the car with Linus.

Damn that Sean Desmond character, Xavier thought. Once his eyes focused he saw the caller ID. What the hell was Dexter hitting his cell phone up at this time of the morning?

He answered and got the shock of his life.

Dex yelled into the phone, "Man, those fools just shot up my house!"

Xavier's eyes opened wide and chills pimpled his flesh with goose bumps. He said, "Dexter, calm down and tell me what happened."

Dexter tried to slow down his breathing. "After we dropped you and Marissa off, Linus and I went down to Greektown. Had a bite to eat, and after that Linus dropped me off. About fifteen minutes after he left, I heard something in front of the crib, so I goes to take a peek out the front door. Saw that GMC SUV stop in front of the crib, the windows rolled down, and all I saw was fire spitting out the muzzles of some weapons, my dude."

"Your parents all right?"

Xavier could hear Dex's mother crying in the background. His father sounded like he was on the phone with the police.

Dexter said, "Yeah, they're cool. Just shook up though."

"I got this handled, man. Don't worry about it."

"X, what are you talking about?"

"Said I got it handled."

"If you know something, come get me. I wanna ride on those fools. This thing is personal."

"You and Linus just fall back. I got this."

Xavier hung up the phone. He got out of bed and flipped on the lights and grabbed the napkin from his jacket pocket.

This was war. He was about to put a stop to these clowns right now.

Xavier dialed Kato's phone number.

*   *   *

The streets were almost deserted at four thirty in the morning. Xavier sat in the passenger seat of Kato's Chevy TrailBlazer. The anger he had for those clowns had led him into doing something stupid, like rolling on them with a cat he no more knew personally than the snakes he'd been researching.

After he'd contacted Kato, Kato had made a few phone calls and got the ball rolling. The lick was going down at Belle Isle, the huge Detroit city park, and nobody could stop it. The GMC boys had to go. Dexter was like family. Didn't bother anybody. The boy could've been killed. Worse yet, one of his parents could've easily perished in that senseless and cowardly attack.

Xavier looked out of his side-view mirror. They were being followed by a black Mercury Marauder; an out-cold, brand-new burgundy Jeep Grand Cherokee; and a newer red Chevrolet Camaro sitting on twenty-ones. Kato had referred to them as his gang.

All four vehicles were now rolling strong down Jefferson Avenue, headed east to the General Douglas MacArthur Bridge. They passed the IHOP, a Mobil gas station, the Jefferson Chevrolet dealership, Fuddruckers, and Wendy's, veering to the right and taking the MacArthur Bridge over to Belle Isle.

At this point Xavier started having second thoughts. It took an evil person to take a life. He wasn't a punk or anything—he was always down for a good scrap—but this was different. It felt different. He felt that lives would be taken behind this ride. And frankly, Xavier didn't know if he had the stomach or the heart to perpetrate such a foul and diabolical act of senselessness.

If he bailed out now he'd look like a punk. Nobody respected a snitch at Coleman, but at least none of the students had ever tried Xavier. But if he bounced on Kato and the treachery got back to the school, everybody and their mamas would probably be trying to step to him.

Xavier's life was passing before his eyes as they kept to the outer road and went by the Scott Fountain. They journeyed deeper into the park's interior through a series of roads until the vehicles reached a huge parking lot, not too far from the giant slide. And there it was, sitting parked in the gloom, like some spectral chariot of death, vehicle idling, headlights on. This was the GMC SUV he'd seen, a little too close for comfort, the night when those goons pulled up on him and his friends and opened fire at LaMarcus's party.

Kato slowed to a crawl, rolled down his window, and stuck his arm out, signaling for his partners to take position. The cars quickly surrounded the SUV. Something wasn't right, though. The boys in the GMC were ruthless. Xavier thought that cars surrounding them would more than likely end in a deadly shootout. But there was nothing.

Kato said to Xavier, "You ready for this?"

Xavier didn't speak at first. Just wished he was at home underneath the warm covers.

He finally said in an unenthused tone, "Let's do it." The butterflies were dancing the hot hustle in his stomach.

Kato reached under his seat and grabbed a gat. He

stuck it underneath his bomber jacket inside of his waistband. "Let's do this."

The two of them exited the TrailBlazer, triggering Kato's boys into exiting their vehicles, flanking the GMC.

There still was no gunfire. It was puzzling, to say the least.

The tint on the windows of the GMC was extra dark. Nobody could see inside.

Kato took his position and yelled to the occupants of the truck, "Y'all can get out now. We have everything handled."

The driver-side door of the GMC opened and out stepped . . . Dylan Dallas, Xavier's old enemy. The dude Xavier had knocked out cold at the soul food restaurant. The chump was also the leader of the former super gang called Straight Eight at Coleman.

I'll be damned, Xavier thought as Dylan walked over to him. Still, there was no gunfire. What was up with this?

Dylan said to Xavier, "'Sup, nephew. You remember me? Of course you do. I'm the cat that twisted your homeboy Felix Hoover."

Things got really interesting when out of the passenger door slid Dutch Westwood, the other slimeball lieutenant from Straight Eight.

Westwood said, "Oh. There's Xavier Hunter. It must be raining Christmas gifts."

Two other guys got out of the GMC's backseat. A cold chill raced up Xavier's back. This didn't seem right to him. The guys from the GMC were now shaking hands with Kato's boys.

Xavier went to look at Kato and homeboy had a devil-ish grin on his face. *Setup.* This dirty bastard had set him up from the jump.

Kato said to Xavier, "I guess every man has his price, see what I'm sayin'?"

Xavier must've missed the duffel bag Westwood was carrying. He handed it to Kato.

Westwood said, "This has to be money well spent."

Xavier just stood there speechless. He couldn't believe the dude had served him up to his enemies on a silver platter.

"Don't look so surprised, nephew," Dylan Dallas said. "I told you behind the school that day that you would have your day in front of my gun. We already took care of the only thing that stood in our way."

Westwood laughed sinisterly. "Like Felix, those two fools from the football team, Ray what's-his-name, and Clyde who-gives-a-damn. See, we figured we'd knock off those who were in the way. Punish you. Save you for last. Don't know if we iced your boy Dexter, but the way his house looked when we jetted, nobody could've sur-vived."

Xavier spoke out for the first time. "Wow. This is how I go out, huh? Let me ask you goons something before y'all punch my ticket."

Dylan said, "Speak your piece, nephew."

Xavier looked around. He was seriously outnumbered. Not to mention the firepower. There was no way he could escape.

He asked, "Slick Eddie, does he have anything to do with this?"

Westwood laughed. "Are you crazy? We don't work for nobody else. This is personal, G. You got in the way of my bread when you and your little Zulu crew tried to regulate Coleman by getting rid of thugs, criminals and hustlers last year. Good people like me and him"—he pointed to Dylan Dallas. "This is payback, playboy."

Dylan Dallas chimed in. "The little goody-goody stunt y'all pulled cut into the profits. In a school where we depended on our fellow students to eat, you and your crew disrupted all of it, with running the so-called 'bad element' out of the school. Time to pay up, nephew."

"Yeah we smoked your homeboys, because we knew that they would have your back," said Westwood. "Now it's time for you to go."

Kato just stood there, grinning. The boy had all the integrity of a snake in the wild.

"Enough of this," Kato said. "Y'all paid me to do a service. It's done. But before you boys take Xavier on that ride, there's somebody I think he should meet first." Kato got on his phone. "Bring it on."

One, two, three—and the whole damn area was flooded with the flashing lights of police units. The officers jumped out with their guns drawn.

Dutch Westwood said, "What the hell is going on?"

Dylan Dallas asked, "What's up with this bacon convention up in here, cuz?"

Kato smiled. He reached into his jacket and pulled out a police badge attached to a thick black cord around his neck. "Dylan Dallas, Dutch Westwood, you boys are under arrest for the murder of Felix Hoover and the attempted murder of Ray Taylor and Clyde McElroy. You two have the right to remain silent. I think you should exercise that right."

The officers converged on Dutch and his crew and slapped handcuffs on their wrists.

Xavier looked at the guys who had driven over with Kato. They were now pulling their badges out of their jackets like Kato had done and were mixing in with the other police. A search of the GMC yielded four AK-47s and two .40 caliber Glocks.

Xavier was relieved. He smiled and told Kato, "Man, for a minute I thought you had sold me like I was a black market product. I'm relieved." He held his hands out in front of him. "Look at how they're shaking. Got my heart pumping Kool-Aid."

Kato laughed. "Didn't mean to do that to you or have you in the middle of this, but it was the only way to bring those bastards to justice."

Xavier exhaled. "It's all good, homeboy. Trust me. It's all good."

Kato explained, "I had to go undercover. Nobody at the school would talk to the police. I got connected and found out through the grapevine that Dylan and Dutch had a price on your head. It took me a while to get past their underlings and get to meet them directly. Got 'em to trust me by doing a couple of jobs"—he used the quote fingers—"to prove myself. Once my street cred checked out, we were good to go. Before you came here I had called them up, told 'em that I had you, and they agreed to meet."

Xavier said, "They sprayed up my homeboy's house. Could've killed him and his parents."

"Oh, they'll be charged with that too. And I'm sure those guns we took out of the truck will turn out to be the ones that murdered Felix."

"That thing with Heather wasn't just some coincidence, was it?"

Kato cracked a smile. "Let's just say, a little birdie told me what was going down." He shook Xavier's hand. "By the way, my name is Sergeant Shannon Tyree. It's been my pleasure. The teachers at Coleman speak highly of you." He went into his wallet and grabbed a business card. "If you need anything, don't hesitate."

Xavier couldn't do anything but stand there. The scene was aglow from the lights of the police vehicles. More had arrived to assist in the arrests. He looked toward the heavens and thanked God. Heather and the GMC boys— well, Dutch Westwood and Dylan Dallas—didn't represent a threat anymore. But Tall and Husky was still out there somewhere. And Xavier bet the farm that he was hand-selected by Slick Eddie or Romello to bring about his demise.

Thank you, God, Xavier said to himself. *There are two down and one to go!*

28

MONDAY, MARCH 2
3:30 P.M.

Samantha was all up in Xavier's mind. Aside from a
few text messages, the two hadn't really conversed
much. Not since Dave & Buster's. The text messages
were hollow at best. Just the standard "Hi, how are you
doing" and "Just to let you know I'm thinking about
you." Xavier was hurting behind it. He missed his Sam.
But he also had his pride and wasn't about to chase after
anybody.

"Dang, can't believe ol' boy is a narc," said Dexter.

Xavier, Linus, Bigstick, and Dexter were standing
around Linus's ride in the back parking lot. School was
letting out and kids took to the outside, happy about the
warmer weather. After being punished by old man winter's wrath with below-freezing temperatures, students

were excited about the warm-up. Fifty degrees was like a small heat wave to them, and some were even walking home wearing short sleeves.

Xavier said, "Man—by the way, for the sake of the officer's safety I can't let y'all know his real name, so we're just gonna continue to call him Kato. But when I saw Westwood and Dylan Dallas get out of the GMC and start shaking hands with Kato, I thought that God was getting ready to call my number."

Linus broke in. "My dude, I know that had to be scary, but I would've knuckled up and fought my way out."

Dexter said, "*Scary* ain't the word for it. I would've gone *number two* in my pants."

Bigstick added, "Before they would've had a chance to turn my lights out, fam, I'd be grabbing the first fool to beat down. Somebody would've been coming with me, that's for damn sure."

Xavier laughed at their ignorance. "If y'all had seen what I did, there is no way you'd be standing here talking gangsta. Guns were everywhere. Besides, I'm not into running. Wouldn't give those snakes the satisfaction of shooting me in the back. These fools had brought a bag full of loot to Kato, to cash out the homeboy for handing me over."

Dexter asked, "How much cheddar did they drop for your head?"

"Don't know. Didn't care to find out either. I just know that Kato flipped the script on those thugs after he took the gym bag. He made a call on his cell phone. Five-o blitzed the area. Westwood and Dylan didn't know what hit 'em."

Bigstick said, "So it was those clowns who murdered Felix and are responsible for shooting Ray and Clyde. By the way, Clyde is back home now, but it's likely he'll never play football again. The doctors said something about the bullet grazing his spinal cord. Fam will be lucky to even walk again."

"Don't forget those chumps were the ones who got to dumping on us at LaMarcus's party that night," said Dexter.

"And it made it tough for anybody to identify them because of the heavy tint on the windows of the GMC," added Linus Flip.

Dexter said, "I'm just glad the whole thing is over. Dutch Westwood and Dylan Dallas will probably draw lengthy double-digit sentences behind this madness."

Dexter is half right, Xavier thought. Westwood and Dallas would more than likely grow gray in the joint, but this thing was far from over. And right on cue, a black cargo van pulled into the parking lot, driving close so that Xavier could see the driver, but not so close as to alarm him. The van was some forty feet away when Xavier identified the creep driving it. He couldn't miss the face that had been stalking him for a good part of the school year. Tall and Husky sat in the driver's seat.

Xavier quickly sized up the matter. Dexter had already been through a terrifying ordeal. Bigstick would have a very promising collegiate career and would no doubt go high in the NFL draft. Linus was a knucklehead and probably wouldn't be graduating, but he didn't deserve for any harm to come to him. There was no way Xavier would alert them to the great white shark that was lurking just forty feet offshore. Now that Xavier knew that the GMC boys weren't in cahoots with Tall and Husky, this hitter had to be compliments of Slick Eddie. While the three of Xavier's boys were still discussing Kato turning out to be a narc, Xavier was staring down yet another nightmare.

And much like the killer had done when Xavier saw him some months ago in the hallway, he made a gun out of the fingers on his right hand and pointed it at Xavier. Then he offered Xavier a diabolical smile before whipping the van around and driving out of the parking lot.

At that moment Xavier was hit by an overwhelming sadness and frustration. But he wasn't going to cry about it. He'd brought everything on himself. The only thing he could do was stay positive and hope for the best.

29

It had taken a few hours before Xavier could build up the nerve to knock on his father's door. He stood on Noah's porch with his back to the door, observing the cars driving slowly down the street. Didn't know if he had been followed. Xavier hated to bring heat to his dad's house. But he had nowhere else to go. Billy really needed him gone so that his baby mama would stop trippin' on him every chance she got.

Xavier knocked on the door, still watching his back. He had his house key. Could've let himself in, but he felt that he'd lost those "open door" privileges when he'd left. The car was in the driveway. The old dude had to be in there somewhere—him and Alfonso. Xavier was getting ready to go around back when he heard the sound of locks tumbling and the door opened.

Noah was standing behind the screen door, smiling. "The prodigal son has returned."

Xavier couldn't do anything but shake his head. "Here you go with the Bible. I can't—"

Noah opened the screen door wide. "Please, son, come in. We seriously need to talk."

Noah took a seat in an armchair in the living room, and Xavier sat on the couch across from him.

Noah said, "You know I don't condone violence, but thank you for what you did for your little brother."

"Where's Alfonso at, anyway?" Xavier wanted to know.

His father smiled. "Since that bully has been off his back, he's been staying after school in the library to complete his homework assignments. The boy has done a complete one-eighty. He loves school now. Happy— grades up. He has his chest poked out now, boasting 'I'm getting mad respect from my fellow students, Dad. Everybody knows that my brother is the man.' "

Xavier knew that he wasn't tripping. But for some odd reason he could sense a change in his father, one for the better.

"That's what's up," said Xavier. "I always knew the boy had brains. Just got caught up with a bully."

Noah exhaled deeply. "Listen, son. Since you've been gone I've had a lot of time to think. And the Lord put it up on my heart to ask your forgiveness. You guys already had it tough with your mother. I guess I got caught up in trying too hard to be a good parent by trying to instill my beliefs in you and your brother."

"They're not just your beliefs. I believe in Jesus too. And even though I was living in your house, you had no right to force it down my throat. As much as I wanted to learn the Bible, your forceful ways were turning me off."

"I know, son. But you have to understand where I just came from. In prison, you either do right or continue to do wrong. I chose the right way. Dedicated myself to the Lord. And I was so happy with my dedication that it was blinding me to how much I was pushing my children away."

Xavier smiled. "You have no idea of the huge weight you just lifted off my shoulders. I don't mind learning the Bible and going to church. I even thought that cleaning out the sister's basement was pretty fun with you and Alfonso."

Noah had learned a long time ago that listening was a process to healing.

Xavier pulled his April report card out of his pocket and handed it to his father.

"This is terrific, son. Despite the adversity you've gone through, you still managed straight As."

"Billy told me to tell you hi." Xavier sat back on the couch. "I'm not a bad teenager. Just need a little room to be me. And I can't do it with you ramming the Bible down my throat."

Noah moved over and sat beside his son on the couch.

Noah said, "From now on I'm gonna back off. You can come to the Lord when you feel the spirit move you."

"And I can still wear my designer clothes? No more referring to them as the apparel of Satan?"

Noah laughed. "I don't believe those were my exact words, but you have a deal, son. Just come back home."

"I'm sorry. You've gone through a lot and I should've been there. I talked to Doug and Billy. Between the two of them, let's just say that I was well-informed—about everything."

"About everything?"

"*Everything*. And I want you to know that whenever you have a problem, come to talk to me."

Xavier laughed and then hugged his father. "You got yourself a deal"—he looked at Noah—"Dad."

Noah broke into tears. For it was the first time he'd ever heard his oldest refer to him as *Dad*.

"Make sure you get your butt up there to see your mother."

"All right, Pops."

30

___

Xavier was sitting in his bedroom with a big smile on his face. He wasn't on probation and the grades on his end-of-the-school-year report card had been stellar. Straight As. The smile on his face increased as he remembered what Ms. Scott had told him a week after he'd handed in his research paper. At first he'd been disturbed by her passing back everybody else's paper except his. Xavier was more disturbed when she called him to the front of the room. He felt that he'd done a good job in researching the deadliest snakes in the world. But being put on blast in front of the class had taken away that confidence.

"Mr. Hunter," Ms. Scott had said to him. "Do you know why you're standing in front of the class?"

He had a dumb look on his face. He didn't have the slightest idea.

She'd continued, "Don't look so frightened, Mr. Hunter." She'd looked out at the students and held up—in full view—Xavier's research paper. "This paper, by far, is the best paper I've ever had the privilege of grading." She turned to Xavier. "I will give you a copy of your paper, but I want to keep the original as a standard of excellence that all my future classes should follow."

Xavier was off of his butt with pure joy. A framed copy of his research paper was displayed on the wall in front of his bed. He'd passed to the twelfth grade with flying colors.

One more year, he thought to himself.

His cell phone rang. To his surprise, it was Samantha. He hadn't heard from her in a while. As far as he knew she was still confused and *thinking*.

He answered nonchalantly, "Yup."

"The tough-guy routine, huh?" she asked.

"What do you want from me? Didn't you tell me that you were confused and needed time?"

"Yes. I did. Do you understand how hard it is for me? Trying to obey my father and dealing with my love for you?"

"Why are you calling me with this?"

She huffed. "My folks are taking me to Disney World to celebrate me entering the twelfth grade."

"What does that have to do with me, Sam?"

"They think it's a good idea that Sean tag along."

"I can see they're already starting to play matchmaker.

Why not hook their daughter up with a potential major league superstar?"

"You're not mad?"

"Should I be?"

"But you know I'll be thinking about you the whole time there, right?"

"Samantha, why are you calling me? Seems like your parents have already selected your mate. Oh, congrats on the trip and I hope you have a nice time—you and Sean 'Hotshot' Desmond."

"You know you really can be hurtful. Xavier, I love you."

"Like you said to me—you have a funny way of showing it."

"I want us to get back together, but—"

Xavier's other line was ringing. The caller showed up anonymous, but he didn't care. He just wanted off the phone with Samantha.

"Aye, I have to answer this," he said, trying not to let her hear the frustration in his voice and betray his true feelings.

Xavier switched over to the other line. "Hello," he answered.

The other end remained silent, but he could tell somebody was there.

"Well, whoever this is, I don't have time for playing games—"

"My time is valuable too, Xavier," said the caller.

The voice was dark, heavy, and chilling. Chilled Xavier right to the bone.

"Who is this?"

"The man who is gonna be responsible for sending you on that one-way trip to see your Maker."

"You're the tall, husky brother with the Rocawear hoodie, the one who tried to send me away during a football game, right?"

"The one and only. Congrats on you passing to the twelfth grade, but too bad you're not going to graduate. I've been given orders to stand down for now. Enjoy the summer, kid, because it's going to be yo' last. We'll send a message that we're not to be jacked with. And having your blood spilled all over the hallways of Coleman will bring the media to our cause. I'll see you next school year, boy."

Xavier sat on his bed, still holding on to the phone.

He thought about Samantha. Xavier loved that girl with all of his heart and it hurt like hell to hear about Sean joining them on their vacation to Disney World. How had their relationship fallen off the cliff? Xavier knew she loved him too, but Sean was standing in the way. Xavier had to do something. He wouldn't be able to make it through his senior year without her.

But right now he couldn't afford to worry about his relationship. Given the last phone call, who was to say that he would even make it through his senior year?

He'd been extremely lucky so far, but in his last year of school, would his luck finally run out?

HOLD ME DOWN

Calvin Slater

ABOUT THIS GUIDE

The following questions are intended to
enhance your group's reading of
HOLD ME DOWN.

Discussion Questions

1. Could you relate to Xavier's reasons for being frustrated with his father?

2. Teenage pregnancy is a serious issue in high schools. What steps could be taken to better educate students on the subject?

3. What was Xavier's reasoning for leaving home? Do you think it was the right decision for him to make?

4. What do you think of the relationship Xavier had with Heather? Do you think it was a healthy relationship?

5. Xavier's English teacher, Ms. Scott, and his mentor, Billy Hawkins, are his role models. Who is your role model?

6. At the end of the story, Xavier and Samantha are just friends. Do you think there's a chance for Xavier and Samantha to ever get back together?

Don't miss the first book in the Coleman High series,

Lovers & Haters

On sale now at your local bookstore!

PLEASE DON'T KILL MY VIBE

The second week of October found sixteen-year-old Xavier Hunter up to his old tricks. It was Monday and he was late to class, but as he nonchalantly strolled into Advanced English with his leather backpack slung over his right shoulder, no one at Coleman High could tell. A huge brown paper bag, neatly folded down at the opening, was tucked underneath his left arm. He was wearing a plain, black, flimsy-looking hooded sweatshirt, faded blue Levi's jeans, and crunchy white, over-mileage Air Force 1 sneakers.

Xavier wedged his big body behind a desk at the back of the room. If tardiness wasn't enough, while the teacher's back was turned to the class as she wrote on the blackboard, Xavier had the nerve to start chopping it up with one of his classmates about the Detroit Pistons' poorly played preseason. If preseason play was any indication of how the regular season would be, Xavier felt that the entire roster—including the coaching staff and front office execs—should be taken out back of the Palace of Auburn Hills, and smacked around repeatedly by the owner until they started playing championship-style basketball again.

For a teacher, Ms. Gorman was bangin', Xavier thought. In her mid-thirties, Ms. Gorman had a honey complexion and always looked fly.

"Mr. Hunter," Ms. Gorman said, "I thoroughly explained that you had one more time to enter my classroom door tardy and you would be sent on a one-way trip to the principal's office."

The assignment on the blackboard was complete and the teacher was dusting chalk residue from her small hands. The class looked on in muted silence. Xavier had been pushing his luck for almost two weeks now, and his fellow students were anxious to see what lie the boy would conjure up this time.

And as usual, Xavier's creative talent for bending the truth didn't fall short. "Ms. Gorman, my favorite, favorite, favorite teacher. If I had to blame anybody for my tardiness, it would be you."

"Oh, I have to hear this one"—she folded her arms and arched her left eyebrow—"and if it doesn't make any sense, Xavier, you are out of here."

All eyes were on Xavier, the class clown. It had become obvious to his classmates that he loved the spotlight. He wiped the sweat from his brow and placed the paper bag on top of the desk. Then he turned around to a handsome sixteen-year-old Hispanic cat with smooth brown skin and keen features. The boy's name was Robbie "Cheese" Gonzales. He was a sophomore and everybody loved Cheese, especially the ladies. Cheese spoke his mind and the females adored him for that.

"Kick a drum roll, Cheese," Xavier asked with a smile on his face.

"Mr. Gonzales," Ms. Gorman stepped in, "that won't be necessary. Xavier, you have exactly one point one seconds to explain to me why you were tardy."

With no further hesitation, Xavier's hand went into the bag and came out holding a fresh, lovely bouquet of flowers.

"Those are for me?" Ms. Gorman asked.

"These are exactly for you, Ms. Gorman. You work so hard and sometimes it seems like we don't appreciate you, but we do. And this is a token of our appreciation." Before he put the bag away, there was one last sumthin' sumthin' left. "While you are sniffing the flowers from your favorite students, please let me finish. You always tell us that an apple a day will help keep the doctor away. So for the rest of the school year I hope the doctor never has to see you, because we don't want any substitutes. Here is a nice, juicy, green apple. Eat it in good health, and remember that your whole classroom ponied up the pennies. And that, Ms. Gorman, is why I was tardy." Xavier's wide smile was charming.

The surprise on the faces of his classmates mirrored Ms. Gorman's. Xavier had pulled off some whoppers before, but this one was so outrageous even Burger King couldn't top it.

Ms. Gorman smiled and suspiciously took the flowers. She knew that the smartest student in her classroom was full of it, but before she could address the con job, one of Xavier's biggest haters, Sally Peoples, butted in with her two cents.

"Now, Ms. Gorman, I know you're not going to fall for that nonsense," Sally barked, dramatically rolling her eyes and popping her neck. She was a light-skinned chick with braces and a ridiculous hair weave that took the shape of a bird's nest. "Somewhere in some alley, a flower vendor is waking up with a powerful headache, a lump on his head, and his pockets turned inside out. And I will bet you a year's worth of nasty cafeteria lunches that this LL Cool J wannabe"—she pointed a finger at Xavier—"is giving you stolen merchandise. And who knows where Mister Steroids got that apple from. Probably snatched it from some kid who was walking by himself to school this morning."

The students were busting a gut laughing—that was until Xavier shot off a response.

Sitting behind the desk, he struggled to arch his back so as to leave no doubt about the point he was trying to make. Xavier thrust his pelvis forward, grabbed the crotch of his jeans, and said, "Get these ba-zalls, girl!"

"Xavier, you know there will be none of that foolishness in my classroom," Ms. Gorman said sternly.

"I know you didn't just grab your *thing* at me, boo-boo," Sally said. "What are you, five? Anyway, you probably need to go and wash those rusty things. If them crusty sneakers you got on look anything like your *ba-zalls*, you need to take yourself and run every inch of your bald-headed body through a car wash."

"That goes for you, too, Ms. Peoples," Ms. Gorman said to Sally. "Quit it."

"You're right, Ms. Gorman. I'm sorry for my behavior," Xavier apologized. He looked over at Sally. "You got me, Sally. You want the truth, you deserve the truth." He dramatically jumped from his desk and shoved it aside, making it screech like nails dragging down a chalkboard. "Those flowers were five-fingered, but not the way you say. You think I'm a low-life thug, so I only did what a petty hoodlum would do: I merely waited till your homeless mama was having dinner in her big cardboard box underneath the freeway overpass and kicked over her crib, and there she was with a nice flower arrangement sitting on top of a milk crate about to eat dinner— a barbecue rat sandwich or some crap—when I grabbed the flowers and ran."

The students were rolling with laughter—even Ms. Gorman was trying hard not to chuckle. Sally was the only one who didn't think the mama joke was funny. But Xavier was about to split her weave with the next crack.

"And as for the apple, Sally, I took a trip down to the soup kitchen and found your homeless father. I traded his desperate, crazy behind a couple of gummy bears and a sandwich for this apple—what a loser." Xavier gave one of his classmates a pound as he laughed his butt off.

The suffocating tension in the room between Xavier and Sally prompted Ms. Gorman to restore peace. "I believe that will be enough from the both of you."

But Sally wasn't done. Her face was beet red and her mouth was clenched so tight it was a wonder that her top and bottom braces didn't interlock. She jetted from her chair and pointed at Xavier. "At least my father is not locked away in prison like some godforsaken animal."

"Ohhs" and "ahhs" went up from the boys and girls who were sitting around the action.

"Sally," Ms. Gorman said, slightly elevating her voice, "if you don't take your seat I will make sure that you are suspended."

"Nah, that won't be necessary," Xavier said to Ms. Gorman. "She got jail jokes—okay, bust this one: What about your uncle who caught a ten- to fifteen-year prison sentence? He's up in the same prison with my father. My ol' man was telling me about how your uncle was being treated. His name used to be Bernard, but now the homeys of C block call him Beatrice—"

"You broke punk! Don't nobody talk about my family!" Sally yelled as she slowly started in Xavier's direction.

"That sounds good coming from a wrought-iron-gate-wearing, trout-mouth chick like you," Xavier cut back, holding his ground. He wasn't about to fall back. If Sally wanted trouble he would have no problem with putting her on blast. Xavier had been so frustrated with life that he was ready to beat the brakes off anybody giving him the business. So he took a few steps toward Sally, down for whatever.

Almost every kid in Coleman High was down with seeing a good brawl between two students—it didn't matter what type of financial background the brawlers were from. In unison, a few students chanted, "Fight, fight, fight!"

Ms. Gorman stepped in and pushed Sally back to her desk.

"X," Cheese said, as he grabbed Xavier from behind to restrain him, "it ain't worth it, man."

The classroom was out of control. Kids were laughing and pointing at Sally as tears made their way down her cheeks. The loud banging of a wooden pointer stick made everybody jump, except for Xavier. He'd never threatened a woman before, but Sally was a heifer—and a smart one at that. The things that he wanted to do to her were not legal anywhere in the free world.

"Sally, sit down," Ms. Gorman commanded. The girl did what she was told, and a girl wearing cornrows seated across from her handed Sally some Kleenex.

"And you, Xavier"—Ms. Gorman pointed to the blackboard—"this is Advanced English. It means that you guys are the brightest of the bunch and you deserve to be here, but what I have heard here today makes me wonder if you really appreciate this opportunity. The world is highly competitive and my task is to equip you with as much knowledge as possible to be able to score high on the SAT or ACT so that you can get into a good university. I'm not beyond expelling a student, but don't push me." She pointed the stick at Xavier. "You, come with me." Before he knew it, Ms. Gorman had Xavier by the hand and was leading him into the hallway. The height difference had Ms. Gorman at a slight disadvantage. Xavier was nearly six-two and the teacher had to crane her neck to look up at her student. "What the hell is wrong with you? I've never seen you this worked up—about to put your hands on a young lady."

"That ain't no young lady. She caught me on the wrong day, Ms. Gorman."

"Is there something going on at home that I should know about? Because this isn't like you."

Yeah, something was going on at home, but it was none of her business. Life at the crib was twisted for him. Xavier was a sixteen-year-old boy with more responsibility on his plate than any of his peers. He stared at a row of lockers that stretched all the way down the empty hallway. His anger was on bump. He needed something to take out his frustrations on. The next sucka who jumped in his face with any type of drama was going to get his eyebrows kicked in.

"Listen, I'm going to give you this hall pass to go to the lavatory and cool off. When you get back here, be ready to discuss Shakespeare's play *Hamlet*."

Xavier took the hall pass and bounced. He was ticked. His next-door neighbor, friend, and mentor, Billy Hawkins, would be upset at him for blowing his cool, especially the part about him almost knuckling up on a girl. Xavier knew how the old man had made it his number one rule to never get physical with a woman. It was a good thing that Billy couldn't see inside Xavier's mind right now. He seriously wouldn't approve of his revenge fantasy against Sally. What had been so jacked up was that the girl had spit dirty on his family. Xavier didn't play when somebody tried to style on his father. Bringing up the old dude was a surefire way of getting him angry.

The truth was that Xavier was a student who was carrying a 4.0 GPA. The hope for an academic scholarship to a promising university was the only thing that was keeping him from playing the ghetto games with those cats who chased paper by exploiting anybody with the ends to buy some product.

He stormed into the bathroom and headed toward the sinks, needing to cool off. He ran the cold water for a few seconds before cupping both hands underneath the faucet and splashing the coldness over his face. He was straight tripping, allowing a nobody with a bad weave to push his buttons. He really didn't know if he was actually mad at Sally because she had been so close to the truth about how he came in possession of the flowers.

Of course Xavier hadn't robbed anybody, but he had come across a crackhead on his way to school that morning who had stuck up a flower vendor. The merchant had just set up shop for rush-hour traffic when Xavier witnessed the jacking. The fiend, who had a long, thin scar traveling from the right to the left side of his forehead, had robbed the vendor using a knife. He had grabbed the frightened vendor from behind and stuck the blade to the man's throat. He then demanded money, and oddly enough, a bouquet of flowers. If there was one thing that Xavier hated, it was a dope fiend who preyed on hardworking people to support his habit. To get the drop on him, Xavier hid around the corner of an apartment building in an alley while the crackhead was busy counting the loot he'd jacked. The junkie never saw him as he took the cash and bouquet. The apple he bought at a fruit stand on his way to school.

Xavier splashed more water over his face and began to feel its calming effects. He glanced down at his body. He wasn't really tripping about the ragged condition of his clothing, and crusty-looking Nike Air Force 1s. But the reflection in the mirror cast no doubt on a boy who was lost inside the treacherous dark alleys of confusion. Sally had tried to earn comical points about him looking like a dark-skinned LL Cool J. The fact was that he did resemble the superstar rapper and phenom actor. But none of that mattered, because Xavier couldn't see past his issues. Without the presence of a father, who had been locked up since he was six, to give him balance, structure, and discipline, his world was filled with utter chaos. His mother's selfishness had forced Xavier to grow up prematurely. He was the older of two kids and the role of raising his little brother fell on his shoulders. At times, playing dad to his brother left him struggling to figure his real role in the family—son, brother, father figure? Could he ever get it right?

He had wondered on more than one occasion if he really belonged to the family. His mother, father, and baby brother were fair-skinned—which left him standing out in family photos like a chocolate dot and feeling as though his mother had had a disgusting romp between the sheets with the mailman. He did admit to himself that Rufus Jangle, the neighborhood letter carrier, was blacker than night. But he'd feel sorry for himself later. He had to pee.

Xavier took the last stall next to the wall to handle his business. He had just finished when the lavatory door burst open like somebody had kicked it. The voices entering were highly recognizable: wannabe thugs.

Xavier quietly zipped and buckled while stealing a peek over the stall door. He knew all four knuckleheads and the dude they were disrespectfully pushing around. Some freshman geek named Sebastian Patrick. The fifteen-year-old boy was in Xavier's fourth-period computer class. He was short and thin, with glasses almost thicker than car windshields. He was shaking so bad that Xavier felt sorry for him.

"So, nephew"—Xavier knew this voice belonged to Dylan Dallas—"it doesn't look too good for you. My homeys here have told me that you don't value our protection anymore. What is it? You think you're too good for us? In this school you will find that freshman life ain't nothing but nine months of bullies and beatdowns—that is unless the newbies get smart and get somebody to watch their backs. That's where we come in. We provide a service and we expect to be paid . . . and you're late with our money."

Dylan Dallas was a seventeen-year-old Tupac wannabe—green bandanna tied around his bald head, oversize hoodie, jeans, and Timberland boots. He even had bushy eyebrows and a nose piercing like the late rap star. He used to drop straight As on his report card—that was until he came up with the bright idea that robbing other students would be easier than graduating high school and going off to get a life.

"That's right, Dylan." This voice belonged to Danger. He was a sixteen-year-old wannabe thug who had grown tired of getting beat up and hooked up with Dylan for protection. "Yup. Sebastian here owes you for an entire month. By my calculations, that's a hundred bones."

As Dylan ran down Sebastian's list of offenses, Xavier stealthily removed his cell phone, ducked back down, and typed out a text.

When Xavier was a freshman, he'd had a run-in with these cats on the first day of school. Words had been exchanged, but before anything could jump off, school security moved in and squashed the beef.

Xavier was careful to peer over the stall door again.

There was a huge seventeen-year-old goon standing behind Dylan. This was his enforcer, an enormous dude who had earned the nickname "Knuckles" for his ability to knock guys out in one shot.

This wasn't his fight, Xavier told himself. If he was going to be kicked out of school, it had better be worth it. He didn't want anything to affect his GPA. Not to mention, being suspended for three days and having to be at home with his nagging mother would be enough to drive him crazy.

"I know about you, Sebastian," Dylan prattled on. "I've been peeping you every day since school started, watched as your old dude picked you up in his expensive whip. . . . What model of Mercedes-Benz is that, anyway?"

"I believe that pretty mofo is an E-Class," a tall, skinny guy sitting on one of the sinks answered for Sebastian. He was bug-eyed, with a huge, pointed nose and dressed in a black Dickies outfit and a Detroit Tigers baseball hat turned backward.

The fool with his baseball hat turned backward had

been the clown who Xavier believed had bumped him purposely on the first day of school. Word around school was that he packed heat. He went by the nickname "Trigger," and rumor had it that he'd spent time in juvie for shooting some dude who was talking smack while Trigger was trying to get the dude's sister's phone number at a house party.

"Now, nephew," Dylan said to Sebastian. "You can't expect to floss like that and not pay us for protection. I don't know what school you came from, but this is Coleman High. And since you've been short with the bread, I've decided that your protection fee has just doubled from one hundred to two hundred. Oh, just in case you don't get the picture"—Dylan pointed to the smallest boy in his crew. He was fifteen and went by the name Dirty—"show him."

At the order, Trigger grabbed and pinned Sebastian's arms behind his back, exposing his stomach. Dirty was wearing a pair of True Religion jeans, a gray Detroit Pistons sweatshirt, and Timberland boots. He stepped up and delivered a menacing Floyd "Money" Mayweather type of blow to Sebastian's midsection. Tears trickled from underneath Sebastian's glasses as the boy fought to fill his lungs back up with air.

"Dirty, I don't think Sebastian is feeling us," Dylan boasted.

Knuckles chimed in, admiring the heat being brought. "Damn, Dirty, I taught you well."

"You ain't seen nothing yet," Dirty explained. "Take his glasses off. I'm about to give him something to really cry about."

Xavier had seen enough. He was not gonna just stand by and let them beat an innocent boy senseless. One thing he hated more than thieves were bullies. He kicked open the door of the stall so hard that everybody in the lavatory almost jumped out of their skin.

"Get off him," Xavier demanded of Trigger.

"Or what?" Knuckles asked, stepping to Xavier. The two boys stood eye level and both were powerfully built for combat. Xavier was looking for a reason—any reason—to just knock Knuckles out.

Xavier stepped closer to Knuckles. "I could say 'or I would beat the ugliness from your face,' but I am afraid that would be an all-day gig. But all the same, homeboy, cut Sebastian loose."

"OMG," Dylan said, smiling. "Xavier Hunter—nephew, why do you want to stick your nose in my business? I mean, we gave your freshman ass a pass on the first day of school last year as a courtesy to your old man. Noah Hunter was a legend in the streets, a true pioneer of the game. I grew up admiring your dad. But your old man ain't in the game anymore—this is my show, playboy. As one last courtesy to Papa Noah, I'm gonna let you bounce." Dylan nodded his head at Knuckles, who slowly and hesitantly backed away.

"Kill that, Dylan," Trigger shouted. He slung Sebastian to the dirty floor and was about to rush Xavier.

"Trigger," Dylan said, "I said let 'im bounce. Now, what don't you understand?"

Trigger went off. "Man, let's do this fool. Don't nobody care about his old man. That junk is ancient history. This chump disrespected me last year—ain't no way I'm letting it slide."

Dirty said, "B has a good point, Dylan. We let this fool get away with dissing us, how long before all these other fools at Coleman start trying us on?"

"Well, nephew," Dylan said to Xavier, rubbing his chin, "the majority has spoken. Looks like Sebastian won't be the only cat limping out of here in pain."

"Let's do this," Xavier proclaimed with no fear in his voice.

Dylan and his crew circled Xavier, but before fists could start flying, the bathroom door opened. In walked three students, two built like apartment buildings; the other one was of average height, wore expensive designer shades, and resembled Usher Raymond.

"Whoaaa, look what we walked in on," Designer Shades announced. "Dylan, man, you're slipping. Four on one—we can't let you get down like that, you feel me?"

Xavier looked at the newcomers and then back to Dylan. "It's your move, clown. Are you gonna let Sebastian bounce or are you gonna make a go?"

Dylan bit his lip in anger.

"Romello Anderson," Knuckles said to the boy sporting the designer shades. "Homeboy, you are biting off more than you can chew."

Romello laughed. "Don't worry about how much I can chew. Like X said, we gonna do this or what?" Romello glanced up at his two enormous companions, sixteen-year-old Ray Taylor and sixteen-year-old Clyde McElroy, and then back to Knuckles.

Trigger looked like he wanted to say something, but the glare from the massive monster on Romello's left side shut down anything cute that he had to say.

Xavier helped Sebastian up from the floor. "Go to class and I'll holla at you later."

Sebastian straightened his glasses, wiped away his tears, and left.

"From here on out your protection is no longer needed, Dylan. And if I ever catch you trying to step to Sebastian again, I'm gonna stick my Nikes so far up your butt, homeboy, you'll have the taste of shoe leather on your tongue for weeks."

"This ain't over, nephew," Dylan ominously assured Xavier. He nodded his head at his crew and they all filed out of the restroom.

After they left, Xavier slapped Romello five. "Man, I thought you were never gonna show after I texted you."

"Dog, I was trying to get up on some honeys in the gym when you texted. Luckily, big Ray and Clyde were getting their sweat on in the weight room."

Xavier thanked Ray and Clyde for their assistance.

Before the two football players exited, Ray Taylor said, "Xavier, my father used to run with your dad. They're both in the same prison and they told me to watch your back. So if you ever need me, you know where to find me."

"Xavier," Romello said, "you owe me. You can start by rolling with me to the State Theater on Friday—teen night, on me. " He started moving his hips. "Dancing, honeys—the whole shebang. And I won't take no for an answer."

Romello was sixteen years old. Xavier had known Romello since junior high, where he had a two-faced reputation around school. Some said that he was only loyal to one thing—and that was getting paid. The boy belonged to Deuces, one of the many gangs inside of Weber Junior High. Dude stayed in trouble. The two had started hanging around each other after Xavier helped Romello fight off three rival gang members. And even though Xavier was up on Romello's shady, ratchet rep, they became friends.

"Ain't nothing to talk about," Xavier exclaimed. "I'm there. Now get your Usher Raymond wannabe butt to class," Xavier joked.

"Later," Romello said.

But it was really no laughing matter. Xavier had just punked out one of the school's shadiest thugs. He knew that someday, Dylan Dallas and his goons would try to return the favor. It wasn't his problem, but Xavier had a big heart and he couldn't let Sebastian get stumped out. If Xavier was trying to stay low key and lurk in the background to keep his grades tight, that plan was dead. Playing the hero had put him on the front line for an impending war. It was time for him to start surrounding himself with cats that would have his back when trouble stepped out of the shadows.

"Mr. Hunter," Ms. Gorman said as Xavier walked back into class to take his seat. "I'm glad that you could grace us with your presence, just in time to introduce yourself to our newest student."

The beef with Dylan was still so fresh in his mind that Xavier hadn't even noticed that the girl sitting directly to his right was new. He was slippin'—a fool like him usually noticed the honeys. The new chick was not only gorgeous, but a dime piece—straight Beyoncé in the face, long, flowing hair, a soft brown complexion, and juicy lips that had been designed for extra intense kissing sessions. Her eyes were her most endearing feature. They were big, brown, and almond shaped, with naturally long eyelashes.

Xavier couldn't see much of her body because she wasn't advertising it—meaning the girl wasn't dressed like a skank. Skinny jeans, T-shirt, chocolate brown UGG boots, same color leather biker jacket, and a nice pair of diamond stud earrings made this girl look like a superstar. A brown Michael Kors bag sat on the floor by her feet. The fragrance that girlfriend was rocking smelled better than any Xavier had ever come across.

"I'm Xavier." He reached his hand out to shake hers.

She looked hesitant at first, but shook his hand. "I'm Samantha—Samantha Fox."

"Fox, hmmm—yes, you are, ma. Maybe we can have some lunch, get to know each other." Xavier was quick with his game.

"Pump your brakes, Romeo," someone yelled from the back of the room. The entire class laughed.

"Yes, Mr. Hunter," Ms. Gorman butted in. "Please try to contain yourself." The teacher went into her desk and retrieved a thin book. "Everybody, can you please take out"— she held it up in full view of the class—"Shakespeare's *Hamlet*." Ms. Gorman said to Samantha, "Looks like we are short one play. I won't be able to get another until to-morrow, so would you mind sharing with someone?"

Xavier saw his chance. "Ms. Gorman, I'd like to vol-unteer my play."

"Respectfully—Xavier is it?" Samantha asked in a se-rious tone. "My father taught me never to accept any-thing from bad boys."

"Ooooh," a few of the male students instigated.

"Oh, it's like that?" Xavier asked, still slyly smiling. "Don't say that because most girls love us bad boys. This school ain't the most secure place in the city for a beauti-ful girl such as yourself to be walking around alone. You might need somebody like me to protect you."

Samantha smiled flirtatiously and batted her long, thick eyelashes. "Your offer for bodyguard services is tempting, but that's why the school has security."

The "oohs" and "aahs" started again.

Cheese butted in, "Girl, the jackers will be off with your goods before these security guards get off their butts to do something."

Some of the students laughed at Cheese's sense of humor.

"It's all good, Cheese," Xavier said. He turned to Samantha. "Security, huh? Okay. But just keep in mind that my door is always open for you, gorgeous."

Samantha blushed, smiling.

"Excuse me, Xavier," Ms. Gorman said. "This is not some mall where you can openly flirt. The only hook up that will be happening in my class is you hooking up with William Shakespeare. Now that you've volunteered your play to Samantha, tell me how will you be keeping up with the rest of us?"

Xavier smiled confidently. "No sweat. I read *Hamlet* this past summer. I don't need the book." He tapped his finger on the side of his head. "Got it all up here."

"The only thing you got up there is a lot of fat," Sally Peoples bitterly cut in, apparently still fuming from their earlier argument.

Xavier turned his back on Sally's comment. The girl was old news and he wasn't about to go there with her again.

"That will be enough out of you, Ms. Peoples," Ms. Gorman scolded. The teacher looked back in Xavier's direction with an inquisitive expression on her face. "Okay, Mr. Hunter, I'm going to ask you to sum up the play, in your own words."

"Oh, Ms. Gorman, you're trying to play a brotha out. I got this." Xavier flirtatiously smiled at Samantha. "Peep this. Prince Hamlet takes revenge on his uncle Claudius for murdering King Hamlet, Claudius's brother and Prince Hamlet's father. Claudius then takes the throne of Denmark by marrying the king's widow and Prince Hamlet's mother."

"Don't let that steroid freak fool y'all," Sally interrupted by snapping on Xavier. "Anybody with Internet access could log on to Wikipedia to print the summary."

"Sally, one more outburst out of you and I'm going to send you to the principal's office," Ms. Gorman scolded. She then returned her attention to Xavier. "Mr. Hunter, would you please be so kind as to tell us what method Claudius used in killing King Hamlet, and what does the third guard, Marcellus, report to Hamlet that he saw one night?"

Xavier had to keep from laughing at the question. He knew Ms. Gorman was trying to set him up. "Teach, you gotta come up with something better than that if you're trying to throw me off my game. Marcellus didn't tell Hamlet anything. It was Hamlet's friend Horatio, who said he had seen a ghost who looked like King Hamlet. And as for the method Claudius used to knock off his brother—it was hemlock, a poisonous plant that he'd cooked into a liquid. One afternoon, Claudius crept on his brother while the king was sleeping and poured the poison inside his ear."

Cheese tapped Xavier on the shoulder and excitedly yelled, "Dazam, my boy's a walking *Hamlet* encyclopedia! That's my dude—y'all get up off him!"

Cheese's energy had sparked a buzz of chatter among the students.

Xavier looked over at Samantha and winked. "Impressed, huh?"

Ms. Gorman said, "Yes, Mr. Hunter, fabulous job. We are all impressed that you took the time out of your busy summer schedule to look over this semester's required reading. So I'm going to encourage you to keep your play in front of you. And, Samantha, please feel free to look on with another student."

The class laughed while Xavier was smiling, hoping that he made enough of an impression to catch him a Fox.

Don't miss the next exciting book in Calvin Slater's
Coleman High series,
Game On
On sale in September 2015!

SATURDAY, JULY 8
8:23 AM

This was too early in the morning for him, and during his summer vacation. At a time when Xavier should've been in his bed, with the covers pulled up to his chin and copping some serious Zs, he was yawning while following a correctional officer with no neck and a butt the size of a small Buick down a drab, dreary corridor.

Xavier still couldn't believe that in another month he would be entering his senior year of high school. Never in his wildest dreams when starting out as a freshman at Coleman High did he ever think he'd make it all the way, given all of the drama he had to deal with in his personal life. But as much as he wanted to celebrate, he knew there were some real hard truths he still hadn't overcome yet. He was still a wanted man with an undisclosed amount of money riding on his bald head, placed there by Slick Eddie, a pissed-off kingpin who at one time owned and operated a multimillion-dollar chop shop out of a huge junkyard on Detroit's Westside. Slick Eddie was now doing a life stretch in prison because Xavier had ratted him and his former soldier Romello Anderson out to the police. Since then Eddie had sworn revenge. Xavier was sure he would never live to see graduation, and Eddie had almost made good on his promise with a couple of unsuccessful attempts. It didn't matter how many hitters Eddie sent Xavier's way. Xavier was focused and he possessed a deep-rooted conviction that nothing, not even Eddie, was going to keep him from stepping across the stage at his graduation ceremony.

As he trailed the correction officer, Xavier had to admit to himself that it took a lot of guts to get him to this point. This was the women's side of Portus Correctional Facility, a place where his mother Ne Ne had been cooling her heels for a little over a year now. There was a time where he didn't care about ever seeing her again, especially after the crazy move she'd pulled at the end of his sophomore year. Ne Ne had breezed through Coleman High's back parking lot in an attempt to abduct his now ex-girlfriend Samantha during the last school dance with her jailbird boyfriend, Nate. Ne Ne was the main reason why Xavier's relationship with Samantha was no longer. But since then Xavier had had some time to think about mending fences with his mother. Although her selfish butt didn't deserve his forgiveness, Xavier's father, Noah, had been instrumental in convincing the boy that nobody was perfect. And everybody deserved a second chance.

That's why Xavier was now sitting down inside a graffiti-riddled booth with a thick glass partition separating him from an empty chair, awaiting the arrival of his inmate mother. He hadn't been able to understand it. Through the first ten months of her sentence, Ne Ne didn't act like she gave a crap about her son.

No letters. No collect phone calls.

But Noah hadn't left her with any room to bring the noise with some weak excuse. Even though Ne Ne had never passed any of the letters that Noah had sent to him and his brother, Noah wasn't about to do the same thing to her. So he had gone online and found her inmate number and mailing address through OTIS (the Offender Tracking Information System) and wrote her, providing the address and phone numbers at which she could reach her boys. But still there was nothing. Then, all of a sudden, three weeks ago, it had been like a switch was flipped when Ne Ne started calling and sending the boys letters like she'd lost her mind. Each letter claimed that she was new and reformed from her old ways. She had found the Lord and became born again and whatnot. Just what Xavier needed—another highly religious nut running loose in the family like Noah. And just when he'd gotten his relationship tight with his Bible-thumping old man, too. Now he had to deal with this junk. But all the same, she was his mother and he respected her.

But nothing surprised him about his mother.

Even as she took her seat on the other side of the glass partition, Xavier wondered if her newly-acquired faith was some scheme she'd cooked up to weasel her way back into his life. To convince him by using King James scripture as some kind of prop to aid in her clever disguise of a woman who'd truly seen the error of her ways.

Ne Ne's looks had changed a bit. Age seemed to set in overnight. Where her face once held the unmistakable arrogance of the ghetto, it now seemed to be home to traces of humility. Gray color showed in the tangles of her hairline. There were bags underneath her hard eyes and she looked to be down quite a few pounds from the last time he'd seen her.

Xavier kept his eyes focused on her face. He wanted to see if her new way of life existed there. But he couldn't really tell because his mother looked to be anxious, shifting around in her seat and avoiding eye contact. It was wrong to judge her primarily on her emotions. This behavior could stem from shame. After all, the last time Xavier had laid eyes on her was when she and her knucklehead boyfriend Nate had tried to get all crazy with it and kidnap Samantha. Xavier surmised that if he'd pulled something so desperate, lowdown, and despicable, he'd be ashamed to look someone in the eyes, too.

Xavier picked up the telephone and waited until she did the same. When he spoke, his voice seemed to be a little harsh. "You know you didn't have a soul back then. The letters you keep sending to the house. How can I believe any of it?"

His mother kept her eyes cast downward. "I didn't know God the way I do now, son."

"Excuse me for not really buying it, but when convicts go to prison a lot of them always come out claiming to be holier than thou, you feel me?"

Ne Ne's eyes kept darting side to side like she was watching a tennis match when she tried to look at him. "You have a right to be angry. I put you and your brother through a lot with my own selfishness. All I can say is I'm sorry."

He had come to see her with the intention of burying the hatchet, per his father's request. But when he finally caught her eyes, something inside of him snapped and he went nuclear. "Are you sorry about hiding my father's letters from us? Trying to kidnap my girlfriend—you doggone right you put us through a lot. Then you had that bum that you called a boyfriend. And don't let me get started on how you threatened to throw me out of the house if I didn't sell drugs to help you—what kind of mother would say such things to her son?"

Ne Ne couldn't answer. The only sign of remorse were the tears sliding from both eyes leaving trails along her cheeks.

Xavier dug deeper. "When I was getting money, you didn't even have the decency, the concern about where it was coming from. All you knew was that you were lining your pockets. You didn't care"—he stopped and looked around—"if I ended up in a place like this, just as long as I kept breaking you off with the ends."

Ne Ne still held the phone to her ear with her left hand as she covered her face, chest heaving and crying into the other.

Xavier knew it was wrong but he felt nothing for her. "But that's okay. You see, even with everything you put me through I still managed to make it through to my senior year of high school. And I'm going to graduate, too. Do something that you never believed in. Despite you telling me that education was useless. 'Member you told me the only way that a black boy could make it out of the ghetto was by selling dope, going to prison, or dying?"

Ne Ne finally looked up, and through tears, said to him, "I've made terrible mistakes and all I ask for is a chance to let me make good."

Xavier was on the blink. He didn't have any sympathy for her. As far as he was concerned, his mother was someone who had profited off the love he had inside of his heart for his family and then busted up and stripped away the one decent thing that was any good in his life. Samantha was gone, and it was all Ne Ne's fault.

"Ne Ne—"

His mother interrupted by saying, "Please, son—I'm your mother, it's okay to call me mom."

Xavier sarcastically chuckled while shaking his head. "You can't be serious, Ne Ne, tell me this is a joke?"—with both hands he flared out his ears—"I'm listening. Is this a joke?"

Tears continued streaming down Ne Ne's face as she tightly held on to the phone.

"*Mom*—that's rich. Whatever happened to 'Don't y'all ever call me *Mama*. It makes me sound old.'" Xavier ruthlessly laughed at her as if her tears were a joke.

"Son, that's not fair. You forgave your dad."

Xavier blazed. "Pop wasn't the one who withheld the letters from me and Alfonso, was he?"

Ne Ne wiped her eyes with the right sleeve of her orange jumpsuit. "How's my baby?"

"You have some nerve."

"Why ain't Alfonso with you?"

"I'm not gonna let you play with his head. Alfonso is doing well. I came here today to see if you were on the level, and I don't know. I don't trust you. Do you know how you affected that boy with your foolishness?"

Ne Ne's eyes were red and puffy. She sniffled. "So now I'm on trial here, is that it? You brought your behind up here knowing you weren't gonna forgive me!" she yelled at him.

Xavier's face broke into a smirk. "Now that's the old Ne Ne I know."

Ne Ne let loose on him, "Look at you sitting there looking like your daddy. How dare you look down your nose at me, you little car thief. Here I am trying to tell you that I changed, but all you care about is losing your little rich girlfriend. You think those rich people in her world were going to accept you? Let me tell you one thing: the only thing all those old snobbish people were going to do for you was put a chauffeur's cap on your head and a broom in your hand."

Xavier looked away and wiped his mouth. When he returned his gaze, there were tears welling up in his eyes. "My dad told me that anybody can change. But in your case, I don't think it's true. I did come to visit you with the hopes that you had changed." He tightened his grip on the phone handle. "But all you are, and always will be . . . is bitter." With that Xavier got up and walked out.

on record as acknowledging confirmation of the claims that the Russian scientists made concerning alien spaceships having spied on the astronauts during the historic Moon landing. "The encounter was common knowledge in NASA," he said. "When the Apollo 11 module landed at the bottom of a Moon crater, two alien spacecraft appeared at the rim."

Chatelain stated that on the third day of the Apollo 11 mission, a strange object that appeared to Armstrong like interconnecting rings was sighted by the three astronauts. Collins expressed his opinion that the UFO appeared to be shaped like a large, hollow cylinder. Aldrin, puzzling over its bizarre dimensions, thought the object resembled a gigantic, half-open book.

Although NASA deliberately interrupted Apollo 11's radio transmissions to Earth to censor the astronauts' reports of the UFO, Chatelain stated that there were a number of other weird interruptions that had nothing to do with Mission Control at Houston. "The astronauts heard noises similar to a train whistle, fire engine siren, or power saw on their radio," Chatelain said. "These sounds were thought to be some sort of code."

Perhaps there exists no more convincing physical evidence of a shadow government, a technologically superior secret society, or a group of aliens who work secretly among us than the mystery satellites and their eerie transmissions.

Although textbooks of every nation credit Sputnik 1, a Soviet space vehicle launched into orbit on October 4, 1957, as the first artificial Earth satellite, mysterious Earth-circling objects— launched by neither the United States nor the USSR—have been detected since 1949.

For at least the past forty-five years, a secret space program originating from somewhere other than the known terrestrial space centers has been placing satellites in orbit around our planet and transmitting bizarre messages to contribute to the conspiracy that cloaks their presence. Some researchers have theorized that the unknown orbiting vehicles (UOVs) are probably launched from bases on the Moon or Mars.

* * *